MID-SUMMER MOONLIGHT

Jo felt she had passed through the very path of a hurricane, turned inside out, revealed and secretless, and now stood in its eye, quiet, excised, changed. How could you know this? she asked. How could you know? Their feet trod out the juice from the old standards, and a sweet fragrance of heady romance filled their lungs, throwing out fatigue and reticence. Jo listened to Jem's words, every one, scarcely believing. Impact was distant, but I know I will remember tomorrow, she thought, listening . . .

Other Avon books by
J. J. McKenna

SARAH AND JOSHUA   41053 $2.50

ASK OF THE WIND

J.J. McKENNA

 AVON
PUBLISHERS OF BARD, CAMELOT AND DISCUS BOOKS

ASK OF THE WIND is an original publication of
Avon Books. This work has never before
appeared in book form.

AVON BOOKS
A division of
The Hearst Corporation
959 Eighth Avenue
New York, New York 10019

First Avon Printing, July, 1980

AVON TRADEMARK REG. U.S. PAT. OFF. AND IN
OTHER COUNTRIES, MARCA REGISTRADA, HECHO EN
U.S.A.

Printed in the U.S.A.

For my father

My thanks to Mr. Howard Burton, M.Sc. for supplying me with bacteriological information.

ONE

CHAPTER
ONE

When Jem Merriman came to Port Penquay, he was on the run. The sea stopped him. The quiet industrious harbor full of sea and boats stopped him. He had the choice of running further, for once upon a time he had been in the merchant navy, but he stopped because of that choice. It would always be there if he wanted it, in time of a greater need. No one knew his exact route from London, and at that time no one knew what he fled, but by some accident or design of fate his ten-year-old Ford arrived in the town very early one Sunday morning and stopped, as it had to, at the end of Victoria Pier. He had gone as far as he could. The stubby thumb of Port Penquay lighthouse and its green wooden door carved with dirty words, initials, and hearts stopped him. It was the most important stop in his life.

Old Sam Antler happened to be in his construction shed that morning. He doesn't sleep so long these days, feels no need to, he says, so he was taking his first cup of tea alone in the quiet of a Sunday morning before the bells began to ring. Through the tea steam he could see the ocean moving slowly and heavily, still sullen after a night of the west wind which had broken the wave tops and flung them against the frustratingly solid granite of the pier. Salt crystals dulled the windowpane. Sam's eyes prodded the sky for weather; the cloud was breaking; a film, more, a two-ply tissue of blue, lay on the horizon. Later the sun would come.

Very little happens in Penquay at seven o'clock on a

Sunday morning, even in May when the tourists are beginning to flood in, and this particular May day was cold and
dull. So cold in fact that Sam wore two sweaters instead of
one, and had drawn his backside up as close as he dared to
the battered electric heater. He was musing gently on the
possibility of stripping down the Transit's back axle, which
was noisy, when into his oily envisagings drove a dirty
white Cortina. It stopped with its radiator grille only
inches from the hedge of green spikes that surrounds the
lighthouse. Sam rested his elbows on the sill and hooked
his nose over the cup, awaiting developments. He wanted
to roll a cigarette, but was afraid he might miss something
if he went back to the kitchen to fetch the tobacco tin and
papers. He waited quite a long time, able to see only the
ill-defined outline of a single figure sitting very still in the
driver's seat. Up-to-no-good thoughts crossed his mind, old-
man-alone-like-me thoughts. Steve was in Sandcliff for the
weekend. His mind's eye checked the lock and bolts of the
wicket gate in the shed doors and glanced in the petty-cash
tin under his bed and in the small safe set in concrete in
the office. The safe contained deeds, insurance certificates,
and two pounds of one-inch copper roves . . . but you
never knew.

Boredom and a craving for the first smoke almost
dragged Sam from his hide, but as his muscles poised, the
door of the Cortina opened and a man stepped out. Old
Sam is no good at people. He would make a lousy witness
to any event, criminal or innocent.

"A bloke got out," he said later.

"What sort of bloke?" asked Ivor.

"Just a bloke. Ordinary enough." And Sam sounded a
little aggressive.

The man he saw step from the car and look about him
was lean and balanced, with dark, graying-over-the-ears
hair and a lined, earnest face. His eyes were blue and
tired, red-blue around the lids, his expression vacant and
the top lip of his wide mouth pinched into small lines as if
he feared some facial reprisal should he let it relax. He
shoved his hands deep into the pockets of his duffel coat,
hunching against the wide-open wind. The buoys awaiting
repair in the yard beside the lighthouse brushed his attention. The boatyard caught more, and for a moment Sam

thought he had been discovered, but the blank eyes moved on over the gray-and-white bulk of the large construction shed with ANTLERCRAFT in plain black letters on the doors, over the smaller hump of the mechanical workshop with its ridiculous window boxes, where mignonette shivered its drab, sweet fragrance, and on, over the stack of timber. The man's line of vision panned like a camera, turning him almost a full circle.

Running the length of the seaward aspect of Victoria Pier is a raised footpath. An adult can see over the top of the wall to the ship-decked horizon, or back inland to Half Moon Bay and the Spit. The stranger mounted the steps to the path, easily but with no spring in his feet. With typical understatement, Sam said he looked fed-up.

He leaned a long time on the wall. The wall is always cold and salt-sticky to the touch, and he stared down at the heavy, dragon-green sea and who knows what serpents haunted there. The clutching bladder wrack sucked noisy breaths through its fronds as the tide slopped up and down, and faint echoes carried over from the bay, of pebbles, sea-rolled, sea-milled, sea-shaped.

Sam's curiosity succumbed to his craving for nicotine and he hurried from the shed to the kitchen, whose window faces the Old Harbor, for the worn and favorite old tin. Sam's tobacco tin was with him in the navy about a thousand years ago. There is a hell of a dent in its lid, but he has never been naive enough to try the old one about it having saved him from an otherwise fatal bullet. As a consequence, his friends believe it did.

When he returned to his cozy window place, Jem Merriman was still on the sea wall, but now facing the town, whose three spires reach up to God. Above his head clouds ricocheted like pool balls and let in the sun. Our small town looks good from the harbor in the sunlight. The visiting yachts and cruisers dance on trot moorings in Days Harbor on the far side of Nash Pier, and the water is thick with orange buoys; the crab and mackerel boats sit more austerely in the Old Harbor with the rowing boats for hire in a duckling clutch, and the Sandholm Island forty-seaters of old oak and new varnish. From the pier the commercial harbor of St. Jude's is barely visible, tucked in behind Angel Point, where the Yacht Club and the sparkling new frozen-ice-cream Hotel Winstone stand. On clear days the small rook's nest of dockside cranes and the two oil storage tanks are just discernible. St. Jude's is generally ignored by the tourists, and why not? Port Penquay has hotels along the front, St. Bartholomew's-on-the-Quay, a riot of twisting, Dickensian streets full of shops selling everything the residents do not need, a very good market, two cinemas, umpteen pubs, a Town Hall of gargoyle ugliness, and a grammar school of extreme granite elegance.

Whether Jem saw the town, only he knows; he might have seen it with his aesthetic eye, or his precision eye, the cubes and the curves and the boxes, the straggly accidental beauty of this place on its two hills; or he might have seen nothing but a black hole moving swiftly before him so that it seemed he was always about to fall.

He stood, Sam said, for bloody ages without a movement except the gusty tumblewind in his hair. It made a halo of dark red-brown around his head, and the sun silhouetted his face so that Sam could not see if he laughed or cried. The old man relaxed as he lit a second cigarette, unfilled paper flaming at the end in the match. No mugger or sneak thief would wait around to be seen, he decided. Perhaps he had come to fish. Sheer nosiness led Sam to saunter across the shed under the two fiberglass hulls that gleamed dully in the skylight gloom. He ducked as he passed through, attuned to the sick-sweet smell of the resin and the angles his body had to follow. He took care to rattle the bolts loudly and wasted a little time in finding the key among a big bunch attached to a chain on his belt. If the stranger had evil intentions, he would be well warned.

But when Sam casually eased the wicket gate open, the man was still standing with his back to the wall, hands in pockets, blank-faced. Sam stepped over the sill, tucked his thumbs in his armpits, and did some breathing exercises, pretending interest in everything but the few cubic feet of pier that held the stranger. There was no response, so he ambled around to the mechanical workshop, glanced briefly at the sheeted timber—teak for deck planks—and wandered back. The man had moved down and was standing beside his car, one toe idly tapping a rear tire.

"Morning!" said Sam, raising a hand in a sort of half-salute, as he does.

"Hello," said the man, quite friendly-like, according to Sam.

"Hoping to fish? Bit of a storm last night. There won't be much feeding here yet."

"I've got a rod in the car," said Jem Merriman. "What do you catch in these parts?" He had a well-bred, deep-soft voice, like water down a mountain, soft to the mind's skin.

"Off the pier? Mullet are good if you can strike 'em. Soft mouth, they say. A young lad caught a ten-pound bass here last week. On a piddling little plastic rod. Some of our local so-called experts were bloody furious about it." He chuckled viciously.

The man smiled. "I must try sometime," he said. "When the weather is better. Do you live here?" He nodded toward Antlercraft.

"Own it," said Sam. He looked down at his shabby clothes, the trousers flannel and split at the knee, the cuffs full of sawdust, and dusty carpet slippers. "I'm a working owner," he added. "Only have four staff. What are you doing here?" He can be very abrupt, Sam can, and he does it purposely to surprise a reaction into the open. If he surprises a lie, he cuts its feet off and smiles to himself.

The man said, "I . . . Is there a café or restaurant open today? I'd like to find a place to stay, but it's too early yet." He looked at the plain, expensive watch on his wrist.

Sam squeezed out his bottom lip and pinched it between his fingers. "There's Pete's," he mused, "but he doesn't open until lunchtime on Sundays. Any other day he does breakfast."

"Never mind. Thanks." The man turned away. With his back to Sam, he added, "I passed a transport café about five miles back on the main road." As he opened the car door, Sam called him. He says he felt sorry for the bloke on that cold morning, but it seems it was more. A memory rang in Sam, though he could not place its source. Memory of hurt, of despair like a tumor, though there was no gesture from the man, no sigh, no melodrama. Nothing. But a hotness at the back of Sam's head, almost a knowledge of pain in the air, fired his tongue.

"Come in and have a cup o' tea," he said.

Jem turned quickly, with a funny look that Sam could not describe. "I'm not very good company just now," he said.

"Neither am I, most of the time. Come on. I was just going to make one."

Two men standing in the kitchen was a crowd, so Jem tucked himself behind the beechwood table and looked around. Everywhere was wood, and not white pine, good wide strips of mahogany making the place dark but rich. By contrast, a cheap round-faced clock with a bent hour hand stood on the mantel over the Aga cooker, alongside a faded photograph of a pretty middle-aged woman in a linen hat; a full ashtray; a miniature whiskey bottle with a sprig of lily of the valley in it, a tarnished pewter mug, a maximum-minimum thermometer and two well-worn books on geology. Pinned to a cupboard door was a reprinted pencil drawing of hands carving a piece of wood.

Sam put the big aluminum teapot, milk bottle, plastic sugar bowl, and two enamel mugs on the table, and sat himself down. "Ah!" he said, as he frequently does. "Ah!" The tea came out strong and leafy, and he left Jem to add his own sugar and milk.

"That drawing is by Arthur Phillips, isn't it?" The younger man nodded toward the cupboard.

"That's him, yes," said Sam, pleased. "It was a funny thing. He sauntered into the shed . . . what . . . four or five years ago. People do when they see us working. Bit of a nuisance sometimes. But this chap, tubby little fellow, took a fancy to my hands. Just stood around and sketched while I was working. I took no notice, really. He told me his name, but it didn't register. Then quite a long time afterward that picture arrived in the mail. Made a good job of it, didn't he?"

"He's very talented," said Jem Merriman. "Very sensitive, though I think he paints better than he draws." He sipped the brown tea, letting the steam condense on his open, tired eyes.

"You know of him, then?" Old Sam was making another cigarette with the ease of a lifetime, thinly, evenly, wetting the glued edge of the paper with the inner side of his bottom lip. He rubbed thumb and forefinger together dryly before rolling, and smoothed the result to a cylinder. As he lit up, flakes of paper ash drifted into the sugar bowl.

"Yes, I know him." Absently Jem fished the ash out with a teaspoon. "It's very kind of you to ask me in," he said. "I've been driving a long time."

Sam doesn't know what to do with thanks. "Where are you from?" he grunted.

"London. Cumberland originally, a long time ago." Sam put him at forty, a slight overestimation as it transpired, but forgivable in the circumstances. "I've seen Antlercraft in several places. A friend in Chatham owns one. They are beautifully fitted, real luxury." Jem smiled a half-smile.

"He must have been a rich friend," said Sam. "We build very few, but I only use the best, and the best workmanship I know. No plastic except the hulls, and no cheap frills. There still seems to be a market, though God knows where the money comes from."

"Have you had any Arabian customers yet?"

Sam thumbed in the direction of the shed. "The express cruiser, not the yacht. I can't pronounce the customer's name, but it ends in oil, the boat's to be a present for his eighteen-year-old son. His representatives came down in dark suits and a bloody great Rolls." He whistled through his few remaining front teeth. Sam could afford a Rolls, but somehow he's never acquired a rich man's mentality. "You like boats?" he said.

"I design them."

There was a startled silence. Sam got his own reaction back. "Do you?" he said. "Who for?"

"Until recently, Simon Wolfe and Partners. I'm a naval architect. I grew up in boats, my father always had one, so it seemed natural to progress from there, university and so on."

"Well, well!" said Sam. "Have another cuppa. Do you know, before I started buying fiberglass hulls I used to get most of my plans from Simon Wolfe. Very, very good they were, too." His hand described the lines of a hull in the air, as if he were touching the body of a woman and the curve of her buttocks. "I miss the timber hulls, you know. Miss 'em a lot."

The men finished their tea in silence, Jem smoking his

own cigarettes, one after the other. Sam does not like to pry, or be pried into, but he could think of no way of making conversation without asking questions. Still, it was his tea, wasn't it, and his home. "Are you on holiday?" he asked. "Bit of peace and quiet away from the big city?"

The man's top lip tightened up again, his eyes sought a safe resting place like a pair of predator-bothered birds. "In a way," he muttered. "If I like it here, and it likes me, I may stay awhile."

"You're on your own, then? No one to worry about?"

"No. No one to worry about."

CHAPTER
TWO

In three months Jo Wilder had ceased to be interested in number 26 Dundee Road, or any other number Dundee Road. It is not easy to distinguish one house from the next, as the whole terrace is rendered in cracked gray roughcast, and she located her home by the street lamp outside, and the ever-open front door constantly blocked by an old pram and a rust-diseased bicycle. In three months Jo Wilder had ceased to be interested, period. She walked beneath the reaching fingers of the past, and the sky above her head held neither sun nor lover's moon. Most of us spend our lives hoping to realize a dream, or a series of small, comfortable dreams—a summer holiday, a new coat, a win on the horses, a child. Josephine Wilder had ceased to dream. Indifference had become the norm. As she climbed the uncarpeted stairs to her tiny apartment, a voice spoke softly in her mind of waste, of uselessness, of being too damn lazy to fight, but it was easily drowned by another, always in her ears. They are dead. Those whom you loved are dead. It doesn't matter. Only things now. Plenty of money for living with. No emotion. Doesn't matter, and keep it that way. But sometimes late at night a high pipe-voice like winds over ice moaned in her ear. You need . . . you need . . . something. . . .

The door opened directly into the living room, small and white-walled, warm from the afternoon sun. Jo tapped on the side of the aquarium and said, "Hello, bubs, fishy-fishy-fish-face." The goldfish, a gift from Irish Steve, swanked his perfect tail and rose to the surface. Jo mouthed back at it. "Greedy pig," she said, tapping in a few grains of fish food.

Outside in the street kids sang "E-I, E-I-O" as they hesitated their way home from school. She watched them from the window. They were brash little tots from Penquay Junior on their way to St. Jude's, wearing plimsolls and anoraks too short in the sleeves. They came from a rough area, the sparrows, homely and raucous and prone to arbitrary bullying. Jo turned away embarrassed as a child raised two grubby little fingers. They resented the eye of interference, however remote.

She carried her shopping bag through to the kitchen, where she unpacked a carton of milk, six eggs, and two packets of dried soup. Her nose wrinkled in boredom as she surveyed the goods. "I wonder," she said, "whether I'm in a good mood or a bad mood. I can't tell unless I talk to someone." She listened for sounds from the rooms downstairs, where Peggy and little Joanna lived, but heard only the drip of her own kitchen tap and the serenade of the evening thrush that crooned all summer long on the television aerial above her bedroom roof. She had leaned out to watch him as he sang, lyrical and impassioned, to an uncaring audience of pigeons and starlings. He was a Samson among the Philistines, a pearl among swine, an original thought among clichés. His song varied but his voice was unmistakable. The harsh "pink-pink" of a panicked blackbird interrupted, and all birdsong stilled. "Peg's Oedipus," said Jo to herself. "The tabby menace stalketh."

In the hallway between the living room and the other rooms of the apartment is a window of good proportions, framed in white-glossed wood with a view across the town to the sea. It was for this window that Jo had rented the place, for this view that she tolerated damp walls in the bathroom, ill-hung doors, and shabby fittings. A redeeming feature it was, and she had written very small on the side of the frame, "Jo's view." Dundee Road runs atop the hill, which slopes steeply to the east and south into St. Jude's, and more gently to the south and west into the eastern area of Port Penquay. In the foreground are the backs of the semidetached houses in Perry Street; in the distance a short rank of three or four buildings, white-walled and steep-roofed, which reminded Jo of France. She bracketed them with flat hands and one squinted eye to eliminate the English view, and remembered Brittany, when she and her mother had been there. A short, recuperative holiday almost two years ago, but Mum had deteriorated when they came home.

Because of the contour, most of the harbor was out of sight, but the pier lay across the center of the view like an arm, bent slightly at the elbow, challenging the western ocean, embracing the town's feet and its huddle of boat children. At the shoulder of the pier, Jo could see the bus terminal with its clock tower and kiosk that she knew would soon be full of vulgar postcards, candy floss, toffee apples, wasps, paperbacks, and cigarettes. Spreading around the elbow was Lawder's Chandlery, which sold everything nautical and nice. The pinhead dots of orange and blue were small speedboats awaiting dashing young purchasers. Jo's eye was ever tugged, with the ritual pleasure drawing on favorite slippers brings, to the last large structure almost at the wrist of the pier. Even from her window a couple of miles away she could read ANTLERCRAFT, the big white letters on the black roof. Beneath that roof were persons very dear, so dear she did not dare dwell upon their necessity, in case, like Denny and Mum, they should meet some untimely end. There was brother Steve, closer now that he had ceased his prodigal wanderings, bending his clever head over his clever hands somewhere under the big black roof. And old Sam, who was her godfather and not obviously lovable, a distant dictator, a grand old man, full of tales.

Gently warmed as if by winter sun, Jo went to the bedroom to change. Beside the bed on a padded stool that served as a table for a clock and a lamp stood a black-framed photograph of a young man, head and shoulders. Jo said, "Hello, Denny," and the picture smiled back. "I watched the children in the street, and they are like scarecrows. I wonder how they will grow? I see some sort of metamorphosis, like butterflies, and they'll come out bright as new paintboxes and knowing all the answers to all the secret questions. It's so much nonsense, of course. They'll be like their mothers and fathers and big brothers." She paused and slowly undressed, removing a cotton shirt, blue jeans. She shivered, but not from physical cold. The voice that came from the back of her neck, just below the nape, and made her head bow, said, "Where are you going?"

"Where am I going?" she whispered. "Denny, where are you? I have walked about the streets of our town and I've never believed you are gone. I always feel I shall walk around a corner, in the market maybe, where you always talked to the flower lady, and you'll be there. . . . I've seen you many times these eighteen months . . . bits of you in other men's faces and backs and walks." She spoke lightly, with no tears, and with laughing in her voice added, "I'm happy to dream, Den. It brings me most of my pleasure."

She turned from the picture to remove, shyly, the rest of her clothes. The body reflected in the wall mirror was pale cream, freckled on the shoulders like nutmeg, and slender with a wiry, unbony thinness. Jo does nothing to deserve or preserve her figure. She lost interest in sailing and swimming, and now moves only in self-restricted areas around Port Penquay. There are borders which she never crosses; never walks the High Moor or the cliff pathways below Fort Hill, never goes into the sea or aboard a boat that is leaving, never uses Pete's Café in Ruby Lane, though Pete and Mrs. Pete miss her. She never even glances along the scarcely noticeable track that once led to the forest of spruces and the place of loving.

She gazed at her reflection without expression. "I would like to feel beautiful again," she said. "Like I used to feel with you, Denny. I would like to strike some sparks from a flinty man." She hugged herself tightly, and her red hair fell across her face.

Five months ago—no, six now—Frances Wilder died and all of Port Penquay mourned in its various ways. Many platitudes were uttered, but nonetheless genuine for being platitudes; grief has a limited vocabulary. It was said, "She was not old," and "Why does it always happen to the good people?" And there was barely enough room in the cramped churchyard behind St. Bartholomew's-on-the-Quay to fit all the people in. Many stood on the ancient flat gravestones of their ancestors. Frances Wilder had been ill for a long time, but very few had known it, not even her son Stephen, who was building boats on the western seaboard of Canada until shortly before her death.

Jo had called him home against her mother's wishes, and he had stood, lean and brown and somehow foreign, very seriously throughout the service, while old friends eyed him sideways and allowed their minds to wander over what he had become and how he had changed. Until the vicar cried "Ashes to ashes" and reminded them to be solemn.

Roland Kemp, in whose grocery and wine shop Frances had worked for many years, broke down and hid his big head in his fat, delicate hands as the earth was cast upon the small coffin. Old Sam, lifelong a friend, stood with his spine straight as a plumbline, now and again rubbing his wet nose on the back of his wrist. Many of the patrons of Port Penquay Cruising Club were there, and many an unspoken question hung in the air as to how the club would ever be so pleasant again without the kind, round face that was always behind the bar on Friday and Saturday nights. Properly, no one voiced the fear, but the shaking heads and indrawn breaths were enough.

Even women had liked Frances, despite the potential threat a pretty widow poses, and over a reviving drink or two they recalled with vague relief that she had never looked at another man in the years she had been alone, though a few had looked at her. And hadn't she been as heartbroken as Jo when her prospective son-in-law, Denny Davies, had been drowned? But never made a fuss. Put a fence around their private hell so you'd never know it was there. Legends are created from such eulogies, and Frances might have smiled. The quiet, decent eyes watched Jo and her brother Steve as they stood, awkward with grief, smoking with sad hands, and speaking together like acquaintances. Folks left them alone but for a squeeze of the elbow, a brief pat on the shoulder, and from Andy Wain, who suffers terribly from depression, a muttered "Keep your chin up, love," to Jo.

Two months later Jo was still waiting for the numbness to dissipate, as it does by excruciating stages after a limb has gone to sleep, but it did not, and gradually she grew accustomed to carrying the deadweight, as a dog will carry a paralyzed leg. Either no one noticed, or everyone politely ignored the deformity, and Jo looked physically as she always had, which made it easy.

She and Steve hovered uncomfortably in Gypsy Cottage, incapable of decisions about a future so miserably tempered by the past, silent in their diverse efforts to accommodate the change, each fearing to distress the other further by the callousness of material planning. But there was a storminess in Jo's brother which fitted their name. He had elbowed about the cottage, uneasy as a threatened dog, and with no work. He had fretted over the possibility of returning to Canada, but the town was strong in his background and Jo was his only kin.

Old Sam rescued the situation—whether inadvertently or purposely, only he knows—by offering Steve a place with Antlercraft. It suited them both, and very soon Steve had converted the old loft above the workshop into a bachelor apartment. It was smaller than Gypsy Cottage, but he felt free in it, though why his always beloved old home should have so oppressed him, not even articulate Steve could explain. It may have been the treacle sadness that filled the rooms and coated the furniture so that his fingertips felt tacky after touching it. It may have been the bare patches in the back lawn, worn by Jo's pacing feet as she stared out to sea and the jagged teeth of Windways Point. Whatever the reason, and not without a guilty backward glance, Steve moved out, and Jo, trusting his instinct, did likewise. Events had changed the easy circling pattern of her life, leaving no way back, as a heart beats. Her eyes gave up with relief the strain of conjuring boats from the tawny-silver crease where the sky folds into the sea. She moved into town and allowed the grass to grow in the lawn again, and allowed Port Penquay to forget its losses and accept its changes as people are meant to do.

CHAPTER
THREE

Pain for Jem Merriman was a thing to be exercised. He could not sit in his single room at the Albion Hotel staring it in the face. It had taken residence with him, and tapped him on the shoulder as he shaved, so that he cut his upper lip and his eyes watered; and it sat in the opposite armchair while he tried to read and distracted his attention with its fidgeting. It was so heavy and fat that the cushions caved under it, and it demanded to be fed with spoonfuls of recrimination and cups of syrupy self-pity.

The old traveling alarm clock that Jem had brought in his one suitcase was showing eleven-thirty P.M. and tripping heavily over the seconds when its owner suddenly threw his book aside and ran from the room, snatching his coat on the way. But the ponderous, whining footsteps followed him down the dark stairs and out onto Harbor Road, and the stagnant smell of its body was in his nostrils.

The air was tranquil down along the front, but high above was a rushing sound that mingled with the clock-clunk of moored boats against the harbor wall, and a north wind, going around to the east, urged the clouds seaward. The town turned its back and drew its houses close. Light still poured from the big hotels, splashing invitations on the pavements, but Jem had no desire for entertainment. He wanted salt on his face and cold, clean, uncolored air. He crossed the road and walked quickly along beside the water. Whiskers of wind at the Yacht Club mooring across Days Harbor set slender masts moving, and rigging at the crosstrees rattling softly. Jem's

companion pain took a step back at such a good memory
sound, old and beloved. The white moon shone out over
the sea, making all the world ghostly. Even Penquay light,
biting at the tide in its steady rhythm, lost its self-
importance. Jem fisted his hands into his pockets, moving
on. He reached the roundabout by the bus depot and
waited while a car turned on to the pier. Mr. Antler's
Arabs crossed his mind, and the taste of strong sweet tea
echoed on the back of his tongue. Last week, only last
week, and it seemed . . . He strode across the road.

On the seaward side of the shoulder of the pier is the
eastern corner of Half Moon Bay. The beach is over thirty
feet down, at the base of a steep landslide of rocks, and
only children and adolescents go this proving way, for it is
both difficult and dangerous. Jem clambered over the wall
at the invitation of the waves breaking in the moonlight
and the breeze eddying down, curling under the main wind
that rustled all the pines in Fort Woods way above.

The moon was just past full, jumping and prancing
through the night, and it was the only illumination in the
niche of rocks below the wall where the soft orange glow
of the town did not penetrate. Jem semi-crouched in the
sinister blackness and welcomed the small blade of fear
that could cut the cord between himself and his fat companion. The stone flats glimmered around him, unreal, and
there was a smell of drains and salt and gull droppings and
last season's thrown-away sandwiches. To tempt danger, to
throw daring sand into its eyes, Jem started to descend
with his back to the rocks, keeping his face to the sea.
There was a determined grimace on his mouth as he
launched both legs out and down. He slid only three feet
before his shoes hit rock, but the jolt reminded him that he
would not be able to walk away from anything with a
broken ankle. Again he pushed off, lying on his shoulders,
scrabbling and fighting and cursing over rocks that were
viciously sharp, or round and slimy and ungrippable, and
his head jerked on his neck as his buttocks banged from
one to the next. The toe of his right shoe caught in a
crevice and stopped him so rapidly he almost toppled.
He'd ripped a nail and skinned the heels of his hands and
was strangely exhilarated. His eyes, too, had widened in
fear and in the darkness of the night, so that he could see

now what lay below. Cold sweat glued his hair to his scalp and his shirt to his back, and a doggedness dragged him toward the ocean.

The lower rocks were in the tideline, huddling beneath clots of seaweed. Jem leaped from one to the next, but momentum got the upper hand and he slipped into a rock pool and banged his head, so that the world went suddenly very far away. Little streaks of white light filled the sky, but they were not of astronomical origin. For a moment the night was pregnant with threat, things hidden in the cracks of the rocks, lying menacing among the weeds with gaping razor jaws and bodies thick as a man's thigh. Jem saw safety in the lonely, moony sea. He jumped the last six feet to the sand and went in over his shoes, then ran through the soft dusty stuff, cracking driftwood and crunching on glass.

There is a bank of pebbles that composes most of the beach; the sea is a builder here. No other sound is the same as feet walking upon beach pebbles. Jem stamped through them, waded through them so that their thin, tangy smell rose with the chafing noise, and so preoccupied was he that the voice borne on the gusting breeze came only slowly to him. He stopped walking to listen. In time with the breaking waves a man shouted, "You're not the only pebble on the beach!"

"Oh, no!" muttered Jem softly. "Other people's insanity I don't need." He peered along the beach and saw a flash of white close to the sand. Carefully, now flinching at the pebbles' rattle, he moved up the beach toward the shelter of the dunes. He held his breath at the loudness of his progress which seemed to drown the sea and all the night. He thought of removing his shoes but remembered the glass, so he went slowly, causing trickles of pebbles that were avalanches and feeling that the world was one big ear.

"Poem!" cried the strange voice, halting Jem as his foot found sand. "If you want to win her hand,/ Let the maiden understand,/ That she's not the only pebble on the beach." Someone kicked hard at the stones, and they flew chattering away like birds.

Jem smiled. Appropriate advice from a disembodied voice laid into his mind like a fish hook. Down by the sea a figure ran to meet the curling waves, a slim, tall man whose hair blew like gossamer under the moon. "Wait, wait!" he called, hopping backward. As he removed his boots and white wool socks, he told the sea, "Keep back a minute!" He ran to the very lace of the water, teasing it to touch him. The sand must have been as cold as ground ice. He danced a taunting dance and waved his arms and sang, "The Pobble who has no toes,/ Had once as many as we;/ When they said, 'Someday you may lose them all,'/ He replied, 'Fish fiddle de-dee!'"

The sea rushed in urgently, but he skipped nimbly away and shouted, "Look! He has gone to fish for his Aunt Jobiska's Runcible Cat with crimson whiskers." The lines ended in a thud as he stumbled over a rock and fell flat on his back in the pebbles. He laughed aloud, then became silent, and instinctively Jem knew he was looking up at the heavens as a primitive man might have done. The moon was behind cloud and the tiny iridescent points that are suns like our own showed in the blue-gray night. Jem felt a tug of sympathy in his heart as he too looked up, and a need to be a significant chip of color in the mosaic of destiny. Ten years, he thought, opening a door in the wall of suppression so that the thoughts trooped in, cartwheeling tumblers, faces in procession. Pictures of places and a lady and a little girl and sails and sunsets, and warm and cold smiles, and empty rooms.

The foamy dark water sneaked up on the strange man as he lay with his head pillowed on his hands. "I am the Akond of Swat!" he announced, and laughed and laughed until there were big tears in his voice. "The Akond of Swat without a Swattery or a Swatdom. What can this fool do?" He giggled gently, like brook water under a bank. "Are you there, Mum? The Duchess of Swat—no, Akondess. Akondira of Swat. I miss you, dear old Akondira."

The moon ran out like a playing child and lit the pewter sea and fell upon the men's faces. The stranger lifted his hands and seemed to hold the moon in his palms. "A giant step for mankind . . ." Then he threw his hands outward, but the moon did not fall. "I love you, moon!" he yelled, and "Bloody hell!" as the sea froze his feet with a quiet kiss.

Jem sat awhile, smoking, after the man had collected his

boots and wandered away singing "Barbara Allen" in a tenor voice that complemented the night. Then his legs got cold, so he moved on through the soft sand with his thigh muscles trembling, following his nose. His heart was a stone and the world was empty and he carried the obesity of pain on his back and it had claws that bit deep into his shoulders. Such are some miseries that even the loss of a total stranger can make a soul sick. So it was with Jem, and his logic loathed it and his common sense tried to ignore it, but it made him ache with emptiness. He plodded in unconscious rhythm with the sea that was waltzing to the "Blue Danube," a sigh and a swish and a four-beat retreat, and he lived with the small things in and around it. The limpets and the periwinkles and sea anemones and rag worms and mussels, who have no self-consciousness and yet are aware. And he wished he could feel the cold rock at his feet and pull his shell down tight around him and have no thought.

Then the air about him was confused by a little dog. It circled him, hopping at his heels, wriggling away in mock fear, squatting at his feet with its tail frantic, speaking in light, happy barks.

"Trix, who have you kidnapped, you canine fool?" said a voice thinned by sandhills. "Come in, whoever you are. She's just a tease." The dog disappeared in a fog of sand. Jem followed, through a gully that widened into a rocky pocket in the breast of the dunes. A fire burned there, well constructed from driftwood and sweet as a pine forest from the dry cones that crackled in it. Gorse bushes with golden flowers overhung the place, so that it was a cave smelling of vanilla custard.

Trix ran to her owner, gently biting his hands as he tried to catch her collar. Jem's eyes photographed the scene. Unbidden, it would return, time after time. The man was sitting beside his fire with the brown-and-white dog playing about him, and they both laughed at a private joke. The man wore a red-and-green-checkered lumber jacket and thick dark pants. His hair was dark gold in the flame light and his eyes were brighter than the dog's.

Jem went closer, finding responses stiff as seldom opened books, deeply buried under the dust of convention. But when I touch it, he thought, it will not be there. It's like neon or glowworms. But still he moved toward the fire and the man and the dog. The man's laugh was sheer delight, with no bevel of hysteria, and it sent the fat companion far into the shadows beyond the firelight.

Trix backed up with a bark and the man said, "Come and sit down, friend or foe. But not foe, I think, or Trix would know it." He squinted across the flames and his face was young, and wise as Solomon's.

"Thank you," said Jem awkwardly.

"Sit! There is a rock for you. What have you lost?"

As Jem sat and stretched his knees and fingers to the blaze, Trix pushed her healthy pink nose under his elbow and into his lap. She wriggled and snuffled and demanded affection. "Oh, I like you," said Jem softly. "You're a proper sweet bundle. You could come home with me." They gazed at each other in instant mutual devotion. "Was it you I heard on the beach?" Jem asked the man, his eyes locating the cider bottle propped up among the stones.

"I'm a little drunk." The man laughed. "But only a little. Two pints and I'm gone. Alcohol and I are ill-acquainted, mainly because I get very ill on very short acquaintance. My mother used to say that I was probably born inebriated, because I'm always like this."

"You are a poet, too."

"No, no. I have a sticky mind for words, is all. There is something in poetry that is more than the juxtaposition of sentences. It sings what I have not the wit to think." His mode of speech fitted him easily. Jem noticed only its lilting cadence.

"I like to listen to poetry," said Jem. "But I don't understand very much."

"I doubt if I do, but it makes me feel good. And yes, sometimes it helps the world make sense to me." He leaned forward, his hands over his knees and his eyes black. "You see, there is so much that is wrong, so many things that men neglect. The sea and the rivers and the animals and birds and . . . Well, you name it. Except money, of course, and the blessed, desirable material things. Men are good, you know, but it seems they have no time to care. They work so hard, and for the wrong rewards. In such a world there is a special need for the values of dreams and poetry." He laughed suddenly. "I bore people to distraction. Old Sam, the darling man, yawns in my face sometimes. But he likes poetry too, and has a complete Shakespeare on his shelf. And Robert Burns. And he quotes bits at me like 'O wad some Pow'r the giftie gie us, To see oursels as others see us!' with a very sour expression. So I say, 'Then gently scan your fellow man . . .' and he gets quite red in the face. I'm sorry, I'm very full of myself tonight.' He opened his arms to the black sky. "It is the fault of the moon and the stars." He stopped and grinned.

Jem and the dog had relaxed together in a blanket of warmth. Jem had not listened to the words, but he soaked up the enthusiasm and vitality of the speaker. "You don't work, then?" he said.

"And why not? I'm young and strong and a fair carpenter. To waste a talent would be selfish. I follow where my abilities lead me. Where else can I go?"

"I'm sorry," said Jem hastily. "It was what you said about working for the wrong rewards. I assumed you disapproved of the whole system."

"You have a tiredness," said the man softly, staring at Jem's face without offense or shyness. "Your mind is very low and your spirit tries hard to pull it up. Brave little things, our spirits, and strong as oxes. Here, have a drink. I don't need any more, as you witness."

Jem took the bottle and unscrewed the cap. He hesitated, wondering whether to wipe the top with his sleeve, then drank anyway. The stranger chuckled and the unspoken thought was known. He said, " 'Stay me with flagons, comfort me with apples: for I am sick of love.' "

Softened by the drink, Jem said, "What does one do with a sadness? Mine only goes when I face a physical challenge like climbing a mountain or jumping a stream that I know is too wide. I think I can get far enough away from it to be myself and come to terms, but it catches up. I'm not coping so well as I always imagined I could."

The man ran both hands through his hair as if massaging his brain. Jem moved Trix's head carefully, then threw a couple more sea-blanched twigs onto the fire. The smell of woodsmoke reminded him of childhood Guy Fawkes parties and huge bonfires. The world was very tall then, and the rockets reached the moon.

"Do you like our town?" asked the man.

"Very much, the little I've seen."

"Be careful of it. We are very insular. When families of families of families live in a place, they feel they own it with an inbuilt deep-down right." He smiled again. Indeed it seemed to Jem that his face could never be sad. "I could quote you line upon line about sadness," he said, "but it wouldn't make you feel better. Or about happiness, but that would be kicking a fallen man. You are alone with it and your light is dim. Would it help to tell?"

Jem played with Trix's ears and became absorbed in the texture and coolness of them. There is nothing that has the same softness and live strength as a dog's floppy ear. Finally he said, "My wife left me for another man. It's strange, but it's not her going, it's my inability to see why that makes me sad. I'm pining for something I probably never had, and I'm quite lost."

"I see," said the stranger gently. "But you have found words for it, and that is a beginning. 'Nothing so difficult as a beginning.' I know it. I have tried so many times to encourage people to conserve the environment, in small ways, nothing that would require great sacrifice or effort, but I get the same response as an encyclopedia salesman." He shrugged. "I will persevere. It is the way of my life and not just a hobby besides. But sometimes it gets very big and I get very small." For the first time he did not smile, and Jem searched for words that would conjure the vibrancy, but none came, and a silence grew.

The night breathed steadily around them, taking the woodsmoke up to the north wind, and the sound of dry sand slithering grain over grain down the dunes was audible between the spittings of the fire. The gorse scraped black thorns together, and there were fainter, unidentifiable creakings and jostlings from other night folk going about their business. From the sheltered pocket the sea was only a faint rumble, felt through the soles of the feet.

Jem took another swig of cider, then eased Trix onto the sand. She eyed him as a pardonable traitor, but not yet forgiven. "I'd better be on my way," he said. "Thank you for . . . Thanks."

The stranger stood with him. "And I must go and watch

the tide," he said, smiling. "I have this perverse notion that it cannot come in without me." They walked single file to the beach, where the wind blew, and they shivered after the heat of the fire, and their fingers searched the deepest parts of their pockets. "We'll meet again," said the stranger. "Everyone knows me. Ask on the pier."

"Who for?"

"The name is Wilder." With a cheerful wave he moved toward the crying silver sea. The moon drowned in cloud.

CHAPTER
FOUR

Our town of Port Penquay is best viewed from the harbor, or from the end of the pier if you prefer a more stable platform. It has a higgledy-piggledy beauty that comes from the blend of original granite cottages, Victorian terraces with austere faces, and a few later additions which shine white and expensive, mostly on the Fort Hill area, to the left of the pier as you look up. The silver-gray slate roofs cover everything. A red tile would stand out like a hooligan in a monastery. The slates originate far away southwest, from a small quarry that has roofed our town since time began. It is still surviving, though by its craftsmen's fingertips, and tourists go to watch the two brown, prune-skinned men who measure and tap and split the slate, so that your eyes bulge at the skill of it. They say little, these two, and what they utter is measured, tapped, and split in the cadence of their work. So is Penquay roofed and repaired with the cold satin from the earth. Except for the Market Hall roof that is new asbestos like corrugated paper, and the Little Theater roof that is brown galvanized iron, and the Pola Cinema that is flat concrete, and the entertainments center that is so tall and complicated as to appear roofless. All the exceptions have occurred, it is said, because of economics.

For all its slate, the town is not gray. It is white and black and yellow and silver like a clean herring gull, and it is green in many parts. Up on the eastern hill above St. Jude's are St. Peter's Gardens, and he would have been pleased to place his feet upon the paths, fisherman or not.

The land belongs to St. Peter's church, which is larger and barer than St. Bart's, and was landscaped by a curate called Simpson early last century. He must have loved trees, for he studied them and collected them from far and wide. The group of horse chestnuts show their crowns high above the houses and are pink- and white-candled, and much besieged in autumn by small boys with sticks. The glossy new conkers in the white pith of their shells are like horse's eyes. There are laburnums, and two pagoda trees with white flowers, and maples from Norway and Japan, and silver birches by the lake in the center, and a may tree that looks so good you could eat it when it blossoms. And on the mound beside the lake is a lofty tree of heaven, with, at a respectful distance, a small, purplish Judas tree. If one knew all the legends of trees, as Mr. Simpson surely did, there would be a tale for St. Peter's Gardens and a story in every step.

Nor are these the only trees in town. London planes march green and flowering in May along the length of Penquay Road, casting green shade. There are cotoneasters and shrubs on the pier roundabout, and copper beeches to decorate Fort Road as it winds upward. The metallic purple-black leaves patter like steady soft rain all summer long. The hotels along the promenade, the front, as it is called, have no gardens but compensate with tubs of hydrangeas, wallflowers, or primulas outside on the pavement, or mossy baskets of petunias hanging from the balconies.

When the sun is right it breaks through two windows of St. Bartholomew's and makes a fixed kaleidoscope on the pavement of every color in the glass-stainer's repertoire. It freckles the seats where the old salts sit, and lies upon their heads and shoulders so that they become harlequins. They sit, these old souls, all season long beneath the stained-glass shepherds, gazing meditatively at the harbor. They wear navy jerseys with their necks loose in their tortoise collars. Occasionally one will light a tarry pipe and point the stem and murmur to a companion, who will nod sagely and wheeze a little and cast a wise, penetrating eye at the horizon. They evoke tall ships, miles of rigging hung about with straining matelots, diving bows under, and Tierra del Fuego and lashings to the tiller. The tourists photograph them, have their little ones sit upon the old knees, ask questions, and try valiantly to understand the answers given in a dialect that is verbal toffee. Often a few coins change hands.

There is a rumor in town about these dear old men. It is said that a minibus collects them each day from Penquay Old Folk's Home, that clothes and packed lunches are provided free, and that the local photography shop, Blenchin's, gives them a percentage. Most of them have never been to sea except on the Penquay Darby and Joan Club day trip to Sandholm, and many of them normally wear spectacles, which may account for the glazed, cogitative stares. But this is only gossip, and there is much of it in Port Penquay.

In the summer it is difficult for residents who like to wander out of an evening for a little entertainment to find a place that is not packed tight as a bale with sunburn and Ambre Solaire. The Anchor and the Black Horse, May's Bar, and all the hotel lounges, so quiet and amiable in winter, become angry as wasp swarms in season. Even the Yacht Club has so many temporary members that its lush blue carpeting gets crushed and sad like grass under a marquee. But Port Penquay Cruising Club is a bastion against invasion solid as Victoria Pier.

At the western end of Half Moon Bay a natural causeway of granite tongues out into the sea, and man has improved upon nature, as he will, by leveling the surface and filling a few holes so that the Spit is a tidy and perfect mooring for the boats of the club members. The tides have scooped a good deep hole on the western side of the causeway so that even deep-drafted craft can lie in safety. The clubhouse stands at the head of the Spit on Gypsy Lane, a rectangular, self-effacing building of stone and wood and slate, with tiny square windows curtained in red sailcloth tied back with white rope so as to be properly nautical.

For those who like to visualize exactly the background against which people move and sit and talk, the interior of the club is so: a foyer with a photograph of the first club commodore, Captain James Hythe-Wick, stern-eyed and so heavily whiskered as to appear to be staring over a gorse bush; a row of fancy coat hooks with plastic knobs

on, and a piece of remnant Axminster donated by Smith's
in the High Street. Turn right through the glass door and
you are in the bar, and a good bar too. The counter is
clinkered pitch-pine and the top is oak plank from the
Sebastian, a gaff cutter that broke up on Windways back
in the twenties. Behind it, Alex the steward keeps bright
rows of glasses, bottles of spirits, sherry barrels with artifi-
cial grapes, pewter tankards, and liqueurs of lurid color,
all reflected in the mirrored shelves. It is a temptation of a
bar, and lighted just right in soft gold, and gives the mouth
to watering just to stand before it.

The room itself is gray-walled, with red bench seats all
around, and plenty of comfortable chairs drawn up to
round wooden tables. Each table has an ashtray dead
center when Alex opens the bar, for he is a tidy man, and
it must be a source of irritation to him that his order is
turned so readily and regularly into chaos. His neatness
extends to the shelves of books about boats, *Lloyd's Regis-
ters* and copies of *Yacht World* that stand in one corner.
The books are arranged by height and date and so closely
packed that the spines have been broken by hard fingers
prying them out. There is a dart board and potted plants
pruned to perfection, display cases of knots that no one
but a boy scout ever ties, and port and starboard lights of
salmon-pink copper and near-white brass. Fortunately, the
atmosphere and the members are neither too polished nor
too disciplined.

At the far end of the bar is a wide archway sealed by a
pair of velvet drapes that gives onto the committee room
cum dance floor. On Saturday nights the music strikes up,
the curtains are flung wide, and the Port Penquay Cruising
Club abandons itself to the quickstep, foxtrot, and old-
fashioned waltz.

And that, apart from the cellar which is behind the bar,
and the bane of Alex's life, being too small to swing a
firkin of beer in, and the powder room, is Port Penquay
Cruising Club. In case there is an eyebrow of query being
raised, there is a gentlemen's room too, but it is of a size to
swing absolutely nothing in, and many gents saunter out
into the night. There is a large and inoffensive oak behind
the clubhouse that bears the brunt of these wanderings,

and a discreet "Visiting the tree" can be heard in the bar after dark.

Like any club, the PPCC has members who regularly patronize the place, and those who come only when their wives bring them. Among the former are Sam Antler and his so-called lads, the men who work for him. It is something to be proud of in town, to be one of Sam's lads. He employs only the best, and several past lads have become noted shipwrights. At least twice a week Sam can be found in his favorite corner, next to the bookshelves, under a sepia print of a straight-bowed, heavy-sailed old ketch called *Eleanor*, and on this particular Tuesday he was joined by Jacko, Ivor, and Steve; and Roger Payne, who is a dental technician and mends Port Penquay's fractured dentures. Pat "Jacko" Brent is Sam's engineer. What he doesn't know about marine equipment, ancient and electronically modern, could be written on a thumbnail. He is an ageless man, plump-framed and thin-haired, and he cannot remember a time when engines have not figured largely in his dreams, waking and sleeping. He handles them with a confident respect that is greater than love, and if he can't make a thing work it may as well be dropped in the harbor. So, although he may have his faults, Jacko is much loved for this talent alone, Not only is he addicted to his machinery, but also to his friends, whom he places only slightly below the Perkins diesel, and this devotion inclines him toward contorted anthills of thought where confusion is master.

Consequently, when, after a quiet quaff of beer, he said, "We ought to do somethin' about Jo," there was a mental union of the group around the table, a construction of soft wary bars, to prevent him barging into fallacy and hurting himself. Old Sam sucked air through his teeth. Ivor Bailey caressed his slim, fine face with slim, fine fingers. Roger Payne pushed his glasses up the bridge of his nose with his middle finger. Steve nodded silently. They had last seen Jo on Sunday night, matching drinks with Colin Whale, who is a ladies' man and a liar. Jo had been laughing, but anyone with an ear for laughter could hear the sigh of high winds on ice behind it.

"She's a good looker," remarked Roger. "I like red hair."

"I don't," said Ivor. "But she's very sensitive, very understanding."

"What's wrong with red hair?" demanded Jacko.

"Nothing, dear boy. I just prefer the quieter tones, the beiges and browns and grays, the colors of winter. Jo is autumn, you know, like a flame."

Jacko glared at Ivor's lifted chin, smooth as ivory. "She's goin' downhill fast," he muttered. "Nothin' inside." He patted his wide chest with a raggy-nailed hand. "Colin Whale, huh!"

Old Sam sipped his beer and licked his lips. His mind skated delicately as a water beetle around the island of the subject. "Wait a minute," he said quietly, commanding attention. In their company he is, well, not God, but not far off Saint Peter. "We should ask someone who knows her best. Steve?"

Steve's face, partly shadowed, bore the deep parentheses of laugh lines, but his forehead creased in a frown. "Jacko is right," he said. "She has the bravery and despair of old soldiers, but even they get shell-shocked. I haven't seen much of her in the past two years, and I am selfish. I don't want to see her ache. Suffering is so raw and personal."

"So how can we put her right?" said Jacko. Of all his friends, he loves Steve the best. His laughing, singing words have woven magic spells for Jacko since they were boys together at Penquay Junior. Steve could solve the riddle of the world, and explain the function of the universe as if it were a two-stroke engine.

"I don't know," said Steve simply. "If the stains of living were so easily washed away, how would we know we had lived? For the present, Colin Whale gives Jo light relief, fun, a totally opposite viewpoint. Could be, he is what she needs."

"I wonder whether he's after her bit of money," said Sam sourly. "That cottage sold for a good price, and Jo got three-quarters of it. I don't agree he's what she needs at all."

Steve smiled. "Be careful, Sam," he said lightly. "If Jo has any fight left at all, it is because she has pulled her world together and has its structure, so." He built a box of his hands. "If we meddle, it could fall apart."

Sam said, "Well, I learned one thing early on, when I

was in the navy. Don't batter your head against a brick wall, there's always a sneaky way round." There was an expectant silence, but Sam had apparently run out of stealth. He fumbled for his tobacco tin and kept his eyes averted.

"We should do something." Roger blew his nose with a sound reminiscent of Penquay foghorn, smoothed out the handkerchief, folded it neatly in the original creases, and put it back in his pocket. Ivor cringed.

"The Brain Trust!" Jenny Stottbury loomed large over them. She is Sam's emanuensis, and ample in every department. She hooked up a chair with her foot and sat, stiff-backed, hiding a large gin in her fist. "What's up?" she asked. "Someone pinched the crib board, or have you all been dropped from the skittles team?"

"This is a gatherin'," said Jacko solemnly. "We want to do somethin' for Jo."

"What's the problem?"

Jacko cradled his glass in both hands. Inside his head all things were clear, oiled, sweet-running, and the problem stood proud as an ill-fitting valve, but he has a block the size of a dinosaur when it comes to articulation. "She's . . . she's losin'," he said.

Ivor intervened. "Denny Davies was drowned, then her mother passed away, and Jo has given up. I sense that aura about her. It's probably a complex defense mechanism." He sipped daintily from his martini, straightened his imaginary pleats, and folded his hands.

"What do you think, Sam?" said Stotty.

"I remember Amy," he said, pinching the thin fold of old skin under his chin. His eyes softened at he looked upon a fifty-year-old memory, a green valley where pain was only dew upon the grass. How his heart had hurt for beautiful Amy. "She was ten years older than me and I had a crush on her, like one does. Lovely Amy. She had long chestnut curls and Irish gray eyes, dark gray. She lived next door in Days Lane, before they demolished it. Now, her fiancé died, TB was a killer then, and Amy pined away. She covered it, laughed, joined the parties, but she was haunted, and her white face at the window haunted me. I can see it now.

"Anyway, she disappeared, and later they found her off

Angel Point. Said it was an accident, but I knew different. I mind my own business, as you know, but I have seen the haunted look of Amy about our little Jo. . . ." He shook his head and huffed a deprecating snort at his own sentimentality.

"Oh, no!" There were tears in Jacko's throat.

Steve patted his heavy shoulder. "I won't let one bad thing happen to my dear sister," he reassured. Jenny was humming "Once in Love with Amy."

"Perhaps she needs a good man," said Roger.

"Ah, perhaps," said Sam. "Whose round is it?"

CHAPTER
FIVE

As May opened the door to June and seasonal rates in the hotels rose correspondingly, Jem Merriman felt obliged to look for more reasonable accommodation. In the few weeks he had spent in Port Penquay he had explored the town and the cliffs and the High Moor thoroughly enough to encourage further exploration in the area. There was nowhere else he wanted to be, except at home with Annette and Susan, which was plainly impossible, and he felt the need for a base and a job. The money was running low, and for a man accustomed to the possibilities wealth offers, it was a nagging thing, like a pea under a princess's mattress. When he saw the advertisement in the Sandcliff and Penquay *Gazette,* he drew a fine red line around it and set off to inquire further.

When the Polytechnic was built—called Pretty Poly because it is—the planners decided to ease the burden on the public of providing lodgings for the student influx by adding self-catering apartments behind the college. Great approval was heard until one voice remarked that these units would be empty during all the vacations and consequently not cost-effective. The plan hung in precarious balance until a bright soul came up with the idea of renting the apartments to tourists as holiday accommodation while the students were away. Hasty sums were done, tenders invited, architects woken from drawing-board dreams, and lo and behold, to use Sam's phrase, a croplet of modern boxes sprang up overlooking St. Peter's Gardens. It was in pursuit of one of these that Jem Merriman arrived at the Town Hall in Upper High Street.

The Town Hall is not easily accessible. Its dull gray face is pockmarked with brown wooden doors, but the spaghetti corridors behind them lead nowhere. There is a dearth of signboards, the commissioner always seems to be on a tea break, and the smoky-cream walls and green office doors are devoid of information. Before Jem found the section he required, he had filled in an application for Council housing, another for rates assessment, and even exchanged a few garbled and cross-purpose words with the Rodent Control Officer. That he still was surrounded by the debilitating fog that emanated from his fat companion did not help. You need all your wits about you in the Town Hall.

He had to wait a long time to be seen, though there was no queue, but finally an officious young man called him to the desk and asked his business. As Jem spoke, the young man was already shaking his head and toying with a thin folder. "None vacant until the end of the month," he said. "Then they're booked by tourists right through to October. Oh, wait, there is one. Suitable for four persons. Just for yourself, is it?" Jem nodded. "Sorry!" The folder slammed.

"I'd book it all season," said Jem.

"I'm sorry, but we don't favor long lets."

"But I'll pay anyway."

"I'm sorry, but it would rob others of holiday accommodation."

"What difference does it make?"

"I'm sorry, but it is Council policy. We must be seen to be fair. There would doubtless be complaints if we let apartments to single people when whole families could occupy them. The rates are very reasonable." He smiled an eyeless smile.

His patronizing tone awoke the anger in Jem. "I'll report you for overcrowding," he snapped. "And for discrimination, and undercutting the hoteliers!" He walked out. He chose the wrong door and had to recross the office. The young man gave him a supercilious smile.

"Fuck you too," muttered Jem under his breath.

He got lost again on the way out.

CHAPTER
SIX

At seven A.M. on Wednesday Steve Wilder woke to the alarm clock, as usual, stretched and yawned, as usual, and smelled the smells of the world to see how the day was. The cold breath of the sea permeated, and the slimy iodine smell of seaweed, and the antiseptic tang of tar, and a dozen other paint, rope, orange-peel, suntan-oil, sand-on-plastic-beach-ball odors. The sun dripped through the skylight in the slanted wooden ceiling above his bed. It edged closer like a shy pup, and he pretended not to notice. The scents of wood rose strong from below, invading the caves of his mind and chivying out memories of travels and friends. Pine was Canada, icy skies and snow, and salmon in fast rivers, and the tough, warm family with whom he had lived, people so much of the Douglas-fir forests that they grew tall and straight like the trees. In his imagination, slow sweet resin would ooze from their veins instead of blood.

Mahogany was West Africa, its heavy strange smell underlying all the others like a bass in a choir, and adding the roundness and fullness of its rich body. It was the devil to plane well, but gave such reward in the pink-striped grain that it seemed to smile upon you for revealing its beauty, like a woman undressed. Oak was masculine, and British yeomanry, solid in tradition, and more than just fine wood. It was a symbol of endurance, undimmed by felling. Steve admired the muscle of oak, the tight-grained stockiness of it.

At seven-fifteen the sun sprawled on its back on his bed and made itself at home. Downstairs, Old Sam began to fry bacon, and the good salt smell of it obliterated the timber and set Steve's senses in a much more primitive key. The empty halls of his stomach echoed with anticipation, and already the edges of his teeth were ready for cutting and the glands in his jaw overflowing to do their duty. He sat up, swung his feet out, and rubbed the side of his heel on the rug that covered the wooden floor. Then he yawned, scratched his ribs with the hardened pads of his fingers, and stood up, pale in the sunlight. In his attic apartment above Antlercraft's construction shed, the walls sloped up to the ridge of the roof. He'd bought silver spruce to clad the rafters himself, and put fireproof insulation behind the wood against the roof. With Ivor's help it was done in three weeks, and was light, cozy, and "a bit bloody inflammable," said Sam. He'd criticized the window in the west wall, too. "A good blow will stove that in, come winter," he said. "Why don't you put it somewhere else?"

"I wouldn't be able to see out of it anywhere else."

"Bloody daft idea," said Sam, because he always has the last word.

Steve was pleased with his window, though winter had not yet leaned upon it. An old pane from Lawder's Chandlery, it was, and distorted so that if he moved his head the horizon appeared to move in steps. It gave the lie to the realities of science and suited his romantic soul. Every morning—and it is true that strong habits develop in short spaces of lifetimes—he yawned at the Atlantic as he pulled on his working jeans, and counted the cruisers moored at the Spit, and yearned to run free along the lonely shore.

Three dull thuds rattled the boards under his feet, shaking the window frame. Old Sam would have that glass out by hook or by crook, and before the westerlies, if he could. Steve found a tidy shirt and trotted out through his kitchen. He had his own cooker there, set in gimbals because it had come out of a boat long ago refitted, but he and Trix always took breakfast with the old man.

The workshop was sawdustily neat, the machines silent

under their hoods; the tins of brass screws, roves, tacks and nails, and hinges upon the shelves; the chisels, hand saws, clamps, hammers, and all manner of tools clipped to the wall above the long bench; the pots of glue and stains and varnishes on the opposite wall under the window. The cupboards and drawers were closed, and the various vises hung down their idle arms. Steve scuffed through a drift of wood shavings, and the sound was like autumn fallen leaves, so that he was saddened, forgetting the presence of summer. He ducked under the spiral staircase into the bathroom. It was big enough only for a washbasin and shower unit, but Old Sam does not hold with too much washing, so the shower runs infrequently for him. Anyway, he never smells of anything but wood and tobacco, and occasionally, onions.

"Morning!" Sam pushed a plate of bacon, two eggs, and fried bread across the table. "What are you doing with that brick?"

"You took it out again." The brick was red and slippery.

"The flush won't work properly. I keep telling you," Sam said.

Steve grinned. "If everyone put one in their cistern, we'd save an ocean of water, and we need to, especially in this part of the country. The reservoirs have deserts all around them."

"I don't want bricks in my lav. Want some bread?" He sawed a slice from the crusty loaf on the breadboard, and the slice was exactly half an inch thick right through. It is against all Sam's instincts to cut a crooked line.

"Please. I'll just put this back."

"I tell you, the flush won't work!" He shrugged as Steve took the brick away. "Did you get these half-baked ideas abroad?" he asked as Steve returned wiping his hands on his jeans seat. "All this saving water and oil and ecol . . . col . . ."

"Ecology."

"That's what I said. It's all very high-flown, but you might as well forget it. If there's no money in it, people won't care." He nodded finally and killed his egg yolk with a jab of the fork. The tines squeaked on the plate and set

Steve's neck hairs on end. Sam chewed noisily, trying to line up a piece of bacon on two of his seven teeth.

Steve said, "I was out till three in the *Maid* with Alan Jones. We sat upon the black ocean and teased the mackerel. It was peaceful as a lullaby, but we took very few fish. The seine nets have had them all, babes as well. Soon there will be none to breed and we shall all be grumbling. You will too, because you like your fish. Conservation is for all of us, Sam."

But Sam gave him a baggy-mouthed look that could have descaled a mackerel. He gathered the used cups and plates, stacked them in the frying pan, and dumped the whole lot under the cold-water tap to soak. "Your turn to do the washing up," he said spitefully.

Later, with his elbows in soap bubbles, Steve heard the organ strike up from Sam's room. Sam bought a Hammond from a lonely man who was taking up the bagpipes instead, presumably to compound his isolation. Sam was essaying Crimond, and Steve tried to sing along in the descant he'd learned as a choirboy in St. Bart's, but the chords were slippery and flew away from Sam's questing fingers. He had to stop to find them, and when he pinned one down it changed its character and brayed at him. Steve gave up his accompaniment. After a pause, Sam started in on "Tavern in the Town," loud and hearty, but his true love sat him down on a bed of mixed sharps and flats and refused to move further. A distinct "Oh, bugger!" came from the other room; then Sam's head was around the kitchen door and Sam was asking, "Are you going to start work today?"

And Steve said, " 'Compulsion doth in music lie,' but that's not quite how I interpreted the line." He wiped his hands and followed the old man out.

An early cool June day it was, and the sun upon the sea, and the keen wind upon the sea and from the southeast. High tide brimmed in the harbor at two-thirteen, sloshed and pushed and persuaded by the wind that trapped the sea and played with it and would not let it out again. A little water even slopped onto the front, and the

children thought it was fun, jumping in the puddles, but
the more mature tourists had sour, discontented faces. The
wind creased their foreheads and gritted their eyes, the
chill made them fractious. High on Fort Hill the copper
beeches blackened and roared in the distorted air, con-
vexed like a lens from the wind and sun. Along Gypsy
Lane, sand smoked from the dune summits and filled the
gutters, polishing the hawthorn boughs of the hedgerows.
On Victoria Pier, sweet and sandwich wrappers whipped at
ankles and lodged in the windowboxes of Antlercraft.

Jem had eaten at Pete's in Ruby Lane, having discovered that it was the only place in town that did not serve
chips, chips, and more chips. Also, Pete's is cheap, unpre-
tentious, and rarely full. He wandered back down to the
High Street with the taste of roast beef and two vegetables
lingering pleasantly on his tongue, breathing deeply of the
salt-edged wind and wondering what to do. He knew he
wanted to work; he missed the absorption, the focusing of
thought upon paper, and the ranging of the mind over new
possibilities. It is good to create, and Jem had created
many beautiful things. He missed the joy of it as he would
have missed daffodils, or the sky.

The old salts were muttering among themselves, turning
up their collars and thinking of cups of tea, as Jem passed.
The tentacle visions of the sea reached for him, prompting
memories of the merchant service. And, unbidden, a small
event jumped from the pool of his remembering, bright in
its colors. He could hear the crackle heat of the day, feel
the stiffening of the skin of his shoulders under the
Caribbean sun. The rod and line gave him an excuse to sit
on the hot deck planking, and he expected no fish. But as
the day held its breath so that he could hear its heartbeat,
and he thought there could never be such heat or such
tense stillness, the reel screamed and the big sea rod
arched against the rail.

They had never identified the fish. It was large and
vertically flat with a coral nibbling mouth, and such colors
as you never saw. A group of men gathered, hard men
who had seen many extraordinary things in the world, and
they whistled and exclaimed as if over a treasure chest of
jewels. It had all the subtleties of a fairy's wing, and some
of the magic too.

So they looked at it, then they weighed it, then they shrugged and went away. In minutes Jem's fish had gone gray. He inspected the pool of water it had left on the deck, half-expecting to see the iridescence there.

A patch of sadness had stuck to his mind, a momentary loss like waking from a sweet dream, and even after the fish had proved to be excellent eating, he was still wondering vaguely where the rainbow had gone.

The keen wind was bringing its tears now, heavy sobs from small torn clouds, with intervals of sun between, and the less hardy tourists went back to their hotel lounges or into the afternoon cafés. Pete filled teapots incessantly from the coughing boiling water tap. The manager of the Pola Cinema looked up at his streaming office window and smiled to think of a full house. The amusement arcade became an ants' nest of penny-wasting activity, and as Jem reached the Albion, the old salts rose from their seats and went to drink tea and play pontoon for matches in the back room of Blenchin's shop.

Sam Antler watched the pier empty with a dry smile. He was kneeling on the deck of the ketch using a making iron and calking mallet with an ease and precision achieved only by means of an elfin spell cast unaccountably over him at birth. Ivor worked beside him, marking and drilling the anchorages for stainless-steel cleats, and watching from the corner of his eye a master at his craft. Ivor never tired of watching Sam, for perfection was rare outside his small, esoteric world. He squeezed the Black and Decker trigger and the bit cut sweetly through the teak, smooth as butter.

They both saw the solitary figure drifting toward the lighthouse, carrying a fishing rod in a canvas case, a bag and a blue bucket for bait. His head was down into the wind and he looked only at his rubber-booted feet.

Sam stopped in mid-calk. "Merriman. Jem Merriman," he said, reaching for the calking cotton. Ivor pushed it toward his hand.

"I know that name," he murmured. "Where from, I wonder?"

"Have a look in the plans drawer. He worked for Simon Wolfe."

"That's it!" Ivor snapped his elegant fingers. "I say, I'd

like to meet him. He must be very talented, his designs are beautiful."

"Not your type," mumbled Sam, tapping with the lignum-vitae hammer.

"Pardon?"

"Nothing." Old Sam has never entirely approved of Ivor, being somewhat old-fashioned in his standards, but he approves of Ivor's work, and that is enough to keep him flexible. But he can't resist the occasional gibe, just so Ivor won't get complacent.

The afternoon rowed itself past easily, with only a squally shower or two like oars catching a crab. Steve sang like a bell in the workshop where he was laying off varnish on locker doors. Trix lay on her old sack in the corner worrying a doggy treat as if it were a rat. Jacko popped in and out, checking measurements in the engine housings of the cruiser. He wrote numbers on a dirty scrap of paper, frowned and whistled a pop tune, and had to stop to exhale because he can only whistle inward. Sam's hammer tapped monotonously and the rain slapped the pier wall, black and cold. At four o'clock Stotty emerged from the office with a tray of tea and ginger biscuits.

Sam dropped his tools and said "Ah!" a couple of times, rubbing his hands. He came down the ladder with knees akimbo.

Jacko was already at the tray. "You look bloody funny goin' down a ladder," he remarked, mauling the biscuits.

"Navy," said Sam. "It's the proper way."

"Looks bloody odd."

"You in a bad mood, Jacko?" asked Steve, coming in.

"Hell, no. Well, yes. I don't know. It's Sam and Amy and Jo. You know, Jo saved my life once, remember, Steve? When I fell in the pond at school. Jo pulled me out."

"And left your brains wet!" barked Sam.

Jacko subsided, but his brains, wet or dry, were painted red with a virgin anguish. In his life many problems had occurred, but never for his solving. Indeed, he'd rarely noticed a traumatic event until its tail was all but out of sight. The burden of Jo and the buzzing of unsolicited bees in his bonnet drove his mind into a corner. He chewed his biscuit, and it was grit upon his tongue.

The four men stared silently out at the rain, Ivor and Jacko side by side on a packing case, Sam on his stool sucking a dunked ginger snap, Steve standing with his head at a listening angle. The wind blew a figure in a navy coat past the door.

"Hey!" cried Sam, slopping tea from the raised mug. Jem Merriman came in, squinting uncertainly in the dimness. "Come and have some tea, lad," said Sam. "Caught anything?"

Jem handed over the bucket. "A dream of a bream," he said.

Sam pulled it out by the gills, a red bream of five or six pounds. He whistled. "That must be the first of the season. They're rare, and good eating. Look, lads. Jem, these are my lads." He made the introductions.

Steve shook Jem's hand. "Good to see you again," he said. "How is it with you?" Jem felt again the radiant warmth that to Steve's friends is no novelty, but Jem was from a nothing's-for-nothing world and sought an ulterior motive. He withdrew a pace.

"I'm fine," he said coolly. Steve nodded, his eyes mild.

Jacko went to find another cup, and Ivor attempted conversation under Sam's hawklike scrutiny. "Sam told us about you," he said. "We built a Wolfe-Antler 46 two years ago, designed especially for us."

Jem nodded. "I was in at the start of that," he said. "But I left to become free-lance. It's risky, but I've been lucky so far, with work." Sam saw the exchange of smiles and accidentally kicked Ivor's ankle.

Steve said, "Are you going to stay in Port Penquay?"

Jem paused before answering, offering cigarettes and lighting them. "I'd like to," he said on the smoke, "but I can't afford to live at the Albion for much longer, and the town is full of tourists. I've tried the caravan site below St. Jude's and every vacant apartment advertised in the paper."

Jacko reappeared with a steaming cup decorated with black fingerprints. "What about the club?" he said. "Someone might help."

"Now, that's a baby jewel of an idea," said Steve. "And maybe it will catch some light." He rocked on his toes with his arms folded, humming a snatch of "The Sailor's

Hornpipe." "What do you think, Jem Merriman? Would you like to join the PPCC and let us help you? Do you want to stay?"

"Uh . . . yes." Jem laughed suddenly. "Yes, I do."

"Oh, good!" said Ivor, and blushed.

"Thank you." Jem emptied his cup and collected his gear. He handed the fish to Sam. "Please take it, Mr. Antler. I have nowhere to cook it."

"Oh, well! Look at that, then!" said Sam in confusion. He walked Jem to the door. "Come along to the club any evening," he said. "Head of the Spit on Gypsy Lane, anyone will tell you."

" 'Bye, Mr. Antler." Jem stepped out into the rain.

Sam's old eyes followed his progress until he disappeared around Lawder's, a lonely, striding man with a privacy about him that was, to Sam, wholly admirable.

Jem had almost reached the shoulder of the pier when he saw a figure approaching. All along the front there was no one else to be seen. The sky above had closed down and turned off most of the lights, the water of the harbor was cratered by raindrops, the boats were made of sodden paper. The cranes of St. Jude's were hidden, and even the Hotel Winstone surrendered some of its whiteness to the squall. The gulls that had planed above the town all day, slicing the sky into portions as they pleased, now stood, each atop its own mooring post or cabin roof. They leaned into the wind, sure as compass needles, and were silent in their scavenging thoughts.

The girl walked quickly toward Jem, and her step said that she did not mind the weather, and the purpose of her swinging arms said that she was no tourist. She wore red Wellingtons and turned her toes out. Because there was no other focus, Jem watched her until she was within eye-meeting range. A few curls of red hair spiraled down from under her hat and stuck to the collar of her coat, seeming childlike, so that he remembered Sue. As they crossed, Jem looked into her face: fair, freckled, nice nose, mouth too wide, large dark eyes a little on the diagonal. A good face, a nice walk, free and easy and leggy.

Jo nodded, with a small, cut-off smile.

Jem passed on with a slight lift in his step, but the fat companion handed him a picture of his daughter, Sue, and the impression of Jo became a winging bird with no shadow and no weight. It flew across the sky of his mind and was gone before he blinked.

CHAPTER
SEVEN

The southeasterly kept up for two days and two nights, as irritating as a bored child. It slept for a fitful hour or two, and folks began to relax on the sun-filled beaches, wrestling deck chairs and removing jackets; then it woke up again. It had cold hands that found the smalls of exposed backs and tickled up gooseflesh on browning thighs, and it threw dry sand in sandwiches (surely this is how they gained their name, with all apologies to the earl). But as a child knows instinctively when it has gone too far, so the wind responded when annoyance turned to viciousness. It went away to play on its own, subdued by much vituperation.

A breathless evening settled on the town like golden syrup. Only the beech leaves moved, trembling on their pinched stems. The sun was in Jem's face as he walked along Gypsy Lane, a red and thoughtful eye watching its child earth turn away to woo the moon. Jem took a deep breath, hooked his thumbs in his pockets, and whistled high and full in the heavy air. He knew there were many ends untied about him, and many futures before him, but yet he had to wait, for the fruit was not ripe on the tree. Those apple steps remaining under his control were few, but juicy now, and he meant to take them. He was headed for the PPCC, and as he went he remembered Sam's craggy face and Steve's warm handshake, and Ivor's oddness, and found his feet hastening. I'm lonely, he thought, and the faces of men and women whom he had called friends, and the child who was his only child and the child of his love, peered between the polished hawthorn boughs as ghosts with untuned eyes.

There was too much distance between Jem and the club to be skated over on the blades of inconsequence. He waded waist-deep into memory that was like a hot bath with cold bubbles. His thoughts went back to a humid October day, a time when he had already known that he and Annette were on a train to limbo. He had walked and talked with her in a false effort to recapture the old sweetness. They had stumbled upon a house once grand and stabled and shuttered and gardened and carriaged. An office now, bare-walled and calendared, whose big windows were uncurtained. But the garden, through some worker-conscious whim, was partially maintained. There was a big cage with several monkeys, though why, or whose, or what for, they never knew. They had guessed quietly between themselves. There was a long brick wall with fig trees, and autumn crocuses blooming leafless among the fallen yellow leaves, and a tree with fruits like massive raspberries, bitter as the betrayal that was already seeded. He had spat out the pith and screwed his face, and been coy because he should have known better than to taste. His wife had laughed, but at him, not with him.

It was old Sam saying, "Ah, how-do Jem," that hurtled him forward through time. They stood at the club door. "I was just going in," Sam said. "Come on, I'll introduce you." He led the way, responding to greetings with his half-salute, to two men seated at the far end of the room.

"Evening! I've got a new member for you. Jem Merriman." He pulled Jem up like exhibit A. "Jem, this is Roland Kemp, our secretary, and Ken Butcher, club commodore. I'll get a drink."

Roland Kemp had a problem in uniting his hands. Separated upon his wide, corpulent belly, they slithered off the sides and lay useless beside him, so he caught the thumb of his left hand in the fingers of his right in a desperate grip. Ken Butcher, by contrast, could have wrapped his arms twice about himself. He had the bland and kindly eye of a turtle, and when he spoke to Jem, revealed a heavy impediment which gave rise to the impression that he was talking underwater.

"Are you new in town?" he gargled.

Jem nodded. "I've been here a month or so."

"Staying at the Albion." Roland Kemp's specialty is being one up.

"Yes, I come into your shop for cigarettes."

Sam brought two drinks to the table and disappeared again. "Know Sam, do you?" Roland relaxed his fingers with a snap and billowed toward the pint mug.

"Not well, but I like him."

"Good chap, Sam. Socialist, but honest, and that's rare these days."

The commodore bubbled in, "Are you interested in boats? This is a cruising club, and we like our members to be connected with boating in some way, even if they're introduced by a proposer as reliable as Sam. Whatever his politics." He glanced sideways at Kemp.

Jem tried not to smile. "I'm a naval architect," he said. "And I own a boat, but she's laid up at present."

"Say no more," barked Kemp. He had a large mustache through which he puffed spurts of air with his lower lip. "Here's your drink. Sam, ask Alex for the new membership cards, would you? I'll take a check, Mr. Merriman. I hope you'll join in the club activities. We have darts, skittles at the Leisure Center, and a crib team. All sorts of entertainments, raffles, dancing lessons, carnival work, regattas, sailing lessons . . . Anything else, Ken?"

"Brass band, we play for all the functions."

Jem's installation as the newest club member was swift and relatively painless. After the formalities, he said, "Can I get you a drink, gentlemen?" and looks of approval were exchanged, the seal set upon the transaction.

At ten o'clock, with the sky framed pale navy at the window and the merriment of glass and laughter defying the coming night, Steve Wilder came to the club. He was followed by Jo, leading Trix, and all three bore the gray flag of concern. They stopped by the entrance and Steve spoke to Alex and Irish Steve, who was as always clinging to the edge of the bar as if the world were getting away from him, and the concern spread across the room from hand to hand. Spotting Sam and Jem, Steve came over. His face was hard and pale.

"There's been a wreck," he said, ice crystals forming

around his tongue. "Some bloody fool ran aground on Five Rocks Reef last night, without a watch and flying a convenience flag."

"That's twelve miles out," said Sam. "What's the problem? Someone hurt?"

"Oh, no, the devil looks after his own. Crew's been taken off. It was an oil tanker, Sam, the *Kimoco*, and she's badly holed. Unless we get a norther, that slick is coming in to land."

Sam shrugged. "You can't do much about that, can you? Are they spraying yet?"

Steve sagged into a seat. "The birds," he said, and it was simple, like a prayer. "Detergent does as much, if not more damage. The poor, poor birds. The guillemots will be going back to sea. They dive in it, fish in it, and they don't know."

Jem felt offended by the man's emotional display. "One small patch in all that sea won't do much damage," he said.

Steve turned with guns blazing in his eyes. "That slick is already four miles long and a mile wide. It's the third tanker in less than six months. The birds can't keep fighting back. Did you ever see what the *Torrey Canyon* did?"

"Did you?" asked Jem. "Most of that slick found its way to Brittany."

Jo brought drinks to the table and sat quietly beside her brother. Sam nodded to her, took out his tin, and began the cigarette ritual, watching the two men as if spectating at a tennis match.

Steve placed his elbows on the table, one forearm over the other. Only his clenched fingers told tales on his heart. "An estimated fifty thousand seabirds were killed," he said, softly hammering. "Our own Half Moon Bay was full of the foul stuff. Our local fishermen lost their living for months, and even the deep-water fish were tainted by oil. You cannot deny the truth of this history, none of you." He stared down like a prophet. "You cannot pretend it doesn't matter. You will suffer from these things, even if you don't give a damn."

Jem played with his glass, head on one side, tight lines in his upper lip. "I think you're overreacting," he said. "Men have to live, as well as birds and fish. How do you think this country would exist without oil? The occasional accident is regrettable, but life survives. It will be recovered in five or ten years." Trix wriggled under the table to renew their acquaintance.

Sam rubbed his chin and winked evilly at Jo, who frowned and turned away. Steve's hair had fallen across his forehead and his eyes were shadowed. "Have you no care, then, for suffering?" he asked, quiet and straight as a stiletto. "Have you never felt pain, Jem Merriman? Does it not sit beside you and block out the sun?" Jem said nothing, and there hovered a shame on the steps of his conscience, kept out by the closed door of anger. Steve continued, "You have the sympathy of all who have burned their hands on the rope of life." He touched the back of Jo's hand with one finger. "These hands, my own, even shady Sam's. Do you truly feel nothing for the thousands of little deaths our greed causes?"

"That's not the point." Jem's eyes, Jo noticed, had blued. Even the whites were blue. "My objection is that people like you exaggerate situations out of all proportion. I walk in the country, I climb mountains, go out to sea fishing and sailing. It all looks good to me. I can always find a clean place. Where people don't go, pollution doesn't go, and most people don't go very far from their motorcars. I can always find a place." He sat back, emptied his glass, and fondled Trix's head.

"I am sorry," said Steve. "I don't know whether, to drive a case home, one is justified in hitting below the belt." He grinned like a school kid. "Forgive me, and allow me to put just one point. The sea is our great resource. Much of what we have comes from it or under it or around it or across it. The birds haven't the brains to look for places that man has not soiled, and they trust in the sea like some men trust in God. We must defend those who have no choice."

Jem had no answering fiber to absorb Steve's words. They waited outside of his appreciation like a short queue for the theater, and though he looked them over, their eager patience, he could not see their faces. "I am sure," he said slowly, "that all this is mere sentimentality, but that doesn't mean I like to see pollution happen."

"Very well," said Steve. "I'll show you. Christ, I hope I

can't show you, but I've a strong and nasty premonition that I will. Tomorrow is Saturday. Come with me, Jem, and open your eyes."

"Where?"

"Lion Bay. The forecast is for southwest winds."

"I see."

"Come. I'll pick you up at the bus depot."

"Yes. Yes, all right," said Jem.

A silence came, and it was a hole in the thickness of the happy, crowded atmosphere. Sam said, "Well, well, well," and buried his nose in his beer.

Steve woke from a trance. "Oh, God!" he said. "Manners maketh man, and I have none. I deserve your doubts. Jem, this is my sister Jo, short for Josephine. Jo, meet Jem Merriman."

"Hello, I saw you on the pier," said Jo, then wished her words were lengths of thread that could be pulled straight again. Jem showed no recognition. "A couple of days ago," she added, glancing at Sam.

Jem looked closely at her. "I am sorry," he said. "I don't know how I missed you. What do you think about all this pollution stuff?"

She smiled and showed big white teeth. "No sides," she said. "But we have seen a lot of it here. I used to go walking too, and sailing, and there are signs, especially if you've known the area for a long time. The changes are slow, but they're here."

"Oh, boo to you," said Jem with a grin, and she laughed with him and he felt good, better than he had in a long time.

Sam's eyebrows raised a millimeter as he glanced across at Steve, but Steve was at the back of his house somewhere, so Sam returned blandly to open eavesdropping.

From above, the sea's edge was moving slick brown, the yellow sand covered to the last tidemark by slick brown, the rocky promontory red sandstone dripping with slick brown. Jem stared down wordlessly. Along the tide's border were lumps, just lumps, rolling with the heavy movement. Steve led the way down the forty-eight steps, counting in his head as he had done as a child, but the old habit did not restore the old beauty. When they reached the soft sand of the upper beach, they stopped and stared about them, stared at each other until Steve turned away. They moved slowly and erratically to the shore. Great clots of the drying blood of industry matted the usual seaweed and driftwood flotsam. As they surveyed the lumps at the tide's edge, Steve swallowed rivers of despair, and Jem frowned in disbelief. The seabirds' heads were thrown back in that unmistakable final relaxation, their wings angled, jammed into unnatural positions, along the tide like broken tents after a campsite storm. Even their poor eyes were coated in oil.

Steve moved along, bent over them in a futile search for life, and the strong promised southwesterly fingered the hair out of his eyes and numbed the tips of his ears. He stayed bent as Jem watched, stumbling along the tide line and mumbling to himself, turning a corpse here and there and rubbing his fingers on the seat of his jeans. At one point he took a pair of glasses from his jacket pocket and peered even more closely through them, and once he took them off and rubbed his stained hand across his eyes. At length he stopped and was still, still as the rock behind him that was the shape of a lion's head menacing the black sea.

Jem followed in his tracks, unaware of the wind or of time passing. He knelt beside the birds and touched an oiled guillemot breast that had been white, rocked a cormorant head that hung so heavy on its neck. Inside, he was still with the cold suspension of shock. As he reached Steve, he realized that his teeth ached from clamping, and he opened his mouth and tasted the oily decay above the salt Atlantic.

Steve said, "There must be about a hundred here. God knows how many altogether along the coast." Jem nodded. "I don't know what to do." Steve spread his hands as if to take all the dead ones in his arms. "We've written a bookful of letters; the laws have been changed over the years; men in high places are concerned. But look. There is a blowout in the North Sea, tankers wrecked all round our coasts, and dozens of mystery slicks sighted every year. And why? Because money buys consent, and more than half the world lives by the dog's breakfast principles of perpetually expanding economies and populations, every one of which demands more and more energy."

"You are losing objectivity," said Jem. "Sentimentality and emotion won't shake commerce. Only money can beat money." He lit a cigarette and looked around the sad bay. A few potential sunbathers had knotted up on the path with their heads together and flies of conjecture swarming around them. One or two came down the steps, stopped, turned, like schoolboys dithering over seats on a bus. Eventually they sat on the steps, looking miserable.

"Poor sods," said Steve gently.

He and Jem stood for a long time, their boots planted in the oil, neither moving nor speaking. It came to Jem that he did not, and never would, care in the way Steve did, and the coming to light of indifference worried him. Am I wrong? he thought. Have I always been wrong? And because he believed in justice, and just in case he had always been wrong, he said, "Perhaps you could get some local interest going—in the birds and fish."

Steve sighed and set off with an old man's gait toward the steps. High above, the pines sang along the Sandcliff Road, and their music was a soft lament as the needles chafed the hurrying sky. "Listen," he said. "Look. That is all man has to do. We had such beauty here."

"You're wallowing," said Jem, finding testiness and using it as a fence between his eyes and those of the birds. "You might as well face facts. You can do nothing to stop the progress of nations, if progress it can be called. Even if you were Jesus Christ you couldn't, though I'm sure you'd love a cross to moan on."

To Jem's surprise, Steve laughed and clipped him amicably on the back of the head. "What gave you the notion that I could have such courage?" he said. "Nobility is dead, and do-gooder is a swear word these days. But come along, alter ego, you've anchored my feet to the earth, now make some suggestions."

"All right." Jem paused to scrape the worst of the oil from his boots. "How about encouraging the local people? Port Penquay, Sandcliff, all the places where your precious guillemots breed. They can't stop oil spills, but they can collect oiled birds and take them to the sanctuary for treatment, they can watch for trouble in the fishing grounds."

"Antipollution vigilantes?" said Steve thoughtfully.

"I suppose so. I just said what came into my head."

"Thank heaven for sensible men," said Steve, his voice like a chuckling brook. "They are worth rubies. We shall apply our joint sense and nonsense, and we shall try. At least that." He paused at the top of the steps and took a long look at the devastated bay. "One day," he murmured. "One day, my little brothers, we shall step up and spit in the face of this rotting world. Then we'll turn our backs and we'll fly away."

CHAPTER EIGHT

Little Joanna downstairs was whimpering, half-awakened by the storm, and Jo upstairs heard her above the raucous howling of the wind. Jo sighed and wriggled on to her back, pushing out her elbows with petty anger at the perverse twist of the bedclothes. The room glared white for a second, the lightning piercing the curtains at the window. Her skin crawled with tiny charges of fear. Normally she liked the crash and moan of storms, the impersonal passion, but tonight's was a different breed. The wind had never torn so hard before, nor the lightning been so constant, like a failing neon tube. She visualized the roof of the old house lifting like a hat, and her lying in bed with only sky and tornado around her. The forecast on the evening news had been of gale-force winds, but forecasts do not tell you how you will react at two A.M. when the assault of wind almost breaks the window and the crying of a four-year-old wrecks your sleep. You are not scared, not scared. Nothing scares you now, remember?

Little Jo's crying subsided and was drowned completely in the noise of the rain. Jo got out of bed, stupidly, feeling the cold humidity of the air on her bare arms and legs, and went to the window. The curtains panted in the draft and tugged her hands as she opened them. She could not remember such rain. It scarcely formed drops, slanted down in thick, jagged lines obliterating the view so that even the near streetlights waxed and waned like yellow will-o'-the-wisps.

Jo glowered at the sky through the four oblong panes with the cross of framework, and a last flash of lightning laid the shadow of the cross upon her. "Thank you," she said quietly. "It's about bloody time I had a blessing." She turned to look for Denny. She could see his face quite clearly in the dark room, though the air between was almost palpable, full of tiny moving dots. She said, "I know you're there with your smile. I tried to tell Sam about your smile, but he thinks I'm nuts. He doesn't say, but he puts on his bland face and he thinks I'm nuts. If I didn't have your changing smile, nuts I'd definitely be. In Bankside with all the others who got their reasons wrong. Night, Denny."

She got back into the cool, crumpled bed and curled her feet into the bottom of her nightdress. It's cold sleeping alone. But the storm would not let her sleep. As if discontented with the first effort, it rolled back on itself, and its internal fight tore the sky open with thunder. "Shut up!" she yelled, but softly. "Don't remind me." It was a storm that got Denny. He sailed out on an April day, the eighth of April, with a stiff breeze and unclouded sun. She would have gone along, but she wanted to shop for furniture and carpets. The *Devotion* was an easy little craft to handle alone.

The thunder ricocheted like a bullet in a gargantuan drainpipe, frightening in its elemental power. A storm such as this erupted in Windways that day, a freak, a specially constructed instrument of death for Denny. Scraps of the *Devotion* were found, barely recognizable and small as firewood. Later, a long time later, they found Denny. Jo screwed her eyes tight and fought the old black wave. It had washed over so often before, but its impact never lessened, and the vacuum it left behind should have been filled with tears by now, but it never was. And he'd kissed her just a peck and said, "See you later."

She edged back from the dark pit where the after-memories were stored. It had taken months to push them in, such messy, spilling months, and now she could usually keep them down, disentangled from the before-memories which floated in and out of everyday thoughts and tinged them with pink, diluting the cold of indifference. Deliberately, she called up his face, his wide penetrating gray eyes, his fine-grained skin. The thunder groaned through her sleeping.

The morning was fresh, wind-chiseled.

Jo walked up the hill to Penquay Road and the bus stop. She nodded to one or two of the waiting faces, daily familiar, but no one spoke to her. Two women berated the cost of butter. She watched the faces from half-closed eyes. Bored, they were. Bored, bored, bored. No animation except for a grimace at the wind, no discontent, no joy, no expression. Bored. With a jolt, she thought: I am like them. All these months of morning waiting at this unsheltered stop, and it had never occurred to her. She had always been different, special because of the past, clutching a self-indulgent awareness of separation from the other mortals who travel on buses. Yet here they all were, maybe all with their own special pain or joy well covered. Jo smiled in amazement. Denny would have known it, he was clever at things like that, he would have told her. She was forgetting, and that was unforgivable, scary.

An old man in a bleached cotton blazer, carrying his lunch in a blue box marked "Lunch," smiled back. Jo looked away quickly. Stranger and stranger, and they weren't strangers at all.

There were other things she noticed that morning, and the noticing confused her. In a garden behind the bus stop stood two pine trees. Pines must be the most talkative of trees. The wind hissed through the needle leaves with a sound like the sea heard in a shell, but much louder. It soothed and sang a pine tune more ancient than time. There were starlings on the lawn behind the wall, gawky strident scarecrows fighting over a crust, with disarranged oil-on-water plumage. A St. Jude's street kid of a sparrow lunged into their midst and snatched the bread from under their beaks. There were forget-me-nots in a corner of the garden, a mist of blue, fragile in the shade of an unused lawn roller, growing beauty out of dank black soil.

She was still staring at them with her heart skipping

from some fortuitous excitement when the bus labored past the Pola Cinema and filled the garden with fumes.

The office was empty when Jo arrived, and that was not unexpected. The office was empty for most of the day. Beside the old Imperial were two letters awaiting typing. Victor Allson, boss of V. Allson, Ltd., Wholesaler, had left them with an "Urgent" note paper-clipped to them. Jo read the large round word. To her certain knowledge they were not urgent, but Vic liked to build his little castles. The firm dealt solely in haberdashery: buttons, ribbons, braids, pipings, cheap laces, stick-on repairs that did not stick, hooks and eyes and needles and pins, fiddly stuffs for dainty fingers. And zips. Mr. Allson prided himself on his zip-fastener range, and a large dusty stock of them occupied the room adjoining Jo's office. They had zips going back to the birth of zips, long smiles full of big steel teeth with heavy black lips whose mouths would never be called upon to open, and nearer the door, on accessible shelves, dainty nylon whispers of zips for the finest of dress material in any color conceivable, except the one the customer ordered.

Day after day Jo spent zipped in with paperwork that was extraneous and stock that was unsalable. She liked the drab, cotton-smelling place, the solitary cell where she could think and make tea and eat her sandwich lunch without critical eyes to observe if she dropped crumbs, picked her nose, or smoked too much. Her room was a square box filled with desk, tea table with kettle, teapot and yesterday's milk dregs, filing cabinet and a malnourished philodendron on the windowsill. The window overlooked the back garden, a high-walled rectangle with a concrete path that led nowhere, bordered on each side by grass and weeds and fallen bricks. It also contained a discarded desk with the veneer arched and buckled by the changing seasons, and a revolving chair without a seat. In a row of similar Victorian, jerry-built houses there was only one garden in a superior condition to Allson's Ltd., and that one Jo could see if she stood at the gray window and pressed her left cheek to the pane, swiveling her eyes to the right. A lady lived alone next door, at ninety-eight years old a temporal monument in St. Jude's, and she tended her plot all year round and made it bloom in the brickdust. She grew tall hollyhocks that peered over the wall at the disgraces on either side, and salvias and daisies and pansies as the seasons rolled. She even had a stalwart rosebush whose blooms were the same pale red as the bricks of the wall. Jo had never spoken to her, never been near enough, but the old lady kept up a running conversation with herself. Sometimes Jo heard her through the lath-and-plaster wall of the stockroom, but never words, if words there were. It seemed to be a song without tune, with no meaning but comfort.

Jo dropped her bag beside the desk and called for Fred. Fearless Fred of Fox Street was his initial name. Fred strayed in one day, a scrawny tabby with evil claws and long black hairs at the tips of his kitten ears. He had been small and scared and bold and vicious, and thoroughly untrustworthy, traits which endeared him to Jo like no amount of affection would have done. Discovering that he would be fed regularly here, Fred took up residence and Jo excused his presence by intimating to Vic Allson that there were mice in the house, probably because he insisted on keeping open packs of coconut cookies in his desk. Fred stayed and in a year caught not one single mouse. One quiet afternoon when work was scarce, Jo looked up from her book to see a small brown rodent disappearing into the stockroom while Fred watched from his sunlit corner by the gas fire. He stretched, rolled over, and slept. Jo admired his mean, lazy personality, his totally self-centered, pleasure-seeking, immoral soul. He was rather like Colin Whale, but he was honest, made no excuses, and had a certain ragged beauty.

Jo did not expect him to come to a call, but she knew he'd be in through the hole in the stockroom window by the time she'd poured yesterday's milk into a saucer. "Morning, Fred," she said as he advanced, his tail vertical. "Where have you been, you randy little devil? It was a catty night last night, you low prowling fornicator. More bits missing from your ears." The cat looked at her balefully, licking drops from his nose. "Don't fret, Fred. Or don't fred, Fret." She reached down to him, but drew back just in time to avoid the five scythes of his claws. "Fred, I love you," she said. "Tell you something, Fred the Red. I remembered to look today. It's the first time for . . . for ages. I saw the wind and the birds living, and I saw life growing under an old roller. And I saw some people, too. The old man with the lunch box has purple veins on his nose and cheeks, and he looked sad to me, as if he'd lost something and didn't know what it was. Fred, have you ever looked at this place? Isn't it just bloody awful? Not for you, I suppose. Wasn't for me until I walked in today. It fitted me until then, so what's happened to change it? Good God, Fred! You can't be purring!" She stopped to listen, and Fred was purring, rustily. "I thought you'd never learned." Jo sat on the desk and stared at him. "Maybe hope got into your dreams as well as mine," she said softly. "Maybe that's it."

The sun broke through the window, sending a shaft to illuminate the brown walls and dark green paintwork. The wind was dropping, and the later day would be hot. Jo moved to put the kettle on, and the dust danced in the air where she had been. She watched her shadow as she filled the kettle, pushed in the plug, and flipped the switch; it was like watching someone else, someone she used to be, or someone she might be. Might be. There was a problem. She shied away from it. No point in considering a future, there was none, and once when she had dared to plan . . . No point. Just day to day to day on your own, in your own little way in your own little job, no fight, no glory, no defeat. She turned away deliberately, saying to Fred, "Hey, cat, I bought you a tin of that chunky fish and gravy like the posh cats have. Just wait while I find the tin opener. . . ."

"Are you talking to that blasted moggy again?"

Jo jumped, cutting her finger on the half-opened tin. "Mr. Allson, I didn't hear you come in."

"So I gathered, Miss Wilder. Tea ready yet? I have to be in Sandcliff by nine-thirty."

"Just coming." She made a face at his back. The seat of his pants was so shiny it reflected sunlight, and the flap of his jacket was concertina-creased. Vic Allson was a poor, aggressive man with fine sandy hair that he combed from one ear to the other, thereby highlighting the fact that he was bald. Had he left his scalp open to view, no one would have noticed, because he was the type of man who is inevitably bald. He was managing director, salesman, and delivery driver, and the seat of his old estate car got far more wear than that of his office chair. Jo ran his business efficiently and could have done so if he had never come into the place, but he insisted on leaving totally spurious instructions on slips of paper torn from old letters, implying that he had no faith in her. He did not realize the implication and Jo did not enlighten him. Good-naturedly she shredded the notes into the waste bin and continued to run the office smoothly.

She took in the tea, as Mr. Allson liked it: matching cup and saucer and sugar bowl with two spoons, and a plate for the coconut cookies, all on a clean cloth on a tray advertising "Brown's Beers." The desk was orderly on top and, as Jo knew, chaotic inside, as were his files and sample cases. He betrayed the shallowness of his character in everything he did. He always wore a fresh shirt, but the same knot had been in the greasy tie for months.

"Typed those letters yet, Miss Wilder?" he asked, making room for the tray. "They're very urgent, you know."

"They'll be in the next post," said Jo easily. "Are you seeing Mr. Carter today?"

"Yes, yes." Allson rubbed his hands together. "We're lunching at his club. Very sound man, Miss Wilder. Very sound. I'm sure he'll give me a regular order and a few new contacts."

Jo put on her impressed face with a skill that was automatic. "We could do with the business," she said serenely.

"Well, I won't deny that. Now, I must pack the new samples and sort out the paperwork before I go."

"It's done. I had a few minutes to spare yesterday afternoon." Jo pointed to two black cases on the floor behind the door.

"You mustn't get behind with your proper work," said Allson pompously.

Jo stared down into his thin white face with its gray stony eyes. He had cut himself shaving again, and beads of congealed blood stood out on his chin. A shabby, shabby little man. The world seemed to be full of them, shabby little rats in a shabby little race. Mr. Allson saw only the big-whiskered racers passing him by, and the pot of fool's gold at the losing post. Jo went back to her room.

Denny used to say that if he had to be in the human race, he'd walk down the track chatting to his friends. And I, she thought, what did I say? I'll walk with you, Denny, I'll walk with you. She blinked at the walls until the bubbles in the plaster became clear again. "Ain't walkin' nowhere, Denny," she said very softly, directing her words to Fred's corner. "I'm standing on the sidelines with a stopwatch in my hand, just observing, not participating. Do I want to get back in, Den?" Fred stared with blank malevolence in his lime-green eyes. "Do I?" And a gentle deep voice like water down a mountain said, "I don't know how I could have missed you."

The skin of her face felt hot against her hands.

CHAPTER
NINE

Sam was frying lunchtime sausages on the Aga cooker, with a tea towel draped over his shoulder to show catering in progress. The pan's contents hissed as he turned and poked, and he slit his eyes against the flying fat. On another burner, a saucepan of boiling potatoes elbowed at their lid.

Steve sat at the kitchen table gazing out at the old harbor. The day was settled and placid in its stomach after the awful indigestion of the night. Dreamily he said, "Shall I make some tea, Sam?"

Sam grunted "Ah!" and shook his pan, but the sausages had stuck firmly and broke up when he tried to dislodge them. "Nonstick!" he said, with enough acid to corrode a shop full of frying pans. Steve found the old square caddy that had a serpent twined about it and "Ceylon Tips" on the lid, almost erased by the fingers of years. Briefly and vividly he remembered his godmother Rose's soft lap, and the old-fashioned scents of lavender and loose face powder, and saw his own chubby hands too small to hold the box. He glanced fondly at her photograph on the mantel.

While he waited for the kettle, he placed on the table a small blue notebook, shiny new with good stiff covers and every page a smooth invitation, a yellow pencil with an eraser on the end, and his reading glasses. The pencil was not sharp enough, so he made it needle-fine with his pocketknife. Thus set, he rubbed his eyes, donned his glasses, adjusted his knees, his cuffs, and his thinking cap, and opened the virgin book. His fingers found much pleasure in folding back the cover, rubbing down over the staple lumps, then fastening firmly upon the pencil. "Plan of Action" he wrote boldly at the top of the first pristine page, underlining it firmly. Then some lines tiptoed into the wide landscape of his head and danced for him such a bonny dance that he had to capture them, for the steps would be the foundation of the plan. He wrote: "Ah, if there shall ever arise a nation whose people have forgotten poetry or whose poets have forgotten the people, though they mine a league into earth or mount to the stars on wings—what of them?

"They will be a dark patch upon the world."

He added, slowly and precisely, "Hassan. James Elroy Flecker." And the first page looked so grand and fine, and full, that he decided to begin the list on page two.

"Kettle," said Sam. He drained his potatoes, added a little milk and a lot of pepper, and mashed thoroughly. The earthy smell tempted the tongue. "What are you up to?" he added.

"I'm trying to construct a plan of campaign against local pollution."

"Oh. Want some sausage and potatoes?"

"No, thanks."

Sam bayoneted the sausages from the pan and brought his lunch to the table. "And what do you suppose you can do?" His voice had glass in it.

Steve shrugged. "Despair obliges men to try," he said. "Silence is consent. We must speak. All we have is a voice and a vote, little enough in the power stakes, but wars have been won by millions of small, desperate men. Your war, for instance."

"At what unnecessary sacrifice!" Sam spoke around a mouthful, and a piece of potato flew onto the table. He retrieved it with the knife. "What would you know?" The steam of his scorn elbowed the lid of restraint. "Millions of men, millions, and for nothing."

"But you went, for a cause you thought worthy, king and country."

Sam killed a charred portion of sausage and inserted it into one side of his mouth. His cheeks bulged and his expression was so at odds with his mood that Steve laughed.

"My God, a hamster!"

"Mff!" Sam was not to be sidetracked. Speaking carefully and slooping back bits of food as they tried to escape, he mumbled, "I went because I was eager for adventure, and bored, and too young." He swallowed as if consigning the Kaiser to the pit of hell, and waited while Steve poured the tea. "If you want to fight, lad, be a general. That way you don't get hurt."

"It's not that sort of war," said Steve. "No one need be hurt. The suffering is there already, borne by you and me and the lesser soldiers of the sea and air."

Sam lit a thin cigarette cautiously, avoiding his nose. His eyes were faded marbles and his voice a cold waterfall. "All war is bloody," he said. "The only way to avoid injury is to stay out." He went away to his room to play "It's a Long Way to Tipperary" on the organ.

Steve's second page took much longer to fill. He chewed the eraser off the pencil, rumpled his hair, and sighed a lot. There were minutes when he gazed through the window and saw only clouds of possibility and the intermittent sunshine of a tenuous idea, but suddenly inspiration rose like a lark and sang exalting above his head, and he snapped his fingers and said, "Yes!" He wrote rapidly before the melody faded. In the harbor the lazing gulls were disturbed by a passing speedboat and wheeled, screaming.

Steve danced around the kitchen singing, "The Poly, the Poly," to the tune of "Keel Row." His spirit writhed in delight, and his candle burned so bright in his house that all the world could have seen it.

The Poly bar at lunchtime is a primitive place, crowded as a souk and dark with denim. The young clever folk seeking to establish their individuality wear indentical blue jeans and jackets and cowboy-style boots, and could be mistaken for an army at recreation.

Steve sat on a barstool and tapped his feet to the jukebox while Ossie Bertram foraged for drinks. Ossie could be a Sassetta saint. He has that fine white unhealthiness, a concave chest and flowing gold hair that is thin and dry. His forehead bulges with brains, and the intensity of his stare has persuaded many a student to shut up and listen. He and Steve had met through the Poly Drama Department, for which Steve once built a mock-up pirate ship. Steve is a good assessor of men, a fine bolsterer of weakness and a sounding board of flat, sensible resonance, and Ossie had liked him right off. And Steve had liked Ossie because he likes all men, particularly those who suit action to word.

"Cheers!" said Ossie, taking Steve's pound note to pay for the beer. It was served in plastic glasses for safety, so light that Steve almost threw the pint over his shoulder. "Now, what's all this about?" A beautiful blond girl wriggled in next to them. "Lie down," said Ossie in her ear. "I think I love you."

It took Steve some time to get through after that. To the back of Ossie's head he said, "I am here to open a door for you to fame, notoriety, praise, and the general appreciation of the public at large with a capital P and a capital L."

Ossie brought his small olive-green eyes to bear. "Oh, no," he said. "We had enough trouble when that group got caught smoking pot in the gym."

"It's a smelly habit," remarked Steve. "This proposition is strictly legal, and wholly admirable. I want to do something about pollution."

"God," muttered Ossie, fingering a spot that hid among the sparse hairs of his beard. "It's all been done, my son, and it's a bit old hat these days. Passé. Nostalgic, even. Has this come about because of the oil slick?"

Steve nodded. "Partially. The problem is so massive, I realize that I'm an ant attacking an elephant, but a friend of mine suggested approaching the problem locally. There are several guillemot colonies along this coast. There is a flourishing shellfish industry. There are many anglers. There are many more tourists. I know that the Council does its best to safeguard profitable industries, and the beaches are being cleaned right now, but they only paper over the cracks. I want all the people in the area to see what I have seen, and feel what I have felt, and speak with one voice against it." He grinned. "I want there to be roses."

"You and every other noble nutcase since Adam. But I think I see your angle. You would like the inhabitants of

Penquay and Sandcliff District to involve themselves in their own area's interests, right? A self-protection scheme?"

"Exactly. It's an isolationist policy, if you like, and not the sort of thing I'd normally support, but it's the only way I can think of to be effective. We need to stir the spirit abroad to whisper in people's ears, 'Be patriotic to Penquay—protect yourselves and bugger the rest.' " He sighed and wrinkled his broad forehead. "Do you suppose that all men who seek after good need to pay the balance in bad?"

"You're a realist," said Ossie.

"I'm a romantic. And our disillusion makes us the best cynics. So, to continue our plan . . . "

"Your plan."

"Our plan, Ossie. You're Penquay born and bred. How about 'Protect Penquay' as a slogan. Be vigilant for our coasts. Stress the fact that we benefit only marginally here from heavy industry, that our livelihoods are based on the natural and beautiful resources of our area."

Ossie ordered another round, and Steve knew he had vibrated a sympathetic string. It is difficult for a born organizer to look a mass of potentials in the face and resist the urge to unravel a knot here, place a handful of similarly colored strands there. Ossie mused on his beard. "Are you coming to drama group tomorrow?" he asked.

"And wouldn't I be sorely missed if I didn't?"

"Sorely, sorely. And I mean it, poet. Let me think about this meanwhile."

When Steve left, it was with the sweet satisfaction of having planted a healthy seed. He was already late, but he stopped in St. Peter's Gardens and sat on a seat among old ladies in flowered velour hats to look at his blue notebook and place a large tick beside a line or two.

Long ago, back in the muddle of adolescence, he had sat on this same seat in the windy black of a Friday night, many Friday nights. His arms had been about a girl with brown hair and soft red lips, and he was hot for her like all passionate young creatures are hot for experience. Mary, Mary. She had straight stick legs and farmgirl's hands, but her breasts were round and tilted up like flowers. She was fifteen, and a nice girl, and in those unpermissive days nice girls didn't, and were respected. But she allowed him to kiss and lay warm heavy fingers upon her body beneath her coat, and he had been in a sticky paradise whose tension could only be relieved in private pounding nighttime, alone. Has it changed? thought Steve, watching the passersby in the park. A group of leggy fauns flaunting their tanned portions giggled and whispered past. Steve's mind wandered to the birds drowned in oil on the beach at Lion Bay, and as if some ghostly bird of retribution cast a dark-winged shadow across his daydream, he saw the tanned and lovely girls with broken limbs and oil-clotted hair cast up on a surrealist shore on the borders of hell.

He shuddered and stood quickly, then ran along the meandering paths, dodging pushchairs and skateboarders, and there was a scent of fear in his sweat that only he and the dogs could smell.

It is both disconcerting and pleasurable that the mind, stimulated by the new, often seeks refuge in the old, and does so randomly, as if to confuse or negate the interloper. Talk of war whisked Sam back to naval colleagues, Georgie Green, drowned in a torpedo attack on a merchant convoy; to Mesopotamia, where he had accidentally broken a branch from the Tree of Knowledge; to his mother's house in Days Lane, and her delight with the sugar and condensed milk he had smuggled home. And to Rose, darling old Rose, whose silver shoe buckle was still in the suitcase under his bed. From Rose to their baby daughter Alice, who died so young and hurt so much. A pale pain now, forgotten by all but himself, but pain triggered pain, and there was Amy, and Jo.

"You're a woman, aren't you, Stotty?"

She looked at Sam as if he'd taken to wearing a long raincoat and dark glasses, and continued to type loudly.

Sam chuckled. "I should have put that better. What I'm trying to say is this. If you were in our Jo's position, what would put you right? I don't understand the ins and outs of women."

Stotty inserted a thumb in the neck of her shirt and heaved up a loose bra strap. "Well," she murmured. "A lot of women need children, or at least a husband to look after. It's a question of fulfillment. Others find that a career is enough, or a creative existence like flower-arranging or preserve-making or throwing pots. Some old biddies like me take to drinking and keeping cats."

Sam winked lecherously at her. He's always liked his women on the generous side. "Roger Payne says she needs a good man," he said.

"They're not exactly thick on the ground," mused Stotty. "Either they're married, or simple, or queer as a bat's eyebrows, not referring to anyone in particular, you understand. But, yes, if there is one to be found, I'd recommend the idea."

Sam nodded, grinning. "Maybe we could turn one up," he said. "Maybe." Aside, he brooded in a chin-scratching way upon the triangle of skin below Stotty's neck, but the flesh is weak, thought he, and mockery demeaning. He patted her plump shoulder as he left the office.

"Your fly is undone," said Stotty pointedly.

CHAPTER
TEN

Friday was ill-designed for work. At eight A.M. it was hot. The heat later in the day would push Sam's maximum-minimum thermometer to ninety-six Fahrenheit. The sky was high and white, and the front empty except for Brian Wills, the postman, pedaling, shirt-sleeved and sedate, toward the roundabout. Soon there would be happy screams from the beach, to hang faint and motionless in the snail-slow air. The yachts in Days Harbor were brittle with reflections, and someone moving barefoot on deck skipped as his skin touched hot metal.

Sam scratched his unshaven chin, stretching his neck like a cat. He and Steve spoke little, their brains still night-browsing, their eyes unblinking and full of vague images: work completed, today's work to be tackled, conversations from yesterday and yesteryear, plans, contentments, smothered troubles. Sam rolled his after-breakfast cigarette and forced his freewheeling mind to mesh with a cog.

"We've another order for a sixty-foot cruiser," he said. "Height of luxury, of course. Keeping up with the Joneses. I'm seriously considering employing a couple of school-leavers. Apprentices."

"Mmm," Steve brooded. "Good idea. Pass on the old skills."

"Ah. And I've had a letter from a chap who wants a carvel schooner. A nice little cruiser, only thirty-two feet, but good. It would be nice to work with wood again."

Steve pummeled the dream dust from his brain. "Wouldn't it, though! Have we any designs?"

confided to Steve and Stotty the threads of his plot, he
chose his words as a gourmet would a trout. Stotty's
approval was instant and wholehearted, rendering Sam's
finesse superfluous, but Steve fidgeted. "You know he's
married?" he said.

"Oh, yes," lied Sam. "But who is getting that serious?"

"She needs it," said Stotty. "Maybe they both do."

"All I've done is open up an avenue," said Sam inno-
cently.

"Okay," said Steve.

Their three heads clustered in collaboration deep into
the heating morning.

Friday night is club night, the night when the week's
troubles pale and the two lazy weekend days stretch tempt-
ingly ahead. Tensions relax, elastic snaps back, clocks run
down. In the haven of the club, legs are stretched luxuri-
ously, bellies allowed to bulge, taut muscles to sag. Fishing
plans are laid, visits promised, TV watching detailed,
cricket matches hatched. The staff of Antlercraft stared
silently into space, easing out the wrinkles.

"It's our Jo's birthday next week," said Sam. "I've been
practicing 'Happy Birthday to You.' "

"Where is Jo, anyway?" queried Jacko.

"I thought we should throw a party for her," continued
Sam. "Mention it to the committee, will you, Steve? Get
some entertainments going."

"Lovely idea," enthused Ivor. "Will it be a surprise?"

"If you can stop your tongue flapping," said Sam dryly.
"She'll be thirty. God, how time flies. . . ."

"Where is Jo, anyway?" demanded Jacko.

"How about Roland Kemp's Barbershop Four?" threw
in Stotty. "They're real hot stuff."

"I'll read some poetry," offered Steve. "And Ivor plays
beautiful classical guitar."

"I didn't know that," said Sam, faintly annoyed at the
dropped stitch in his general knowledge. "Anyone else? Do
you do a snake dance or something else I don't know
about, Stotty?"

"Plenty you don't know about, but not in public."

"Andy Wain plays cornet," said Steve. "I wonder whether Jem does anything musical. He'll have moved in by next Friday—part of the team."

"Get it organized," instructed Sam.

"Where is Jo?" Jacko thumped the table.

Sam gazed upon him in offended surprise. "Coming with Jem. I asked him to give her a lift."

Jo was sitting on the front wall in the hot, bright evening, swinging her feet in dull contentment. Expecting to see the lumbering old Antlercraft van, she ignored the white Cortina pulling into the curb until it beeped at her. Jem got out and opened her door, saluting like a chauffeur. "Hello," he said. "Sam asked me to collect you."

"Did he? I mean . . . thanks, it was nice of you to come." As she squeezed past him, his warm body smell reached her, mild, attractive, twanging a chord. They say we find a mate by our noses.

The car moved slowly down into the town. "Your brother is giving me a home," said Jem. "And Sam is giving me work. I'm very glad I came here."

They smiled mutually. "We're not too provincial for you?" asked Jo.

"Not at all. I wasn't born in London. One just gravitates toward work. And people. You look very pretty tonight."

"Why, thank you, Jem. You too." They laughed, and Jo felt good. She glanced unobtrusively at his hands on the steering wheel, very brown, at the cloth of his shirt, muted and expensive, at his curling strong hair, moving in the breeze from the open window.

"It's a fascinating town," he said as they slid into Upper High Street. "I find something new every day."

"So do I, and I've been here all my life." Jo wondered whether that was true. It should be, she thought, but have I closed my eyes?

"I'm very glad I came across you," said Jem lightly, flicking his eyes from the road to the woman.

"But you missed me first time." Jo grinned.

"Then I'm delighted to have been granted more than one chance."

"What a charmer you are, Jem Merriman."

"I mean it, Jo," he said seriously. "It really makes me happy."

As they entered the club together, laughing, Jem's hand politely on Jo's waist to negotiate the door, Sam caught Jacko's eye and winked.

An angelic chorus burst into song in Jacko's ears.

TWO

CHAPTER ELEVEN

The skylight over the landing gave a good north light, and Jem had arranged the big drawing board to catch it. Against the inner wall stood a hastily constructed cupboard and bench with a roomy paper drawer and a shelf for books and pens, inks and pencils, erasers and curves. Jem used the kitchen sink for soaking paper to stretch onto the board. To be back at work set a spark in him, and as he began nervously to toy with ideas on scraps of design paper, a glow of release began in his gut that for hours at a time drove out the cold that greeted his morning waking. To begin was to dive into a swimming pool with the intention of executing the perfect length, smooth and elegant, fast and flowing; so he teetered, fearing the threshing and splashing and ignominy of panic. Yet designs tumbled from his mind so fast that he had to take the plunge, and his swift fingers could hardly keep pace.

"I feel," he said to Steve, "like the man who found the lost crapper."

Steve chuckled. "I have dreams like that. I'm haunting every building in a city for a toilet, and just as I find one and prepare for action, I discover that there's a great hole in the wall, or the door won't shut, and there's a crowd of people staring at my backside. Grim, they are, and good to wake from." He sorted through some rough drawings. "You're clever, Jem. How can you draw like this?"

"I learned. I've had a lot of practice. What do you think of this?"

Steve took the sheet that showed three cutaway views

and a small, sketchy sail plan. "I wish I could dream on paper like this," he said. "I see you've made the cockpit quite small. That's good. A large open cockpit can be a downright disadvantage for cruising."

Jem was quietly proud, grateful that his abilities had not deserted him during the enforced layoff. "I'll start on the preliminary drawings this evening," he said. "Then Sam can comment."

"Not tonight," said Steve. "Tonight we celebrate."

"Jo's party—of course. I'm blind from work."

"Indeed, and I've had news from the Poly. The students are to support our antipollution campaign. The good, good souls are organizing a march, and the fishermen's cooperative is backing us to the hilt."

"Oh, God," said Jem. "Steve, do you realize what perils that could hold?"

"No," he said happily. "But if you do, you'd better come and tell us when we discuss it. Also, they have actually given me a speaking part in the end-of-term play. They had to, really. The fountain ghost thinned away, as it were, and I know all the lines. I feel good. Come on, get your money, we have presents to get." His long legs were folding down the stairs before Jem could answer.

"Best bib and tucker by eight o'clock!" Steve was calling to Sam.

"Aye!"

Jem crossed the workshop in the wake of a whirlwind. "Don't forget the party!" Steve was telling Jacko, and "Stay, Trix!" to the dog.

"Oh, a present, a present . . ." Ivor was panicking as they left. "I forgot while I was practicing."

As Steve roared the Transit along the pier, Jem said, "Have you a girlfriend to bring to this party?"

"Not at the moment. My lady love is far away, and I don't know if I shall ever see her again, Jem, though she is lovely as a rainbow, and quiet and tall. She is an Indian, a Mohawk from the east and from time out of mind, and her name is Degonwadonti, which means 'many opposed to one.' Her race is, I think, a casualty of civilization, but she has pride and intelligence and holds the secrets of the woods and waters. There is a silent, ancient strength in her that puts me to shame and gives me courage."

"But you left," said Jem, and there was an envy in him with no name and no home.

"How could I stay away from a dying mother? And my girl was wise enough to realize she would not make the transition. Maybe I'll go back—someday."

Up the High Street they drove, left into Market Street, and around the fountain and horse trough, neither of which had passed water since the local shortage began, and into the car park.

The Market Hall is divided into many parts, a town under one girdered arching roof. The greengrocers occupy a section near the main doorway and have wooden boards with their names, and such lines as "Penquay's Oldest Merchandiser" with most of the last "r" missing. Their goods are like gems in a crown: the gleaming ruby apples, sleeve-polished, each in its own tissue setting; fat tomatoes, even as pearls; great suns of grapefruit and planets of oranges; and boxes of phallic cucumbers laid like fertility symbols to catch the eye and lead it to beds of lettuce so crisp and green you could eat the color and taste the sap of life. In sacks behind are the staple, desirable potatoes, local grown and with good brown dirt on their skins. They are so necessary they need little display, except when the new ones arrive, small tender pretenders to the throne of King Edward. In season they have carrots in one-pound bunches with the green tops uncut, and leeks of a size and proportion to support the roof of Chartres.

Jem wanted to pore his taste buds over the stalls for a while, but Steve strode on. "Flowers," he said. "They have blue carnations."

"No such thing."

"You wait."

"They're not natural, then."

"Maybe not, but they're blue."

And they were. Pale turquoise with darker blue spots at the pinked edges. "How do they do it?" Jem asked the flower seller.

"Trade secret," she said, then grinned. "Tell you the truth, I don't know. I only sell them."

"They're a bit showy," said Jem. "I'll have a bunch of those yellow daisy things."

"Food for us next week!" cried Steve, tucking the mixed

bouquet under his arm and leading the way from the arcade that was so full of flowers in green buckets that Jem was reminded of the carnival he had watched in Trinidad. The scent was as heavy and the colors as bright. He hummed a snatch of calypso.

The fish market was quite a different kettle of fish, so thought Jem, smiling. The thin metallic smell clawed at the clothes. It had been fresh in the dawn but was getting rich now. A fishmonger screeched the lid from a steaming copper pot and with a long-handled basket lifted out large red lobsters. He called, "Hiya, Steve! Got a couple of beauties if you want them. Last for a while. That bloody oil."

"How much?"

"Usual."

"Okay, I'll pick them up later. Thanks, Artie. You and me will have lobster salad for dinner tomorrow," he said to Jem. "Wait till you taste it. You will be dissatisfied with other lobster forever and ever, amen."

Jem managed to prevent his friend buying skate, gurnard, plaice, John Dory, cod's roe, mackerel, herring, finnan haddock, and whiting, on the grounds that they would hardly need to feed the multitude, whether they had five loaves or not, but condoned smoked eel, kippers, and local prawns.

"Oh, but the fruits of the sea, aren't they just something!" said Steve, eyes bounding like brown deer over the iced and parsleyed display. "I've had a love affair with fish since I can recall. A love-hate streak, maybe, but I like to catch 'em and eat 'em, and I like the evolutionary mystery of their strange shapes and colors. Do you know, a plaice can make a passable imitation of a Scottish tartan? And how, with no brain to speak of? And John Dory, such a spiny, dinner-plate character, and yet he bears a mark they call Saint Peter's thumbprint. We had a funny thing at Sandcliff a time back, also fishy. If you've ever caught skate or ray, you'll know they have protuberances of rather a compelling nature. Would you believe it, a large sign appeared on Sandcliff Pier requesting that anglers catching skate remove the offending articles before bearing their proud catch back through the town. I understand that two or three old ladies complained to the Council."

He laughed loudly for a moment, fetching up spontaneous grins around him. "I've often wondered," he added, "how they worded the complaint."

Bert Lark's in the market is revered in Port Penquay. Not only is Bert a master butcher whose meats are of a quality and tenderness to tempt confirmed vegetarians, but his cold cuts and pies and sausages have won prizes up and down the country. He makes liver and bacon sausages that are long and dark, and hot spicy sausages with chili, and red Northumberland sausages that hang from hooks like sore scrubbed fingers. His pork pies are packed with real pork, and the hot-water-crust pastry, made by Mrs. Bert Lark, bears no resemblance to the rubberized paper pulp of lesser pies.

Jem and Steve stood long with their elbows on the counter, pointing first to one delicacy, then another, kids in a sweet shop. "Bath chaps," said Jem. "Let's have some of that."

"And a whole pie," breathed Steve. "And Scotch eggs. Scotch eggs. You won't believe them."

Bert, having developed an excellent sense of timing, popped up as Jem looked for service. Not only did they buy for tomorrow, but for breakfast all week long and lunch on Sunday. They also bought a side of smoked bacon to suspend from the kitchen ceiling and hack, romantically and inexpertly, into slices fresh for the pan.

Three boxes landed in the back of the van. "Now," said Steve. "Presents. Let's go to Bryght's."

Bryght's is the only department store in Penquay, and correspondingly expensive. Steve hovered. "What do you want?" asked Jem.

"Uh . . . Christ knows. What do young women like?"

"Perfume?"

"No. Jo is fussy, and I can't remember the names she uses."

"Lingerie?"

"Don't know her size." Steve stretched his hands out, cupped. "About that."

"Thirty-four?"

"No. Arthritis."

They strolled among the holiday spenders, chuckling and winking at the salesgirls. Jem felt lightheaded, as if he were nineteen again, and because they were shopping for her, Jo crossed his mind time and again. He found that he needed a reacquaintance with her face. Her eyes were clear, and the color of her curling hair, but her features blurred and became Steve's. "I'm looking forward to this evening," he told himself.

"Good," said Steve. "Your spirit is lifting its head to look at the world." He added seriously, "Don't expect it never to bow again. If a sorrow is real, it will die only when you die. But sorrow can be tamed and taught not to run riot through your living, and as time goes, it lies quiet beside you." Steve spoke as if of cabbages or rainfall. "Say, that's pretty." He pointed to a silk scarf patterned in the shades of a desert sunset. "Or the green, how about the green? My, how do they create colors like this? I've only seen that in a dawn sky after the northwest wind." He fingered the scarf gently.

"Is Jo like you?" said Jem. "Does she take such pleasure in all the things about her? I find it very refreshing."

Steve threw a quick straight look. "She used to be," he said. "I was away when her fiancé was drowned, so I can't place exactly when she withdrew, but she has changed, Jem." He was about to add more, but let it lie. "I think I'll buy the green one."

"What can I get?" said Jem.

"She loves plain chocolates."

"Right. A big box."

They panted up the several winding flights of steps that skirt the shops and give slices of harbor views, back to the van. Old gas streetlamps, now converted to electricity, straddle the alleyways on ornate wrought-iron arches painted black and picked out in gold. Penquay is good at that sort of thing. It also has a gentlemen's convenience of the same era, dark green and of tantalizingly lacy iron-work, preserved and pretty but totally redundant, since the planners altered the road and left it inaccessible on a traffic island.

"What's all this nonsense about a march?" asked Jem as they squeezed the Transit past suicidal pedestrians in the High Street.

Steve was silent for some moments. Only as they idled along the front in a queue of traffic like a row of hot loaves fresh from the oven, did he show any sign of having heard. "Will they all think like you, I wonder?" he said. His eyes were hidden behind sunglasses. The glare from the water and the sky and the sun-beaten chrome made the very air shine.

Jem felt defeated, and victorious, and wanted to apologize for both. "Will it do any good?" he said. "Will it change anything?"

Steve crunched through second. "I believe we are all changed, by everything. We see a thing, or feel it, or meet a person, and we carry away a little bit with us as if we'd brushed against burs. I met a girl in Canada and now we have created loneliness. I bet you've a whole mass of habits and attitudes and mannerisms picked up from your wife. After this march, things will not be as they were before, however minute the change."

Jem saw then the profile of Steve, the always-smiling, ever-buoyant Steve. His nose was muscled and firm about the nostrils, and the wide mouth, for all the laughter, was sad at the corners, like a clown's mouth under the makeup. "I hope it achieves what you want it to achieve," said Jem.

"It's going to be a real slap-up, humdinger of a party!" announced Steve as they stopped outside Antlercraft. "I'm first with the shower."

"Oh, no, you take so bloody long!"

They raced through the workshop, leaping trestles and setting Trix to barking like she does after rabbits, and Ivor cried, "Be careful, boys!"

Steve got his fingers to the door handle first, but the door didn't give.

"What the hell's going on!" demanded Sam from inside, above the noise of running water.

"A real humdinger of a party!" said Steve. "A proper shindig!"

CHAPTER
TWELVE

My birthday, thought Jo. My bloody birthday, and an important one at that, leaving all those roaring twenties behind, and only one card, from Aunt Ruth, who wasn't a proper aunt and lived in Glasgow. Huh! Old Sam wouldn't send a card or a present. A ten-pound note folded small and tucked into her palm in private, that was Sam and always had been. But Steve . . . he'd always remembered from wherever in the world he had been. And Peggy . . . but Peggy had an empty head and would be artificially abject when she remembered.

Doesn't matter. Her chin wobbled with it. Doesn't matter. Balls to the lot of them. Knickers. Nuts. She'd even been tempted to tell Vic Allson as a sap to her disappointment, but let the moment pass. She'd told Fred the Red instead.

Rather than allow petty anger to degrade into depressing thoughts of birthdays gone by, Jo marched downstairs and around to the back of the house. Half of the garden was hers, and noticeably more verdant than Peggy's half, where the lawn was full of weeds and anemic patches where little Joanna left toys and bits of wood to rot. The one old rosebush was cat-draggled and rich in greenfly.

Jo found a spade in the coal bunker and attacked her disappointment. It was the wrong time of year to dig, but therapeutics have no season. It took her way back to a safe time. When the rhythm of right foot on spade, push, heave with shoulders, red sod over, right foot on spade, was established as background music, the old memories came rising up as if released from the shiny clods under the spade.

It was years since she had been really close to the earth, looking down into it for pink worms that the hens loved. Mum had kept a few hens for all of Jo's childhood time, and she used to help dig the garden just to find worms and long white grubs for them. She thought she must have been more aware of growing things then, perhaps because she too was growing. She had looked into the eyes of daisies and touched the dust of buttercups and had seen, really seen on one occasion, an elf leaping among the runner beans with one of the red flowers on his head for a hat.

She and her friends stole Mum's peas from the plants to eat the sweet green smiles inside and use the pods for sailboats on the rain barrel. Where have all the rain barrels gone? she wondered. Tiny animals had lived in theirs, and she'd never known how they got there, nor what their names were, but some larvae figure-of-eighted just below the surface, and some ran on the face of the water, scared of the pea-green boats. Mum had always filtered out the wildlife before she washed their hair in the soft water.

It began to drizzle then, just a cool reviving breath of it as the evening closed over. Jo dug on. Drizzle feels good when you are hot and untidy and dressed for gardening.

She thought she must have been about seven when she discovered geography and realized that there were more places in the world than just her little place. She and Steve had determined to dig to Australia, and as they had yet to get to geophysics they did not know the enormity of the task. With a small metal spade, last used for sand-castle construction in Half Moon Bay, they began, at the edge of the path by the compost heap. On reflection, she doubted that their small square hole ever exceeded two feet in depth, but the tales they told each other, my, they were tall as tall, big as trees. They were "going into the second earth now" and they might find gold or diamonds or rhinestones, because Mum had a brooch . . . or maybe pale maggots three yards long, or a purple centipede, or an underground cave to hide in, or, glory be, bones!

"Where has all the wonder gone?" said Jo aloud to the thrush who had assumed his aerial stand and was clearing his throat. "I don't want to watch the ants in the wall, or pick blackberries, or count the stars."

Faint and high, the telephone started ringing, and Jo ran to answer it, leaving the row half dug and the spade blade deep in the earth.

"Jo? This is Jem Merriman."

There must be processes that go on deep inside of us without our approval or consent. Jo's heart kicked unexpectedly and knocked her breathing out of time.

"Uh . . . hello, Jem Merriman."

"Steve asked me to call. He's had to go out."

"Oh." A sadness came, uninvited.

The chuckle on the line warmed her. "Happy birthday," he said. "A party has been arranged in your honor at the club. We'll collect you at eight-thirty."

"Oh, God! Oh, sorry. No, I mean thank you, Jem. From the bottom of my heart. What's the time? You should see me. I've been in the garden. It's a lovely surprise, I thought everyone had forgotten me."

"No. Never, Jo."

She stood beside the telephone table for quite a time after he had hung up, wondering at the quivering of her knees and the leaping excited throb of her pulse. Then she told the goldfish, "I'm having a party, fishy-fishy-fish face," and she laughed as she ran to the bathroom with a light and happy tread.

In small towns, coastal or otherwise, where people work hard on sea or land, the excuse for a party tends to be grasped in both callused hands. Port Penquay has more entertainments available than most, but the residents regard these tourist traps with little affection. There is a common sense about the people of the granite moors which is not eroded by the pretty streams of novelty, and a party at the PPCC was always a solid, value-for-money affair.

Now, parties have peculiar effects, as varied and interesting as the characters who are going to attend. Some, like Steve, relish the anticipation of an entirely unknown evening, a spot of profligacy on the clean and predictable lapel of daily life. In his mind he refuses to entertain any possibility whatsoever, and makes the whole thing arrive fresh and unexplored as new snow.

Some, like Ivor Bailey, allow their imaginations to run on like strong horses. He had been practicing his guitar every morning from six till eight, and every night from ten till twelve. Jacko loved to hear it. He nodded his big head and waved his arms clumsily in a bliss that held no envy. Jacko can't play a kazoo, but he loves music and singing and dancing. The fingertips of Ivor's left hand throbbed with practice so that he could barely hold a chisel, but he was note-perfect and poised. He had chosen a part of Rodrigo's Guitar Concerto as being neither too highbrow nor so plebeian as to offend his own good taste.

If he was happy with his party piece, that was about the only peace he had. If you asked him, he would say he adores parties. The truth is that they worry the pants off him. First came the question of what to wear. Casual, so he could unwrap the blue cashmere sweater; or collar and tie, so he could don the exquisitely ironed cream shirt and matching velvet bow. And coming to no decision on that, the next anxiety was Jo's approval of the present. Cookery books, even large color-plated ones, seemed so banal . . . By the time Jacko knocked on his door on the evening of the party, Ivor had worried about which after-shave, what to drink, to whom and about what to talk, what to eat, who to dance with, whether someone would bring the music to dance to anyway, how much the liquor would cost, how drunk he might get, and who would put his new shoes on the stretchers if he should be rendered incapable.

Jacko had bathed and washed his hair in toilet soap and scrubbed his grained hands till they cracked, and scraped his nails with the point of a kitchen knife, and shaved twice so that his smooth cheeks shone tight and sore. His plain white shirt was new out of the box and creased precisely, but he wasn't sure he'd taken all the pins out, so he moved stiffly, like a wooden soldier. Parties worried Jacko too, but not for the self-conscious reasons of Ivor. Understanding was his problem; the questions, the jokes, particularly the jokes, for they gave him the disquieting feeling that there were hidden worlds whose existence was known only by slit glimpses through green curtains.

Old Sam, having jumped the gun with the shower, was ready an hour early. He sat in his bed-sitting room with his gray summer pants pulled up at the knees, his tie pin horizontal, and his soft straw at a sedate angle over his eyes. The room is shabby, the only haven where Sam allows himself to be untidy. The books in the dusty bookcase have a gritty feel, and the stacks of old *Motor Boat* and *Yachting* magazines sprawl in a corner like drunks. Even the valued Hammond normally wears a bloom like a grape, but by now it was polished and positioned at the club. Sam could practice "Happy Birthday" no more. He has never given a party in his life, but he is a great attender. He likes the music and the company of ladies and the whiskey, and he loves to talk.

He sat quiet and peaceful, with the cowbell sound of wire rigging tocking against masts that had so long been the background of his life that he heard it in his bloodstream. No worries had Sam. In his time all things under the sun had happened to him, and knowledge blunts the capacity for angst. Even Jo, whom he loved, caused him only marginal trouble, for he had matured into a contented old man with enough wit to realize that all things pass and are as dust before the wind.

However, when he recalled, as he did every five minutes or so, that he was to perform musically in public that very evening, a finger of apprehension poked him hard in the ribs.

CHAPTER
THIRTEEN

Anyone seasoned in parties and their phases knows that they cannot begin stiff and cold. They must be brought to a suitable pitch before launch time, rather like an orchestra needing to tune up and loosen its fingers before the opening bars of a symphony. And speaking of bars, Sam, Jacko, Ivor, Stotty, and Roger were already propping one up at seven-thirty, assuring a nervous Alex that the dance floor and stage looked fine, the records ideal, the buffet superb, and the quantity of toasting wine sufficient.

There was no official guest list, but a party, like kerosene, gets everywhere. Irish Steve arrived wearing a tie, and no one offered him a drink because they didn't recognize him. Mick the Artist had unearthed his best floppy cravat and cleanest jeans, and brought as a present a small sculpture from his hairpin period. Mick is a painter too, but he has to paint signboards and houses during the winter. In summer he sits on the pier and turns out masterpieces for the tourists, who seem to like his work. Miss Vine at Vine Galleries has to double-order French Ultramarine especially for Mick's season, and has been heard to utter remarks studded with spines such as "pap" and "masses." Still, chacungasongoo, as Sam would say. Sam leched his way around Cherbourg one week in his springtime. Mick's studio is in the drabbest part of town, up behind the Little Theater, and his rooftop patio used to be the scene of intellectually wild pot-smoking parties until Mick read a book on heart disease and got into the physical-fitness thing. Now he jogs every morning and wears a sweat band on his brow, and still has a pale and concave aspect.

Irish Steve bought his own beer and told Alex a joke while waiting for the froth to settle. "There was this Paddy," he began—Irish Steve is a true Irishman—"who went into a bar and asked for a Scotch on the rocks—wit' ice!" Alex chuckled politely. Sam commented that no whiskey drinker worth his salt ever took anything with Scotch but another Scotch. Stotty ordered a round and discussed pig breeding, a career she had followed as a young woman, with a morbidly fascinated Ivor. Jacko laughed a long time at the joke, which he actually understood, apparently holding a melon under each arm. He was still waiting to discover pins.

Jo was at home in bathrobe and makeup. "I want to look nice, Denny," she said, screeching the hangers in the clothes closet. "What did I look nice in? A dress. You always liked to see my legs." She grinned over her shoulder at him, caught his expression, and looked again. "Den, is it all right?" she asked softly. "I don't know him, yet I'm touched by him. Can you tell me?" The picture smiled on. "Oh, Denny, I didn't know I was so lonely. I don't want to be anymore."

She grew restive under his placid gaze and turned away, slicing through the hanging clothes. "Don't help me, then," she muttered. "I'll decide for myself whether he is to be trusted. I believed you when you promised never to leave me, so where's the merit in any promise? I'll just let things come and go, and be as polite at their parting as at their meeting." She pulled out a cotton dress, sniffed it, laid it on the bed. The room was hot and still; no breeze played in the curtains at the open window. No answers came to unspoken questions. The thrush had stopped for breath. Jo scratched gingerly at the sunburn on her forearms.

It-doesn't-matter had a lump of caring in its throat, and there was a pause, a total silence in the melody of Jo.

Scared, she ran to put some music on the stereo.

The breathy sound of the Pan pipes ran clear as a rock-hindered stream, up and down the simple scale that is basic to life; Jo remembered a squirrel in the beech woods of Fort Hill, scampering along a wire fence like written notes of music. She said aloud, "Denny," because he had been there and now his presence was gone for all time.

She took the record from the deck, holding it like a precious stone. The titles were Romanian and unpronounceable for her, but the pipes of Gheorghe Zamfir needed no translation and could have been played no better by Pan himself.

A familiar squeal of brakes banished Arcadia. The gray Ford Transit waited at the curb, rattling gently.

The drizzle had done no more than turn to steam in the evening. There was no freshness; the street had the atmosphere of a laundry. Sam stood sweating by the open van door. "We're in for some thunder," he said.

"Happy birthday, Jo!" chorused the van. They had all come, Jem and her downstairs neighbor Peggy too. Ivor sat on a white handkerchief. The journey was laden with laughter and comments of such subtle delicate humor and wit, that the speakers could hardly believe their own brilliance. Of such stuff are parties made. A sheen of magnanimity graced every phrase and gesture. Jo smiled, and kept smiling. She smiled so much her face ached.

Borne on the froth of impending joy, the party floated into the club, laughing a little hysterically, high on adrenaline. The bar glowed, the dance floor where a few couples already waltzed glowed, Alex glowed, Roland Kemp in his secretary's position near the door glowed so red and puffed so hard that Jem pondered briefly on his first-aid training. He found himself chuckling, but no one asked why. They all chuckled their way to the first, or third, drink, battling with exaggerated gentility to pay.

"Jo, you look good enough to eat," announced Mick, dumping the sculpture in her arms.

"Oh, Mick! How nice . . . what do you call it?"

"Cactus sodomizing a jellyfish."

"Say . . ."

Ivor nodded seriously. Roger blew his nose explosively. Steve whistled softly through his teeth, and Jacko stared from face to face before catching Sam's wink.

Someone put an old Beatles number on the phonograph, and Jo, tapping her foot, said, "Come on, Jacko, dance with me."

Jacko was overcome with shyness and gratitude. "Blimey," he said, "I've got two blinkin' left feet." He allowed his arm to be taken, but inspiration, like a piston, caught him somewhere behind the left ear. An incredibly crafty expression widened his eyes and mouth, blatant as a bomb. "Why don't you ask Jem!" he said. His transparent maneuver and obvious desire for approval were met by a total blankness from his friends that Jacko felt and resented. Jo glanced up at Jem and in that particle of time she read his thought and it hurt and was irrevocable. You are wrong, she cried silently. How could you think this! "I asked you, Jacko," she said firmly. "Be a gentleman and don't refuse." Her sideways eyes at Jem as she walked away could have soured milk.

On the dance floor, moving her legs at forty-five degrees to her body to avoid Jacko's feet, she said gently, "Dear Jacko, are you up to something?"

It was beyond Jacko's ability to resist such pressure for long. The beans spilled profusely. "Did I do it wrong?" he mumbled at last. "Christ, Jo, I wouldn't hurt you for the world. I'm not very bright, am I?"

Jo kissed his cheek affectionately. "You're my best friend," she said. "Come on, I'll buy you a drink to prove there are no hard feelings."

Steve was standing slightly apart from the crowd at the bar, nervously running over the lines of the poem he had composed. It was written in his blue notebook, at the back, upside down. Jo marched up to him. "I suppose," she said sweetly, "that it was your idea. Manipulator."

He looked down at her for a moment, into brown eyes that were images of his own. "Does it matter whose idea? We conspired for love of you. Jacko loves you best of all, but you know the good Jacko . . ."

Jo's anger washed away, leaving the bare stones of depression. "I know," she said. "I feel so ungrateful now. Mean. A mean little self-centered person. But, Steve, Jem read us all like books, except he included my name. He will think wrong of me now, and none of us can tell him the truth."

"Jo, come and open your presents!" called Roland Kemp.

In a dream from which there was no escape, Jo opened

parcels containing handkerchiefs, perfume strong enough to anesthetize a cow, a corkscrew, a toby jug that frightened her with its malicious leer, a pair of earrings for pierced ears, no use to her, Steve's scarf that she tied on straightaway, Ivor's cook book, and Jem's chocolates. Sam had already made his usual secretive gesture.

The guests became very quiet, watching the small woman in the pale unfashionable dress. Her face and arms were pink, her thick hair shone gold, she stood with her toes turned out and thanked each giver with a grin, but her smile of thanks to Jem went over his shoulder.

Irish Steve sat on the arm of a chair and broke it. Above the ensuing roar, Ken Butcher burbled to Steve, "Shall we start now, before they get too, uh, uncontrollable?"

Seats were taken for the entertainments, and willing, breakable attention paid.

"The first item in our . . . uh . . . little show tonight is Andy Wain and his hot cornet!" cried the commodore. In the pause that followed, very little happened. Jacko belched magnificently and said "Pardon."

"Andy Wain!"

No Andy, and rising titters from the audience. Ken held a hasty muttered conversation with Steve, who departed rapidly. "In the absence of our good friend Andy, who I'm sure will be with us soon, we'll continue with Mr. Ivor Bailey and his classical guitar!" announced Ken, and Ivor, calming his nerves with a large vodka in the wings, started like a rabbit, stubbed out his cigar, and ran.

The quiet notes were pure as rain and the audience loved him. Applause and howls for more rattled the glasses on Alex's bar. Feet stamped and Jo threw some flowers from her bouquet. Ivor left the small stage after two encores upon a euphoric cloud known only to the talented few.

In the absence of both Steve and Andy Wain, the commodore continued the program with Roland Kemp's Barbershop Four. Their close harmony was a little nerve-frayed at the start, but as confidence grew, their tenor, baritone, and bass voices wove together as smoothly and evenly as strands in one of Sam's ropes. They hit the audience with "Swing Low," "Carolina Moon," and

"Down by the Riverside" with their striped waistcoats bulging and their straw hats jaunty on their heads or covering their hearts. The climax of "My Grandfather's Clock" with accompanying tick-tocks brought the house down.

Jo clapped and clapped until her hands were sore, and the building seemed to be splitting at its old seams. Jem, sitting a few seats away, returned her smile, surely without malice, and Jo, who had closed the door of hope, yet felt a draft of warmth.

At last Andy Wain was found wandering around the tree looking for his cornet. Unless it is at home, locked in the closet under the stairs, it is never parted from him. The temporary loss of it had thrown Andy into the pit of despair from which he could not be dragged even by its recovery. Tearfully he said he would go home. Patiently Steve persuaded him to have a drink, dry his eyes. "Don't let our Jo down," he pleaded.

The chant of "Why are we waiting?" echoed weakly, then with more relish, out into the hot, throbbing night. Thus cajoled, Andy played. Not his best, for his lips were too trembly for proper triple-tonguing, but well enough to please the bandmaster, Mr. Gregory, and amply well enough to please the well-oiled audience. Steve had to wait a long time for the rowdy sector to quieten and declare itself ready for poetry.

"I'm not a very talented disciple of Thespis," he said. Hoots and giggles. "But I'll try." He held up a hand. "This poem is by Michael Drayton, who lived from fifteen-sixty-three to sixteen-thirty-one, but despite its age it is in no way out-of-date." Clearing his throat, he recited "Since there's no help" without gesture and with just the requisite pathos. His voice shone clear to every corner.

The audience was silent. Here and there a sniff, a sleeve to the corner of an eye. "Lovely!" said a spontaneous voice, and appreciation broke out. Jo was proud of her brother. Through full eyes she watched him, smart in his new blue suit, shoes polished, head bowed. What a good man he is, she thought. Good through and through like gold. Not like me.

He looked up, grinned. "This," he said, "I wrote myself, and believe me, there is no comparison. But I wrote it for

Jo after watching the gulls fly inland, because I thought
she would like it."

"Go ahead, lad!" called Sam from the back by the bar.

> "Seagull carving at the clouds,
>   Peeling wind-rind with his wings,
>   Blades, kukri-shaped.
>   A stranger over drab roofs
>   Beaconed from above the tide,
>   I watch from a window.
>
>   He's an adaptor,
>   Preyer on man's waste.
>
>   Came of a time when Earth was tidy,
>   Clean, cluttered by Nature.
>   Came with silver petty rage,
>   Always uncooperative.
>   Herring gull, brainless beauty,
>   Unconscious of yourself.
>
>   He should have a mirror
>   To act as he looks."

"Well done!" said Sam, coming forward, walking not
unlike a herring gull. "Beautiful," sighed Ivor. Jacko ap-
plauded for all he was worth. His jacket and tie were off
and his white shirt was limp.

With much ceremony Sam crossed the floor, sat at the
organ, and arranged his fingers. Despite a couple of forti-
fiers, they were damp and shaking. He need not have
worried. After the first three notes the whole assembly
except Jo joined in with that oldest of tunes and rendered
Sam superfluous. He even stamped hard on the swell
pedal, but those eager, full voices swamped him. And he
got every note right.

CHAPTER
FOURTEEN

As the evening flowered, the party's petals unfolding their pure red color, dancing continued, lights dimmed, eardrums cowered under the onslaught of decibels. From outside, the club seemed to swell and settle like a partially inflated rubber dinghy. Jo watched Jacko dance by with Mrs. Roland Kemp, a dainty butterball woman in perspiring pink, whom Jacko held like a stick of gelignite. Before the unreality of the scene spiraled into hysteria, Jo took her muzzy head out for a breath of air.

The Spit was almost too solid after the rhythmic sagging of the club. Alan Jones's *Maid* was moored there, cluttered with rags and newspapers and old fishing gear. Roland Kemp's Meridian 24, called *Aniseed*, lay alongside, with three Mirrors owned by younger club members who liked to race. At the very end of the Spit a big cat, the *Alhouette*, swung heavily, uneasy in the humid night. Jo knew she normally lay in the old harbor, owned and skippered by Terry Nash and used all season long for fishing trips. Vaguely she wondered why it was here, and some suspicion stirred the bottom mud of her glazing mind, sending up tendrils like smoke, but they failed to reach the surface. Lightning speared the horizon, and faintly, later, the rent of thunder rolled across the sea, bringing a flat smell of acid and oil. Might break up the slick, thought Jo, turning away. The rocks of Windways had shown vividly in the green flash.

She walked back, musing. It's a shame that now I hate all boats. Used to love them, the lift of sail, the quiet hiss

of water at the foot, the silent speed and need for judg-
ment, hard work, responsiveness. Denny like an accurate
cat, gray-eyed and serious. And now I dare not see, or
hear the vocabulary of boat sounds; their beauty is forever
tainted by my own sickness. She'd heard a man once say,
of the conditions just hours before an earthquake, "There
is a yellowness between us and the sun."

And now her friends, doing only what friends are supposed to do, had set that familiar yellowness between herself and Jem, just when she had thought to see the sun
clear again.

Jo returned to find Steve and Jem waist-deep in alcohol
and argument. It was a calm sea full of unseen circling
sharks. "I'll tell you who is going to come to this demo,"
asserted Jem. "Freaks. Layabouts, idle rich with nothing
else to do, louts, students, all bandwagon jumpers who see
seals and birds and think 'Oh, isn't that pretty.' They're
just good-cause hunters. No government will take one iota
of notice of them. It's just so much sentimental slush that
bears no relation to the realities of nature."

Jo flared at him with more violence than was warranted.
"I am going to the demo, and Steve, and Ossie, and friends
of ours who are fishermen. Ordinary people, Jem, who
work hard. If it's freakish to care, then we're freaks. If it's
foolish to try, then we're fools. But if your world is wise, I
would rather live in mine!"

"Would you, Jo?" said Jem softly.

"Indeed I would." Her eyes were fierce in the lie.

"I like foolish things," said Jem.

Jo glared and walked away. Steve tapped his glass
thoughtfully. "I think you are like our old Sam," he said.
"He has an abhorrence of sexual perversion, particularly
homosexuality. It has caused friction at Antlercraft, though
the morals of those you know are always more acceptable
than those of strangers. Still, Sam hates queers with a
strong passion, very noticeable in a man so curiously
close with his emotions."

Jem had been ordering two more pints, listening with
only one ear. He put his elbow in a puddle of beer on the
bar. "You think I'm gay?" he said, chuckling.

"No, no. You're not hearing. I thought at first that you

considered yourself as rather outside the human race, nothing could touch you except perhaps personal loss, and you do not regard pollution as that. But now I'm wondering whether you are not like Sam. Why should sentimentality and even outright sloppiness get your dander up, anyway? Is it a stab at your manliness, a threat? I ask myself, why does it frighten you?"

"I am not at all frightened, just bored." Jem shook his head. "In fact, I feel rather sorry for you."

"You do?" Steve drank from his pint and knew it was one too many. But he refused the bait to defend himself. "I think," he said carefully, "that you are a real romantic at heart. Like Sam and homosexuality, you know that you could cross the border into sentimentality and be as sloppy as the worst of them. And hence trapped, liable to be used or committed. So you must defend very forcefully against it."

"I feel sorry for you," said Jem, "because you are as trapped in your loneliness as I am, as Sam is, as Ivor is, and all this love for humanity and ecology is so much padding, just insulation to keep you from yourself." He offered a pack of cigarettes, and Steve, rarely a smoker, took one.

"Are you right?" he said, coughing on the smoke.

Jem nodded. Somewhere was sorrow, but deep-buried beneath the cold sands of his truth. "What's all this about Sam?"

Flatly, his mind elsewhere, Steve said, "He joined the navy very young, and Kitchener believed his age lie. The lads all missed their mothers and needed comfort, you know how these things can start. Advantages are taken, little abuses . . . They were inexperienced in temptation, and they were scared of war."

The men drank in silence, swamped by the din. Steve stared about, his eyes heavy as ball bearings, rolling together. Irish Steve was leaning on Jacko's shoulder, retelling his joke. "There was this Paddy who went into a bar and asked for a Scotch on the rocks—wit' water!" Irish Steve neighed like a horse, and old Jacko joined in, but his eyes were dark in perplexity.

When the buffet was unveiled, everyone declared himself unable to eat a morsel, but in less than ten minutes all that remained of the filled rolls, dips, quiches, crisps, Bert Lark's pies and sausages, flans and cakes, were crumbs. Paper napkins and plates lurked in every corner. Alex was well satisfied and the guests were well fed.

A sense of slightly pop-eyed well-being percolated through the company, the party petals curling at the tips with the first harbingers of wilt. One or two guests, nonstarters, left; the rest succumbed to the demands of working gastric juices and slumped into chairs and amiability. Ivor and Mick the Artist pecked at tidbits of Van Gogh data, feeding them to each other with ecstatic chirps, each politely waiting for the other to finish, so that he could regurgitate yet another, even more tasty delicacy.

Jo was still smarting with sunburn, indignation, and resentment. The thunder-chased wind was rising outside, loud enough to be heard above the clamor. She resented and resisted that too. She hovered on the rim of a deep construction debate between Steve, Jem, and Sam, and jabbed meanly barbed remarks into each of their sentences, though she said no word aloud. Steve said little too. Jo could see he had overstepped his rather low liquor threshold.

The rain began, a sharp patter becoming a relentless hammering. Irish Steve started a fight with his longtime friend and neighbor Browny Law. Or it could have been Browny who started it. These dark red men swung haymakers that would have demolished barns had they connected, and they broke some furniture, and they swore a lot, locked in weary, puzzled combat like a pair of drunken warthogs. Alex, smaller than both, evicted them with ease and much scolding, and they rolled around in the mud for a while, encouraged by impromptu seconds. They were later discovered, slimy and obnoxious, swinging their feet over the Spit, singing "Good Night, Irene" like lovers.

The party was groaning, browning at the edges. Several couples left, to be replaced by diehards sniffing out a late drink. Oxygen was at a premium. Time passed recklessly. Colin Whale arrived. He clapped Roland Kemp on the back, made Alex laugh, bought Roger Payne a drink, all while his long green eyes scanned the cluttered room, pausing at every woman. He is tall, black and green, lizardlike, heavy-lidded, always suspected, never caught. When Sergeant Cassell has a stolen car reported, Colin Whale crosses his mind.

He spotted Jo, waved, and moved toward her, easy and sinuous through the crowd.

"Jo darling, why didn't you tell me it was your birthday? I'd have brought you a little something."

"From Woolworth's?"

"From the chemist, sweetie."

Jo laughed brazenly, catching Jem's steeling eye. "Colin, you're incorrigible."

"But I get so little encouragement. Do come and dance, so I can lay legitimate hands on you."

"Why not live dangerously?"

As they went, Jo saw Peggy signaling all sorts of disapproval, but she winked and kept going.

The couples on the floor smooched oily together, close as sardines. All those still capable of stance had left their seats for the final slow waltzes, and Ken Butcher as MC was selecting records and conducting with a drinking straw while swaying perilously on the edge of the stage. He wore a strange blue paper hat, too large and supported only by his ears.

Jo seemed to be dancing with an octopus, and was relieved when Ken announced an "Excuse me." She brushed the creases from her dress, only to be bear-hugged by an enthusiastic Jacko.

"Excuse me."

The new arms were slim, cool, firm, but not grasping. "Hi," said Jo, suddenly evacuated from bleary indifference.

"Hi, yourself. You dance well, Jo."

"Thank you. There's not much room, is there?"

"You didn't seem to need much with that Whale character."

She laughed. "No woman does. Colin is our local Casanova. He's kind of a permanent hazard, an accident black spot, but more predictable." They waltzed and turned, drifting, enjoying the mutual balance, knowing exactly where the next step would lead. Jo said, "Jem, do you really think that Steve's demonstration idea is so haywire?"

He said, "I'd rather talk about you."

"You're not another seducer like Colin, are you?"

"Infinitely better. He'd bring you flattery and candy and have a flashy car, and he'd try to get you drunk."

Jo nodded. "That about fits. And you?"

"If I wanted to seduce you," Jem said softly, eye invading eye, "I would take you walking on the High Moor in the midsummer moonlight, and I wouldn't talk to you."

In the big, brash brawl of a party, then there were only two. Jo, with her face a little shiny and rumpled, a smudge of black at the corner of her eye, and the gentle wave of hair back from her forehead that would never change, etched in Jem's memory, a beautiful fine sweep of gold lines. The tip of her nose whitened as she smiled, revealing good broad teeth, fan-shaped, and "You have eyes like brown marbles," Jem was to say.

Jo felt she had passed through the very path of a hurricane, turned inside out, revealed and secretless, and now stood in its eye, quiet, excised, changed. How could you know this? she asked. How could you know? Their feet trod out the juice from the old standards, and a sweet fragrance of heady romance filled their lungs, throwing out fatigue and reticence. Jo listened to Jem's words, every one, scarcely believing. Impact was distant, but I know I will remember tomorrow, she thought, listening.

He said, "Lovely, lively woman, you've been so much in my mind, I can't put you out now." And he said, "My life has always been a dumbbell shape—office, home . . . home, office. Now you have given me another dimension." And he said, "I'd like to throw you in the river and pull you out again." He kissed her mouth, once, and she tasted salt and soft.

"How did you know?" said Jo.

A cry from outside, from the Spit, came urgent and long, carried in on the wind, now a Force 7 southwesterly backing the tide. To Jem, to Steve, and to Sam and Jo that cry penetrated. It was starkly real. Steve, stiff with beer for so long, leaped like a hare and was first to the head of the Spit.

He fought the wind to the end, where Jacko and Roland Kemp, bursting with effort, were trying to fend off the catamaran *Alhouette*. She flopped like a bucket on the plunging sea, threatening to swing on her forward warp and crash into both the *Aniseed* and the *Maid*, which rolled and rode steadily, moored secure.

"She's lost the aft anchor!" bellowed Roland above the wolf wail of the wind. "If we can't keep her off, she'll break up on the Spit or wreck my boat!"

Jo and Jem panted down, hearing the words. Steve yelled, "Just let her come in against the Spit once, near enough for me to jump! I'll take her out."

"I'm going to help," said Jem.

"Oh, no! No!" Jo was ill with fear, suddenly stabbed in the guts with it. The spray of the cold sea hit her in the face, got in her mouth. "You must not, Jem, not in this storm! No!"

He hesitated. "Why not?"

"Not you too. And Steve. You'll all be gone. I couldn't stand it!" Her face was livid white, glowing with fear. She tugged at his arm.

"I'm quite able," said Jem, colder than the spray. "I've been to sea before."

"Oh, I didn't mean . . ." But Jem had gone, running to where Steve, hauling like a winch on the forward line, was trying to pull the bows around to counteract the sideways swing of the bucking cat. Roland and Jacko thrust against the rubbing strake with an oar apiece, but they could not hold both tide and wind. As she swung, the cat came close enough for Steve to jump, and after him, Jem. The boat ground against rock, shedding yellow fiberglass.

Steve dived for the flying bridge. At the second touch the twin Volvos crackled to life. He reached for throttles, clutch, and wheel as Jem leaned out dangerously on the port hull that kicked like a mule only inches from the granite Spit, pushing off with a boathook that bent under the strain. As the power took hold, he yelled, "Cast off that line!" and someone obeyed swiftly, throwing the warp haphazardly.

The engines held her against wind and sea, but remooring would have been impossible. "We'll ride this one out!" cried Steve. "Let Terry Nash know!" A wave from a black-wet figure, and the cat's engines roared, making steady headway, bows into the wind and fighting every inch of the way. It was like pushing through molasses, but she was a good boat and happy to be free, and she made it.

Terry Nash had to be forcibly restrained from committing grievous assault on his schoolboy brother, who after a row with Terry had moved the *Alhouette* from the harbor to the Spit to fake her theft.

Sam took Jo home to Antlercraft for the rest of the night, but she was strung out on the nails of anguish and could not close her eyes. There is a torment that cannot be worded, so enveloping it is, and each crash of the storm, each bellow of wind, had to be climbed like a mountain.

As soon as it was light, she took the Transit up to Fort Hill, left it on the road, and ran between the squat, fashionable houses to the cliff path. She moved as a prayer, muttering and crossing all her fingers on both hands, feeling only a tinge of relief that the wind had dropped.

At first she could see nothing. The sea glared, broken-mirrored in the early inclined sun inside the floating oil booms. Then, through the dazzle, a small white wave, and behind it the yellow hull and white superstructure. The catamaran was making easily for the old harbor, arcing wide around the fist of the pier.

Jo sat down and lit a cigarette. Then she cried a little, remembering what a fool she had made of herself, turning Jem away on the bulwarks of her fear. But relief was greater. They were safe, and her soul was quiet, with no weight dragging at its coattails.

"What a hell of a birthday!" she said aloud; then she sneaked away home to Dundee Road to sleep until evening.

CHAPTER
FIFTEEN

The talk in the town was still of the wrecked oil tanker, and more indignant protest than Steve Wilder had thought existed was voiced in the pubs and clubs and shops and hotels. Many proprietors of holiday accommodation were incensed by cancellations, and manifestly, loss of income was the needle of outcry. The District Council was doing its best to clear the affected beaches, now five miles of them around the Sandcliff area, but it had retreated into a corner behind a web of red tape in an effort to fend off claims for compensation from both fishermen and hoteliers. The television teams came and broadcast nationwide the news that booms had been placed to protect Penquay harbor and neighboring coastal beauty spots, but still the tourists doubted and did not come. Mud, and oil, sticks.

Steve and Ossie Bertram took a dozen students to Lion Bay, where they donned masks, waders, and protective clothing, and staggered about in disgust, scraping up buckets full of pollution. The oil was evaporating slowly, having the consistency of unset jam with the pips of dead birds embedded in it. All the limpets were dead, and the sea anemones and little gobies and small green crabs.

They worked alongside the Council operatives, scraping and slopping into a collecting tank, with the rank flat smell in their lungs and their mouths, so that they tasted it for days in every meal. It got into their hair and their skin too. In a short time words were lost. The men and women worked and worked, but still the beach was laden. It was like attempting to vacuum the moon. Each face was set and pinched and dogged, cold even under the sweat.

At one o'clock they broke for lunch. Ossie, gleaming like the monster from the bog, drank tea from a thermos flask. "What a bloody, bloody mess," he said. "I've never seen this in real life. It looks so different on television. I was right to organize this demonstration, Steve. Practically everyone in town will support it, they can't ignore this. Two buses are coming from Sandcliff, and the TV cameras will be here too."

Steve nodded. At his side lay a heap of slick refuse, funereal feathers and beaks and claws. "There was a man I knew," he said slowly, "who drank a copious amount of wine and often imagined he was Jesus Christ. I shall never know whether the illusion grew from the drink, or whether he drank to drive away the enormous weight of responsibility. It is an awesome thing, to fly in the face of all that man has come to hold dear. The money lenders are back in the temple, voted there by popular assent. I know we are beginning at the bottom of the pyramid, carefully and wisely, but at the top is fiscal power, and that is as well protected as a queen bee. I have a sudden premonition, Ossie, that after all our protests—and they will be vociferous enough to catch attention—the result will be promises. More care, more policing, more attention to navigation et cetera, but these substandard charter tankers will sail on, because they're cheaper. The owners can even insure against fines for pollution. Great, isn't it? There is to be an international convention on crew training sometime in the future, but meanwhile . . . Unlike Jesus Christ, we haven't the stuff of miracles at our fingertips."

"Should we not bother, then?" said Ossie, acid in a cut lip.

"But of course!" Steve laughed. "I wouldn't slit my throat now, just because I know I'm bound to die one day. We should all have our glory times to show a little light to the world."

One of the girls came up the beach, feet heavy and dull. By its beak and one spread wing she pulled a cormorant, carefully, so its dead body did not bump too hard upon the hidden stones. "Come on," she whispered. "Come

along, poor little one." She knelt in the oil beside it, and it
settled on its back with its breast sacrificed to the sky. Her
gentle finger made furrows in the blackened feathers, and
as she stroked she made the wuther sound of mourning.

Ossie beckoned to one of his team who carried a camera
to photograph the extent of the damage. "Her," he said.
The young man nodded and went to work. As the shutter
clicked, the girl looked up, anger catalyzing pain and pro-
ducing the face of outrage. The shutter clicked again.
"You low-down, prying, unfeeling bastard," she said
lethally, but the boy only nodded.

The photograph appeared in the Sandcliff and Penquay
Gazette and was sold to the dailies. Steve had a blown-up
copy made for the club, to pin above the Royal Society for
the Protection of Birds collection box, and on the strength
of it the commodore instigated a raffle, proceeds to the
Sandcliff Bird Sanctuary.

It was as well that the demonstration had not been
planned as a surprise, for it is impossible to keep such a
thing under one's hat, or even a collection of hats. The
Poly vibrated like a hive. Lectures were poorly attended if
not abandoned altogether, but as the end of the term was
drawing close, the appetite for learning was already on the
vacation slopes. Young women from the home-economics
program were busy for days with needles and black cloth,
and young men from the Arts Department were applying
their skills to huge sheets of stiff white card and black
paint. The party that had helped to clean the beaches
brought back buckets of sludge and poured it into a glass
tank embellished with a white skull and crossbones. They
brought birds too, and made a pall for them, to be carried
by mourners in black armbands and hats appropriated
from the drama section. Photographs of the broken-
backed *Torrey Canyon* and Amoco *Cadiz* were sought out
and mounted on placards with the slogan, "Fifty thousand
seabirds killed," alongside similar prints of the *Kimoco*
and "How many this time?"

The ripples, as they will, spread and engulfed the divided reef that was Antlercraft. Old Sam hedged himself
about with indifference. Outwardly, to Steve in particular,
he was amenable, ready to defend the fishermen, ready to

agree that he would not appreciate the jeopardizing of his own livelihood. Ready indeed to complain if sea trials on the ketch had to be postponed. But to Jem, in the privacy of the drawing-office landing, sensing he had found a kindred soul, he confided his doubts.

"I'm too bloody old and I've seen too bloody much," he said, propping a skeletal thigh over a stool. "It'll do no good. All these demonstrations cause is trouble."

Jem laid his Rotring pen down. He and Steve had done two hours on the *Alhouette*, all that was necessary when dawn came so early, and snores had been more prevalent than conversation. But since, he had sensed a coolness, no, less than that, a wariness when Steve and he spoke. None of the laughter had gone, it seemed, yet some of the joyful quality was missing, the moment when the sun goes, yet still lights the sky. All references to the oil slick and the demonstration had dropped from daily exchange, which satisfied Jem, but he felt that he had somehow harmed and tainted a fresh and free thing, and only because he wanted it to recognize him.

He heard himself say, "I suppose it can do no harm, Sam. The Jarrow marchers achieved something."

"Ah, maybe, maybe." Sam sounded unconvinced and had that I've-heard-it-all-before crease about his mouth. "But there's no political meat on this one, Jem lad. Nobody starves anymore."

"Are you going to watch, Sam?"

"No . . . no. Got better things to do. The masts have arrived, and the suits of sails for the ketch. Want to come and look?"

As the two men descended the stairs, each in his nautical fashion, Sam mumbled, "Enjoy the party?"

And Jem said, "Yes, very much, even the seagoing part."

While the masts and sails were being scrutinized, Jacko sat in his workshop in front of a brand-new Marine Dieselite 6MLD, with eyes that were blank and befuddled. It was not the impending demonstration that bothered Jacko, for he believed in Steve. No. And it certainly wasn't the generator that caused concern. Of their own accord his skillful fingers checked the belt tension, flew among spanners and screwdrivers, accurate as bats. No. It had come to Jacko that the aftermath of Jo's party, despite his own blundering, should have been fairy castles and sunsets. Yet what had happened? Nothing. He had screwed up courage to ask Ivor, but to no avail. "Why not ask Jem?" he'd suggested tartly, and Jacko had gone away still uneasy.

His attention evaded him easily, as it was accustomed to doing, and wandered around the shop to find comfortable old niches. The welding and metal-working area, the steel fortresses of oxyacetylene bottles, the electric arc, the mask and solders and fluxes. Into the small store, poking in neat files full of neat drawers containing nuts and bolts and washers and screws. Under the bench around reels of electrical cable of all colors and amperages. Across to the Harrison lathe in its concrete bed, back to the big central bench. Jacko recaptured it, writhing under the pressure of keeping it contained. Small sweat droplets burst upon his cheeks, and his shoulders bunched with tension. Someone had to do it.

The struggling birth of an idea was a new sensation to Jacko. He reddened, squirmed, squeezed, wriggled his ears, pinched his nose, embraced his knees, and curled his toes. The pangs were no less great than those of the borning of a baby. When it lay, beautiful and pink upon the white rumpled sheet of his mind, Jacko was overcome. It scared him yet was so formed and perfect that, like God, he saw that it was good. He wiped his face with the back of his hand and relaxed heavily upon the stool. His knees shook. Maybe God felt like that too.

After a short interval it dawned upon Jacko that having an idea was one thing, applying it quite another. Momentarily he longed for the coddled warm time before responsibility had raised its head and put him in charge of Jo's happiness. But a pride was about him too, a new father's pride glowing with the white light of rectitude, and he knew that he could do no more.

He found Steve in the ketch, lying on his back with his head in the saloon bunk locker. He kicked the prostrate legs urgently.

"Christ! What is it!" The voice was hollow.

"Me," said Jacko.

Steve slid out and sat up to rub his shins. "Mashallah!" he said. "Are you mad at me?"

"Listen . . ." Jacko babbled on incoherently, holding his hands out to Steve as if they held a parcel.

"My dear Jacko, you're like a party balloon. Say it slowly."

Jacko moved a roll of green upholstery leather and sat down. The gist of his speech was that Steve should persuade Jem to take Jo out, preferably to the Poly end-of-term play. Steve patted his boot kindly. "You are a good fellow, Jacko."

Jacko wriggled with pleasure. "Will you do it?" he said.

"No. I have already done those things which Jo did not want me to do, and there is no health in me. Now I will leave it to them, to Jo and Jem. If they don't, they don't."

"Steve, you've got to, you can't refuse!" He stared down at the body of his friend, whose eyes were closed to pleas. "Get up!" he shouted.

"No, Jacko, believe me, we put our collective foot in it, right up to the crotch. Jem is clever, and he hates to lose."

"He ain't lost nothin' yet!" Jacko stood, menacing.

"If he lets us manipulate him, he will lose. It's hard. I can't see a way. Leave me alone, Jacko."

"What about Jo?"

"Ask Jo. Our attempt was vain and fanciful. Let things take their course. I have my own problems."

Jacko stared at the impassive face with the bewildered anger of the teased bull. "Hell!" he said, and kicked Steve's shin, but Steve only groaned, and Jacko stumbled out into a wilderness.

CHAPTER
SIXTEEN

The day before the demonstration was of a kind that astrologers and augurs circle large and black upon their calendars, so that they can say "I told you so" afterward. The signs were all there. Mars in the ascendent crossing Saturn's path. Geese flying in a Y formation over the town, presaging depressions of all hues. Roger Payne saw a lone magpie, a rare bird in his garden, spit and crossed himself to avert the ill luck. At Sandcliff a little girl pointed out a strange phenomenon in the sky, and people said, "It's a blue moon!" In the harbor a porpoise jumped once, and was not seen again. There are such days, and it does no good to ignore or argue them. It behooves one best to keep the lowest of profiles and endure with patience, but in the roles of men it is not always possible to stay in bed all day, or to avoid contact with humanity.

Jo woke, and the waking surprised her, for she had not known she was asleep. In a dream she had lain awake, watching the room through closed, storm-bound eyes. Unnamable horrors leered at her from behind the walls, squeezing obscenely through the fine cracks in the plaster to circle her bed. She drowned in terror, calling Denny's name through the black wave and committing herself with the apathy of the vanquished to his ghostly decision. And as she woke, a voice said, "Be still . . ." and it commanded, and it was not Denny's, nor Sam's, nor any voice she knew. The peace of defeat invaded.

Jo began to cry, great heartbroken sobs, for in her early dreaming Denny had lived, large and real as the pier, and holdable, so she remembered his arms. And the night had been paved with gold and there had been great swaths of blue in the sky, and laughter, and the roaring of the pines above the place of loving. The old Jo had been there, with hope and sparkle and the joy of kings with golden crowns.

It had gone in the false waking of black things behind the walls, and gone more definitely with the real waking. The memories drizzled away, leaving a low gray sky and a lonely woman with her fists bunched into her eyes.

The old lady in Fox Street next to Allson's heard the thud of her letterbox and shuffled from the grimy kitchen to fetch her mail. The hall linoleum was cracked along the lines of the floorboards and the backing showed through in a bald patch where the letters had fallen. The old lady stooped to pick them up, and put her back out. Locked at ninety excruciating degrees, she groaned to the nearest chair and sagged into it under a shrieking of sciatic nerves that was almost audible. It was a long time before she could open her mail. One was an electricity bill, the other a leaflet advertising a new brand of toilet tissue, singularly inappropriate, as the most the old lady could afford was the Sandcliff and Penquay *Gazette* torn into squares and hung from a nail in the outside lavatory. She closed her eyes and whimpered.

Irish Steve woke with a hangover, a relatively normal state of morning affairs for him. His tongue was huge and dry, lodged in his mouth like last week's bread, and his skin did not fit him. As he rolled from bed a smell assaulted his tired nostrils, a smell such as requires immediate investigation. In his pajamas, concertinaed in the legs and arms, he pursued it.

There is an unkempt sink in the annex to the aquarium hall, and Irish Steve assumed the odor must come from there. Muttering all sorts of slander against the Sewerage Department, he made straight for it. On his way through the aquarium hall it came to his attention that all the water snails in one of the tanks were climbing out of the water and up the glass as fast as their feet would carry them. Intrigued, he looked closer. The goldfish floated flat upon the surface, last gasp long gone. The stench of hydrogen sulfide was awful.

Steve breathed in through his nose and out through his mouth several times; then he cursed, made a cup of cocoa, and sat down to think.

It was the sort of day that turns even the mildest man aggressive, so that Sam Antler, always a touch crotchety, became positively ferocious. Ivor, suffering dreadfully from something he called "environmental neurosis," stormed out of the workshop after Sam called him a pansy. Sam's thumbnails had just been rendered black and blue and bound to come off by Jacko dropping half the weight of a diesel on them. Jenny had a headache because her cat had kept her awake all night, yowling after the female in heat next door, and she refused to type because of the noise.

Jacko sat in his workshop with his chin in his hand and his eyebrows forming a furrow across his kindly face. For a week he had sat thus, in between necessary jobs, quiet and hurt, yet brave and steadfast, keeping Jo to himself in his mind, guarding her from loathsome indifference. He was at a watershed, and a bridgehead, and it was to be his rising or his falling. Poor Jacko, never alone in his life, could not comprehend the retirement about him, and he ached for the laughter of Steve Wilder.

Ivor came in, slamming the door, and Jacko looked up with a smile, but Ivor was outraged, trembling, pale. He lit a cigarette and glared. "I'm not staying here," he said. "Not after what he said."

"Who?"

"Sam."

"What did he say?"

"Never mind, but it cut me to the quick. I'm really very upset. He has no sensitivity whatsoever."

"Oh, he's all right," said Jacko comfortingly. "I dropped that bloody engine on his fingers and he didn't say a word."

"I'm leaving!" said Ivor suddenly. He crushed out his cigarette in Jacko's brass ashtray and rubbed the stub fiercely across the engraved pattern in its base.

"What, now?" Jacko was shaken from isolation.

"Right now. I'm going to ask for my cards and go to work for Nash Marine. They offered me a job long ago. I'll go where my talents are appreciated."

"But Ive, you can't!" Jacko stood up and placed himself between Ivor and the door. "You're not goin'," he said solemnly. "I'll get Sam to say sorry, but you're not goin'."

Ivor hesitated. "I can't work for a man like that," he said with quiet certainty. "You don't understand, Jacko. He's offended my mortal soul." He made to walk past the shorter man, but Jacko had resentments building like steam in a boiler. Ivor should stay until Sam had been consulted and this mortal-soul thing figured out. It hurt his sweet good nature a good deal to do it. After all, a friend is a friend, but great troubles require great remedies, and there was no time for thought. As Ivor tried to pass, Jacko hit him solidly under the left ear with a fist like a train.

"Hell, Ive," he said. "Hell. Now, you stay till I get Sam."

Ivor uttered a surprised, strangled protest and lay feebly back in the cotton waste on the floor.

Jacko found Sam in the kitchen, soaking his thumbs in cold water. He sat upon a low stool with his hands over the lip of the sink and his forehead resting on the edge. He was gray and sour. "Christ," he muttered, his knees squeezing together. Immediately Jacko's problems became multitudinous. Guilt and sympathy for Sam struggled with stern compassion for Ivor. Words finally burst from the fecund jungle of emotion. "Sam, Ivor wants to go. You've got to stop him."

Sam groaned, rolling his head against the steel sink as if to cool his mind. "Go away," he said feebly.

"You've got to come," insisted Jacko. "He won't stay down long."

There was a tight silence. "Down?" muttered Sam. His thumbs throbbed purply with the steam hammer of his pulse. He lifted his head until his eyes focused on them. The lurid bruises were bulging under the nails and a thin string of blood ran from one, brown in the water. "Down where?" He squinted at Jacko through a fog of pain.

"Come on." Jacko tugged urgently at Sam's suspenders, which he wore outside his sweater. "Oh, come on!"

It took Sam a while, months it seemed to Jacko, to grasp the strange and terrible situation. Visions of Ivor's pale face under the green harbor water crossed his mind.

They were enough to get him to his feet. "What's happened?" he asked, his lower lip almost touching his nose in an attempt to control the pain.

"Come on!"

They found Ivor seated in Jacko's chair dazedly fingering a lump on his head, which the mirror in the first-aid cabinet had assured him was as big as two eggs. His dark eyes bulged at the recollection of the assault. His whole demeanor told of the enormity of his shock and outrage. He looked, thought Sam grittily, like a nun trapped in an orgy.

It took much smoothing to sort out the morning, and afterward Sam was exhausted and demoralized. He even forgot to take pleasure from the graceful hulls in the construction shed. Ivor went home anyway, to recover, but promised to return next day, cut to the quick though he would remain.

Poor Jacko talked to himself all day, even though Ivor had forgiven him. "I had to do it," he said often. "Bloody day, awful day . . ."

Jem Merriman received a reply to the letter he had sent to his daughter. Susan had painstakingly copied down her mother's dictation, the pressure of the childish pencil so hard that in places it had torn the paper. He could see her blond head bent, a strand of hair chewed as she concentrated. She had written:

Dear Daddy,

Thank you for your nice letter. We have a dog now, his name is Spiro and he eats all his food. I was in a puppet show at school. Mummy says I can come and stay with you soon. We are going to France with Uncle Arthur. Mummy will write to you. I have got a Bionic doll and her arm comes off because I had a good school report. I love you, Daddy,

                                        From Susan

She had added three big crosses at the bottom.

Jem's loneliness became a lump in his chest so large that it pushed out all the air. As he walked the streets of

Penquay in the refuge of anonymous faces, his breath came so tight it made his eyes water and his nose run. All feelings lose their immediacy in time, and the impact of Sue's letter, folded carefully back into its pink envelope and stowed in his wallet, lessened as he walked. But the exclusion of himself implicit in her simple words hung heavily on the fingers of his soul, and all day she was like a kite, tied to his loneliness, casting a shadow on his face.

All over Penquay, people put the lid on the day early and with a sigh of relief. For many, sleep came easily, and was welcome. For others, it teased at the door like a stripper. Sam's thumbs throbbed dully and peopled his dreams with torturers. Jacko slept like a turned-off engine, and Ivor read Goethe through ten cigarettes, the ceiling above his cot draped in curtains of smoke. Jo slept with the picture of Denny beneath her pillow, but he did not come back that night.

CHAPTER
SEVENTEEN

The babes in arms and the old and house-bound of Penquay might have been unaware that the demonstration was taking place on Saturday, but everyone else knew and reacted accordingly. The procession was to follow a route from the central building of the Polytechnic, along Penquay Road past the Odeon Cinema and down to the bus terminal. There it would circle St. Bartholomew's, cut through the lane into Market Street, and from there to Upper High Street for a stop and dispersal outside the Town Hall in the car park, where marchers could rest their weary feet and sing "We Shall Overcome."

Pete in Ruby Lane heard about it and analyzed the hunger of marching youth and interested bystanders, and ordered two hundred extra croissants and currant buns, margarine and cheese and shoulder ham, doughnuts and fruitcake and other stomach fillers. He polished his coffeemaker that looks like H. G. Wells's time machine, and relinquished teapots in favor of the big urn. He and Mrs. Pete rearranged the price list and sat back to wait for the influx.

Elsie Payne told Roger to do the weekly shopping on Friday and stay indoors all day Saturday. She regarded marching students of any race or creed, whether bellicose or meek, as Maoists. She is a lady for labels and selects them at random from the news media, sticking them with plenty of verbal glue, ample predjudice, and little discretion to anyone whose ideas are not her ideas.

Ivor and Jacko decided not to march; rather, Ivor de-

cided. Jacko, still ostracized, concurred. Contrition was
strong, so that he followed Ivor and patted his shoulder
whenever he could. Steve was still slumped on the couch
of self-mockery, so that he forgot to ask Jo to march with
him, and said to Jem only, "I don't suppose we can rely
upon your support?" and Jem, unthinking, replied, "No."

Old Sam, having refused to go, and hating weakness,
could not change his mind. But he reserved a private possibility of sauntering to the church and watching the ban-
ners flutter by, after all the others had gone about their
business.

The folks up on Fort Hill would relax in their leather
armchairs and watch TV, or maybe drive down to park
their Jaguars on the front and feel they were slumming.

At Penquay Police Station things had been plodding
along for the past week. The total staff of the small brick
jail with its curly portico at the end of Days Lane is seven,
and bearing in mind shift work and overtime, Sergeant
Cassell decided he would need extra help from Sandcliff.
They could spare him only three constables, making his
Saturday presence eight, including himself. It worried Sergeant Cassell. The demonstration was supposed to be
peaceful, but if it got out of hand . . . if marchers began
insulting townspeople . . . if townspeople became irate and
threw back more substantial items than rude words . . .
if he ended with a riot on his hands and the High Street
looted and the Town Hall stormed and Port Penquay on
the ten-o'clock news . . . It made the stiff collar of his blue
shirt damp to think about it, and played up his incipient
ulcer. Ossie Bertram received four phone calls from Sergeant Cassell, each to ensure that the demonstration would
be absolutely quiet and peaceful.

So it was that Port Penquay made its various plans
about where to be and where not to be, what to see and
what not to see, whether they would laugh, jeer, or simply
stare, whether it was a success or a flop. If it wasn't for the
way things have of collecting their own momentum, of
coming alive and developing unexpected personalities, it
would hardly have been necessary for the demonstration
to happen. Fortunately, there is always the unforeseen.

At two o'clock precisely, the principal organizers of the
march, Ossie, a representative of the fishermen's coopera-

tive, and a councilor who also owned three hotels, led the way around the grassy oval in front of the central building and out of the open iron gates. As they moved, the lovely human sound of chattering and laughing by a mass of nearly four hundred persons quieted, and the uneven soft thunder of walking feet took over. Black armbands were in place, and many faces frowned earnestly under black hats. The sky was white and hard to look at, and a small summer wind scurried between the slow-moving legs. Right at the front went the tank of oil with six bearers, and their shoulders a little crooked, and behind them a banner held by two strong men, "Ban the Tankers." Several older lecturers from the college carried heartrending photographs of dead fish and whales and seals, and birds with their wings glued together by oil. The coffin of the birds was most poignant. The young people carried it as if it held a child. And so, down the whole column, were placards hating pollution and placards loving mankind and animalkind and placards telling and placards asking. But the marchers themselves were the real show. Halfway along Penquay Road they encountered the shoppers and the beginnings of a crowd out to watch, and they became aware of their audience. The heads bowed, though no word was given, and "Save our wildlife," rumbled ominously and sadly from the leaders. The chant was taken up and passed from mind to mouth along the column, and "Save our wildlife" echoed from the chins on the chests. It was at once pleading and angry. The short queue for the Saturday matinee at the Odeon turned to look as one man. To them the marchers seemed to stretch forever into the distance, and they were a multilegged insect and their low cry was frightening.

Sergeant Cassell had directed that traffic be excluded from the lower end of Penquay Road for the afternoon, so that when the procession arrived tourists were wandering in the middle of the street. The column came around the bend and the shout went up, "We hate pollution!" and the bowed heads raised to the hot, uncaring sky, and the arms spread, palms upward in supplication. The onlookers scattered, and those that could climbed steps and gained vantage points in shop doorways. The walkers came on slowly, slowly. The heads bowed again simultaneously and with great dignity, and in total silence but for the quiet foot thunder, the column filled the road and moved toward the sea. The great silence perplexed the crowd; the column became a thing, a dark shape. They looked at the placards and they pointed out in whispers as if it really were a funeral, and they saw the sad young faces and the older stern ones of Steve and the fishermen, and wondered how it felt to be inside their heads.

As the tail of the column wound past, a clear strong voice called, "Join us! Protect Port Penquay! Join us!" and some of the crowd did, and others hurried away.

Old Sam watched from a seat by the harbor wall as the dreadfully silent marchers emerged around the bus terminal and turned in front of the church. The glass saints seemed to have compassion in their thick-lidded eyes, and pity on their ever-smiling mouths. Should have had a band, Sam thought. For marching you need a band. Like when Georgie Green and I joined up. He smiled. Not even of age, and we had to go, longed to go, couldn't wait to leave those good, ill-paid apprenticeships. God, we thought we were dashing young chaps, uniforms smart as tacks, your country needs you . . . all that. And he and Georgie Green, five-minute recruits fresh as cabbage, had marched down from the recruiting office, now the Sandcliff YMCA, behind a bloody great brass band blowing its heart out. And weren't there some ladies waving encouraging hankies from a window, and just he and Georgie and all that bloody great band.

Suddenly a ringing came, a buzzing, unresolved ringing of voices, and "Join us! Save us! Join us!" shone clear out across the harbor and made the sea sing as it does in the sun. Half a dozen other tones began, "Steve, good old Steve! Ossie, good old Ossie!" and the column took it up, though they were not all sure of the names. And as Sam watched, Steve was lifted shoulder-high behind the leaders, with his head touching the "Protect Port Penquay" banner, and he smiled and clung on, and some of the students wept, though they did not know why. Old Sam knew why. He knew the wonder and the glory of an army, the way it is proud and terrible and sad and useless, the way blood sings and throats tighten, the thrill of a cause that is right and a uniform that symbolizes the claim to right, even if it is only an armband or a hat. He swallowed away the tightness of his own throat, and shook his head, and deep in him felt a foreboding. Then he shook his head again and muttered, "Load of nonsense. Just a lot of kids having a bit of a show." The cries hung in the air long after the procession had disappeared into Market Street.

There must have been more than half of the town population out to watch, and a good proportion of them lined Market Street and Upper High, all the way to the Town Hall car park. The walkers flowed into the street and the constables marched alongside them, excited and watchful, but with faces that were impassive. Their blue helmets came well down over their faces and their eyes gleamed warily in the shade.

Everyone in the street saw Steve upon the shoulders, and many remembered his smiling, intense face, and those who did not know him asked his name. There seemed to be a light about him, and it lay around him and on the heads of the walkers behind. They spread their hands, palms outward, and cried, "We hate pollution! Stop it now!"

The long winding insect coiled itself into a ball before the Town Hall, and around it gathered a ring of watchers. But they did not mingle. Always there is them and us. Always. So there was a clear space, a person wide, between the campaigners and the campaigned upon. Ossie Bertram climbed the steps beneath the portal and raised a megaphone to his mouth.

"Friends!" he cried. "We are so pleased you have come. We are sure you know about this oil pollution and will want to stop it. We want to begin here in Penquay by protecting our coast, our fish, our birds, our citizens! The supertankers must be prevented from perpetrating such devastation upon our coasts ever again!" A cheer rose from the crowd, like a flock of doves. Ossie continued, "Here is Steve Wilder, who helped to organize this campaign."

He stepped down to another cheer, and a dozen hands propelled a hesitant Steve into his place. He took the megaphone self-consciously and waited several long seconds while the crowd's hum dwindled to expectant silence. Then he lifted the megaphone and heard his own voice magnified and running away, and it sounded like a stranger's.

"Many of the marchers here today have a personal and very important interest in our protest against the tankers," he said. "They are fishermen. They enrich this town to a large extent by their trade. They are at present without a living." Cries of sympathy and waved fists. "Another sector to suffer is that which promotes and supports the tourist trade, our largest source of income. Hotels and guest houses are half-empty. The holiday makers have not come. You," he said softly, pointing at the crowd, "have vested interests. You are important in the function of this area. Without you the town will fail. Undoubtedly you will claim, and receive, some monetary compensation, and you may think that sufficient. But I ask you, I beg you, to look further.

"We do not replenish the seas. Dead fish are dead and gone forever. We cannot force the tourists to come. It can take years before people trust an area again, once oiled beaches have soiled its reputation. And finally, because they have no claim to recompense, no tongue, I ask you to remember the wildlife of our coasts, the rare birds, now rarer, and the marine life of the shores that is not essential to our survival or economy." A cheer, small and ragged, from a group of ornithologists and conservationists.

"We are going to form a Standing Committee on Pollution," announced Steve. "Its function will be to make representation at the highest possible level in the Department of Trade to encourage controls on tankers, their owners, skippers, and crews. It will work in this way. Any club, committee, institute, or group may hand us its voting approval. In this area there should be at least thirty thousand members of various organizations, and that is one very large voice. Please give us your support!"

An unexpected volume of approval met Steve's speech, for it had been too short to cause boredom. He jumped down, to be shaken by the hand by men he knew and men he did not know. Promises of help fell upon his ears, and compliments and questions, but Steve was thinking: Padding, is it? Do I really do this only for myself? And in truth, there was no answer. Or it lay, undivined, beyond his grasp.

He paid avid, forced attention to the others who spoke, but he caught sight of Jo, who had marched at the rear, and a leaden screen descended, leaving him alone with festering doubt. His sister smiled at him, raising a thumb.

She, too, stood alone.

When a large and spectacular event occurs, it is quite reasonable that other concurrent and smaller events will go unnoticed, or at least be relegated to the bottom drawer of the day. The demonstration was not entirely without incident, though none was as a direct result of the march. Five students, enchanted with success, decided to extend the enchantment artificially and ended by having a drunken brawl in the public bar of the Stag with a party of fishermen from Barnsley. Sergeant Cassell was obliged to dust off a couple of cells for the night. And during the afternoon of turned heads it was hardly remarkable that the amount of shoplifting and petty larceny had doubled for a Saturday. One old lady died in her bed while her daughter was out watching, but she most probably would have died anyway. Two babies were born in the absence of the midwife, whose car had been boxed in the market car park for two and a half hours.

While the march was wending through the town, four young women who preferred sunbathing and water sports to anything as unsettling as a demonstration gamboled in the sea off Half Moon Bay. They were lithe and tanned and happy, with not a pimple among them, and they swam like mermaids. They had medals from school for lifesaving; confident, go-ahead, girly girls. The threat of oil bothered them little; they had seen no evidence and believed the new sign staked above the beach that read "Safe for Bathing" in big red letters.

They were quite a way out from the Spit when one girl muttered quizzically and trod water, staring around her. Another noticed, and she too raised her head and peered closely into the milky aquamarine water.

With a yelp that sounded clear across the sea, she made for shore, breaststroking to keep her face out of the water.

The others followed, all the way keeping their beautiful eyes peeled, and in the shallows stood and shook their arms and turned each other around for close inspection. The smallest, who had black curls and a firm eye, said, "That shouldn't be there. I'm going to complain." She marched up the beach.

"Who to?"

"I don't know. Who deals with . . . with sewage?"

They were all mystified. "I'll ask the police," said the girl with black curls.

So it came about that Sergeant Cassell, satisfied by the pacific nature of the demonstration, felt an inclination to be helpful to the pretty young ladies and immediately passed the buck to the District Engineer at the Town Hall, who acts as agent for the Regional Water Authority, thereby doing his bit for public hygiene and decency, and concluding a well-organized day.

He saw fit to be amicable with a young constable colleague, telling him the story and elaborating the distress of the ladies, and the constable found it meaty enough to pass to Roger Payne, who happened to be drinking in the PPCC that very evening. It was not long before the news had spread almost as far as the effluent from the sewage outfall.

But although the crowd below the print of *Eleanor* heard the snippet, so saturated were they by the events of the day, turning the demonstration like a crystal to marvel at all its facets, that, like full sponges, they could accept no more. Even Steve Wilder forgot what he had heard.

Later, he was to remember, and even later, to wish he had not.

CHAPTER
EIGHTEEN

While Port Penquay rattled and swayed to the demonstration, Jem Merriman climbed a mountain. As always, with one or two isolated exceptions of late, he stood apart from, above perhaps, the daily concerns of his fellow beings. The notion of a demonstration bored him, he felt scathing toward its enthusiasm, its aims, its lost causes. They do not, he thought, live in the real world. I will go and conquer something of the real world.

He rose very early, cooked porridge and ate it quickly, leaving the bowl for Trix to lick clean. Steve in the next room did not stir, and Jem congratulated his own swift and soft movements. He packed his old rucksack, bleached from many years of rain and sun, collected his small folding easel and handmade wooden box containing paints and brushes and palette, checked the car, and drove off along the empty pier just as the sun caught the topmost jibs of the St. Jude's cranes.

He drove fast, thinking of nothing but the road and the car and the gradual warming of the day, and he drove far, way to the north to a range of hills that are budding mountains, whose highest peak is Ply-Tor. By the time he arrived, some early walkers were about, casual sun-and-air folks. Jem ignored them as he laced his climbing boots, and attacked the high-domed hill that is like a green breast with as much enthusiasm and determination as the levelers of Everest.

It had been different last time, conditions almost unimaginable now under the rising sun. Last time was twelve years ago, before he married, before he met Annette, and it was midwinter and snowing. In the valley the snow slushed quickly, but up on the mountain it lay loose and freezing, scything on the buffeting wind in crystals that were sharp as sand. It had been impossible to keep one's eyes open, the tears froze and cracked, and on the exposed northern edge impossible to stand or even to breathe. The passing wind vacuumed the air from his lungs, and the blizzard scoured the skin from his cheeks and forehead. He remembered the thrill of combat, the glow of achievement on crawling to the summit, and remembered too that on such expeditions he always felt the lack of a companion, someone close to share the battle, not just a friend, another half.

Pacing steadily up now, the rucksack straps cutting through his summer shirt, he re-experienced the loneliness and emptiness, but where it had been pale then, and liable to relief in later life, it was brightly colored now, red and blue; and not so much later life left. Annette should have filled the vacancy in his soul. She liked to be in the country. She did not baulk at mud or snow or water. She walked at his side. So where had the chasm opened, and when? The bare rocks of the track gave no answer. Jem did not know. "We did not care enough," he said in a whisper with the even rhythm of his feet, watching the toes of his boots come and go, come and go.

It took him two hard-driven hours to reach the summit, unsympathetic to the pull of tendon against muscle, relishing the pain, allowing the sweat to run into his eyes and to drop from his chin. Even on the stillest of days a wind inhabits the heights of Ply-Tor. Jem rested against a granite outcrop and let the wind dry his face.

The view was arm-stretching, commanding, a view to arouse a conqueror's obsessions. The valley, splashed with cottages and farms, was squared into fields of ripening maize, grass for hay, vegetables. The fields are small, the land ungenerous. Mostly there are sheep, spreading up the hills like browsing stones. And the hills themselves, starting small and round, rising, expanding, breaking through the grass of the summits like cakes baked too fast. The summer had bleached the land, and the air above it, so that the sun was too high to see, and the landscape faded purple-blue into distance beneath it.

Jem sat and opened his rucksack. He had a thermos of tea, sweet and strong, a pack of raisins, some dry smoked sausages called Chausseurs, crusty bread wrapped in a clean white handkerchief, a toothbrush, a pencil, a spare pair of heavy woolen socks, and of course, maps; half a dozen of them. He poured his tea and took out a map. He enjoyed the feel and folding of a map, the precision, the lines and contours, the ability to locate. At all times Jem needed to know his spatial position. He shuffled around to face Port Penquay, lost in the miles, and his thoughts dwelled upon his life there, and a smile crossed his face.

After a small meal he unpacked the folding easel and the watercolors, set up the drawing board on which he had pinned a sheet of fabriano paper, sharpened his pencil, and hesitated. Creativity is never easy. The first stroke may be the wrong stroke and may irretrievably point an unsatisfactory conclusion. Carefully and faintly he outlined the far hills, suggested the position of fields and cottages, and a nearby clump of heather. Once started, he worked quickly.

The sky was very pale, a blue never seen in the dark frosty skies of winter. He mixed a very thin solution of cobalt, loaded his number-ten sable brush, and began to wash.

While he waited for the paper to dry, he stared hard at the colors of the local world, the tones, tints, shadows, trying to detect the precise shades of each. And Jo walked into his thoughts. I wish you were here, he thought, I wish you could share this with me. It was a very natural thought, just came in like a friend. You are a country girl, a coast girl with a soft-wide accent. Perhaps you would understand. But perhaps you are not so clever. He smiled savagely. Hypocrite. What is it I need that I degrade a lovely woman for it? Sex, maybe. He considered it, mixing Alizarin crimson with the blue for the far hills. There is a pub in Penquay called the Royal Oak where the local ladies congregate. Jem had been there, had been tempted there, but had gone on his way alone. No, lust was not

among the colors of his palette. "I'm lonely," he said aloud
to the hills.

When he had completed his painting, he sat back to
criticize, lit a cigarette, and took up the sharp pencil. On
the back of a map he began to write, very small, very neat,
in his architect's hand: "I did this painting for you. I
thought of you while I did it, so you are in it for all time. I
would like to keep it to remind me, but it is for you.
Strange girl, strange Jo, you seem to have so much potential. You are often in my head now. I see Steve, and there
you are, same eyes, expressions. It is impossible to avoid
you. I should have stayed in the merchant navy, a lone
roamer. I long to burn up, do outrageous things, swim in
the Atlantic surf in winter, dance, fight, lose control. Are
you with me, Jo? I would like to find a pocket in this
hillside for us, bare my soul, and swipe at gnats in the
evening. I shall have to come to you, if only for comfort."

It took him a long time to write those few sentences,
and when he had done he could not define the emotion
that had nagged him to start. "But I started," he said to a
sheep that passed below him, looked up, wandered on. "I
started," he said to a wheeling rock. He drank the rest of
his tea slowly. The sun was at its zenith, fanning the
midday breeze. Jem lay back, put his head in his hands,
and dozed.

It was a full-blown afternoon when he woke, and a
boiling of children was wending up toward him under the
guidance of an organizer with a knobkerrie and a strident
voice. Jem hastily packed his things. He took a long,
steady look at the painting and realized it so excelled his
usual standard that he did not want to part with it. On the
descent he bargained with himself. If you keep it you will
always have a piece of Jo. But you promised to give it. She
doesn't know that. But you do; a present is a present.
She probably wouldn't appreciate it, and anyway she
would think you presumptuous to offer. Nonsense, you
gave her a birthday present. That was her birthday.

When he reached the car the ridiculous argument was
still unresolved, and he felt rather silly about it. "Juvenile,"
he said to the rearview mirror. He placed the painting on
the backseat and looked it over again. The color of the

heather, so hard to capture because it is strong but not gaudy, was to his eye damned near perfect. And the light, better than he had ever painted. I could show it to her, he thought. But she might praise it so much that I would be forced . . .

He sang "O Sole Mio" in a very loud voice to drown his cheese-nibbling mind. He drove slowly through the butter-yellow evening, and the picture bounced on the rear seat.

It was only as he eased down the Penquay Road, cosseted in homecoming feelings, that compromise raised its head. I won't give her the picture, Jem thought. But I'll make up for it.

So, without nudging, persuasion, or collusion, he accorded with the garbled machinations of Jo's friends, and he sang all the way back to Antlercraft.

Implementing the compromise was, as Sam says, "as easy as falling off a log." On Sunday morning Steve said shyly, "Jem, would you like a ticket to see our play, *Hassan*?" And Jem said, "I'll take two, please." Steve, smiling, said, "Who will you bring?" And Jem said, "Your sister, if she'll come."

As it turned out, Sam came too, having a consecutive ticket, but "I won't be with them all evening," he said.

Jacko, earning overtime, was working on the cruiser's prop-shaft gear when Steve made his sale. He ran over to Steve when Jem was out of sight, took his hand, and wrung it. "I knew you'd do it," he said. "I knew. Christ, I knew you couldn't give up on her."

Steve closed his eyes. From the wicket door Jem said, "It's all right. No one would have made me ask her if I hadn't wanted to."

"Mashallah!" said Steve helplessly, his eyes to heaven.

"Christ!" said Jacko.

In whatever theater, wherever in the world are raised a proscenium arch and a curtain, be they of plywood and blanket or gilt and velvet, there is always a hush and a solid expectancy in the auditorium as the entertainment begins. We wait like spies. Jo even forgot for a moment that Jem sat beside her, collared and tied and polished.

The Poly theater curtains were of drab red stuff, and the

college orchestra clustered below them on the level of the stalls, partially obscuring the view with its spidery gadgetry and dog-eared parts. The members had at least abandoned jeans in favor of suits that did not fit well enough to be their own. But they played the notes of Delius with a passion that transcended the prosaic, and the audience rustled and hushed, even the hardened laughing lecturers at the back.

The curtains parted, a breath-catching moment, to reveal Hassan and Selim seated upon a beautiful carpet in an otherwise impoverished back room in Baghdad. A very realistic caldron produced steam in the background, threatening to engulf the actors in a fog.

From her left-hand side Jo received a loud conspiratorial whisper. "That fat chap is Phil Tudor. I used to play crib with his father, years ago. Didn't know they acted, though."

"Yes, Sam. Sssh!" said Jo tightly, wincing apologetically in Jem's direction. But soon Sam became entranced by the words and laughed first and loudest at all the amusing lines, even at some that weren't.

There was an interval after Act One, and Sam found the bar like a bloodhound. Getting served first from behind a thirsty crowd is one of his many talents. He and Jem and Jo lounged against the wall, Sam rolling a cigarette with one hand. The young couple were glad of his presence. Through him they talked to each other.

"Ha!" said Sam. "I liked that rescue scene. 'O thou maggot!' " He snorted amusement.

"I liked the poem," said Jo. " 'Shower down thy love, O burning bright! for one night or the other night Will come the Gardener in white, and gathered flowers are dead, Yasmin!' " She stopped, blushing.

Jem smiled at her and Sam said, "Ah!" a couple of times.

"Where does Steve come into it?" asked Jem as the five-minute bell rang. "He's been muttering all week about souls of unborn children, and comets."

"He's the fountain ghost." Jo laughed. "In Act Three. I feel quite nervous for him."

"He'll do fine," said Sam.

But when the time came, Jo almost missed him. The

play had swung from comedy to tragedy, and the suffering of the lovers cut a deep parallel so that she had to fight with the lump in her throat. When Ishak spoke the lines, "His life is rhyming like a song: it harks back to the old refrain," she was clutching Jem's sleeve and too scared to let go. No, she said inside. It does not have to be, nothing is ordained.

Steve appeared beautifully ghostlike from his bloodred fountain, which was in the form of a naked boy laughing in artistic symbiosis with a dolphin, and the mortals fled in terror. Jo jumped at the familiar yet thinned voice and settled herself to be objective, but her imagination was a sea of subjectivity. Steve's form flickered so that one had to blink to focus him, and the spirits of Rafi and Pervaneh, the lovers, were almost transparent. There was a brief smatter of applause for the electricians.

Pervaneh was speaking. "There is a faith in me that tells me I shall not forget my lover though God forget the world. And where shall the wind take us?"

The ghost replied, "What do I know, or they? I only know it rushes."

"How do you know about the wind?"

"Because it blows through the garden and drives the souls together."

"What souls?"

"The souls of the unborn children that live in the flowers."

"And how do you know about the passage of ten million souls?"

"They pass like a comet across the midnight skies."

"Phantoms shall not make me fear. But what of Justice and Punishment and Reason and Desire? What of the Lover in the Garden of Peace?"

"Ask of the wind."

"I shall be answered: I know that in the end I shall find the Lover in the Garden of Peace."

Jo missed a few lines because she was obliged to find a handkerchief, and she caught Jem smiling at her. She said quietly, "Aren't you watching the play?" It seemed he was not, and she avoided his eyes.

Steve delivered his last line: "It is the wind. I must go

down into the earth." He vanished behind his voluptuous fountain.

Pervaneh spoke: "Ah, I am cold . . . I am cold . . . beloved!"

Rafi trembled, insubstantial as a mirage: "Cold . . . cold."

"Speak to me, speak to me, Rafi."

"Rafi—Rafi—who was Rafi?"

"Speak to thy love—thy love—thy love."

"Cold . . . cold . . . cold."

The wind swept the ghosts out of the garden and the bells of the caravan rang wildly.

"Is it over?" said Sam.

"Not yet," said Jo. "There is a little hope left yet. The Golden Road to Samarkand."

CHAPTER
NINETEEN

Jo and Jem drove to Sandcliff, to the Blue Bowl, a famous sixteenth-century pub with flagged floors and plain wooden settles. Locals played shove ha'penny on a chalked board. A few tourists joked at a corner table. The couple sat side by side, and Jo glanced often at Jem. He had a good, strong profile, straight-nosed and with little hairs growing out of his nose that needed trimming. It is said that ante-bed he looks at her, post-bed she looks at him, but Jo looked and Jem did not. But he did laugh, and was delighted, and did not listen to her words. She eased him with her glow of liveliness, and he toasted his fingers at the flame and thought, how warm, how good, how pleasant not to feel the hand of winter at one's back.

And suddenly, out of nowhere but the mind's treachery, he was telling her about Annette and Susan, especially Susan. Words gushed and dribbled from his mouth, and he was at a distance from himself, joking at the table with the tourists. To his ears his voice was soft and unemotional, and he saw Jo listening with her lips closed, her eyes huge and her expression blank.

"Do you miss them?" she said, after the wash of words had subsided.

"I miss Susan. She has a cheeky, sweet face."

Jo felt cold as he spoke, living in puckered seconds the getting-to-know, the knowing-and-loving, the loving-and-losing, the loss. But firmly she reined in her galloping mind and said silently, it cannot always happen. Don't run the gamut of you and him before you have started. The unknown Annette, whose power was still great enough in distance and time to soften Jem's voice, stabbed panic through her chest and forced her to call up the old tune: Doesn't matter. Have fun now. Learn the sums of him that make a man. Forget your sad bloodred uncertainty.

She played with the diamond ring that had been Denny's gift and that she wore on her right ring finger now. It was loose because her hands were cool. "Do you like sharing with Steve?" she asked lightly. "It's so long since I lived with my brother that I have to force the memories. He used to be too big, sometimes. Not in stature, though he did have to duck at the kitchen door, but full-wide of ideas and talk and politics and causes and fishing—you name it. He was always generous, too." She laughed, and Jem watched her big white teeth. "He gave away anything that wasn't nailed down. He was always coming home from school with less clothes than he went in. Poor Steve, he's gold, pure gold."

"Why *poor* Steve? He's one of the happiest people I've met."

Jo shook her head. "I don't know. Is he?"

"He's a very enthusiastic person," said Jem, "but his feet don't seem to be quite on the ground. He has a magic quality like mercury, which fascinates me because I feel he inhabits a different world, but not so different that I don't recognize it. Do you understand? I'm not being very clear. I feel the same charm in you, but you seem to know this world better."

"I wish I'd known you long ago," said Jo. "Before any of the spoiling things happened. I had a lot of confidence then, and trust. Too much, maybe. Go too cocky by a long chalk." She grinned. "Steve is somehow stronger. He knows all about the spoiling things, but he won't be beaten. He's a gardener, and the wings of the storm bird may break his roses, but he'll plant more, and wait." She glanced away, embarrassed.

"So you are alike, Yasmin," said Jem, taking her hand. "Strange, nice people you are. And you have good little working hands. Have another drink?"

"Please."

Jo watched him at the bar, the way he stood, flat and firm, the angle of his neck, the way he used his hands. He liked his hands, she could see. The glasses stood proudly in them and would have felt, if they could, the warmth and slightly callused dryness of them. Jo's breath caught. But he's not like Denny. Denny was taller and fair and long-faced, but . . . he had the same high-carried shoulders and a way of turning his head. Jem smiled at her as he returned.

She took a little Dutch courage, then said, "I wanted to apologize, Jem, for my behavior at the party. It probably seemed disproportional to you. I guess it did to me, afterward."

"That Colin Whale chap?"

"No, no." She smiled and made a note, as women do. "When you and Steve took that damned boat out. I'm very scared of the sea now. A few years ago you couldn't keep me off it, or out of it, but it claimed someone I loved, and I've lost all trust."

"In people too? Poor Jo, I heard about that."

"Then Mum died. I can see it rationally, you know. Coincidence, horrid coincidence, explains it all. But I live alone and I think a lot, too bloody much, Sam says. It gets to seem that all I've loved and wanted, I've lost. Is that self-pitying? I don't feel that way. It's simply this, now. I don't try for anything anymore because the possibility of losing saps all my confidence. When you and Steve went out on that boat, I got a phobia that is like screaming. I panic and say crazy things when it overtakes me, but I can't stop it." She smiled halfheartedly. "So now you know what a mess I am."

"Jo," said Jem gently. "You can come under my coat anytime."

Can I? thought Jo. Oh, can I? It would be so good.

Their journey home was dark and quiet, the elderly engine humming and chittering smoothly. Sandcliff Road follows the coast for two or three miles, clinging to the edge of the cliffs, and there is a strong fence to prevent overenthusiastic drivers going for a high launch. The moon tangled in its wires, netted like a fish.

Jem stopped the car. It ticked as it cooled. The filling moon cut a golden road to the end of the earth. "To Samarkand," said Jo. "I've never forgotten how lucky I am to live here. Even working in St. Jude's isn't so bad when I have all this beauty."

"Even the sea?"

"Oh, yes. To look at. A love-hate relationship." She grinned in the dark, moving toward him. He took her head in his hands. It was the holding of a warm, round cup and the tasting of sweetness from its lip, though her mouth, as before, was a little salt, a little wine. A sudden passion warmed him, ran quickly to his arms, his thighs, left them aching. Jo whimpered. "I'm sorry," he said, releasing her.

"I've enjoyed this evening more than any I can remember," said Jo.

"And I," said Jem. "For a long, long time."

Jo wiped the palms of her hands on her dress and breathed a long, silent breath. Inside she was singing so loudly she thought he must hear, and perhaps he did, for he said, "I would like to dance with you, Jo, and swim, and laugh, and quarrel and make up, and take you to dinner, and to Capri, and throw you in the dustbin, and be a whole human being."

She chuckled. "I think that would be nice," she said. "But at the risk of being a wet blanket, do you know me well enough? I'm both awkward and independent, of necessity. It has worked out that way. And you have a wife who might want you back—then where would we be?"

"You must trust me, Jo." Jem felt his grasp slipping.

"I have trusted others," said Jo. "I'm only being realistic."

There was a silence, and Jo watched Jem's silhouette against the golden moon road. It looked absurdly young, unlined, crisp-haired. She wondered whether he was angry, but when he lit two cigarettes and passed her one, his eyes were soft in the lighter's flame. "We have a key," he said. "that gives control of our relationship. I see it pass from me to you and back, Yasmin, and whichever of us holds it has the upper hand and feels safe."

"Yes," she said. "I understand."

CHAPTER
TWENTY

With rarely a backward look, for his conscience lay clean beside him, Jem Merriman embarked upon two of the most delightful months of his life. Apart from Jo, with whom he was as an explorer on a new planet, constantly discovering flowers and birds, lights and shades, fungi and butterflies, his new design was blossoming. For hour upon hour he measured and drew and traced. For days he sat in Penquay Library checking and referring to tomes of math related to naval architecture. The excitement of creation is hard to describe. He smoked one cigarette after another with the tension in his gut that is like gambling or high diving or driving too fast on ice. He longed to finish, yet extended every detailed moment to its limit so that it would be the best, the supreme.

He designed the schooner with a shallow fin keel with some internal ballast which gave a draft of only four feet, and a skeg-mounted rudder well aft. The prospective owner had given a free hand, but for the stipulation that accommodation should be roomy, and that he intended long-distance sailing. Consequently Jem laid out a real cabin in the forecastle, six-foot headroom, a partly enclosed huge double cabin opposite the head, which incorporated a shower unit, a living-sleeping saloon, all with plenty of under-bunk lockers, and a neat, well-equipped galley. After discussions with Sam, he decided to rig the prototype as a Chinese schooner, with options for sloop and conventional schooner. Work stretched before him like the Golden Road to Samarkand, and as a woman said of all men, "They have their dreams, and do not think of us." But in the moments of lapsed concentration that come in any hard-work day, Jo's face materialized on the drawing board.

The Arabs came and took the express cruiser away on an enormous low-loader. Her design was established, tried and true, and she was to be sent to the Middle East as deck cargo. Quite a crowd gathered to watch. She was, after all, a thing of great beauty, fifty-three feet long, white as a swan waiting for freedom, fast as a bat with two eight-hundred-horsepower diesels, and on the trailer, high as a house. The last thing Sam had done to her, a little tradition he keeps like a promise with all his boats, was to stencil upon her bows below the rubbing strake the stylized antler, and to paint, freehand with a sable brush, the thin red line that all Antlercraft carry, "Like Balaclava," says Sam.

It is always a sad and proud moment, to lose a child you have conceived and furnished with good things, and for which you have given time of your life. Sam watched the boat go, slowly along the jostling pier, wished it well, knew it was right, and felt no doubts. He said, "If you've got those drawings for the hull completed, Jem, we'll get over to Robin's first thing in the morning to collect the wood. Can't afford vacant space for long. By the way, Stotty has a couple of letters for you—requests for plans. You'll be making money yet."

Jem laughed, a pure happy laugh, as he went.

"He's changed," said Steve.

"So has Jo," said Sam. "Not that I've seen much of either of them." He winked. "Does he say anything to you?"

"Not much. I think he would, but her brother is perhaps the wrong ear. He hasn't been home for quite a few nights."

Sam grunted. "As long as it's not under my roof," he said sanctimoniously. "Now, this boat's supposed to be in the water next week. Shall we get on?"

The ketch's design had been thoroughly sorted, but Sam hadn't been at the tiller of a yacht in a long time, and having made a few alterations and minor rearrangements, he took the excuse of a trial gladly. A splendid day it was, with a good force-four wind from the southwest so that they could tack out close-hauled into it, run by the lee and downwind, under a sun that would make the white sails glare like snow.

Jo arrived at Antlercraft at nine o'clock on this Saturday morning, eye-catching in tight jeans, carrying a picnic basket. Her hair was cut, washed, and burnished. Sam smiled at the sight of her happy face and shining eyes. She kissed his cheek. "Where's Jem?"

"Upstairs. Coming with us?"

"Are *you* coming with *us*?"

"I just said that," Sam huffed through his nose, a laugh for Sam.

"We're going for a long walk and a picnic. I have a bottle of white wine."

Sam frowned, thumbing at the harbor where the new boat lay, barely moving at anchor. "We're taking her out for trials. I thought Jem was coming."

Jo was silent, glancing around the pier, at the boat, up at the big shed, biting her lip. "Oh," she said. "I didn't know."

"Let's ask him." Sam led the way. Jem was just about to leave. He came toward them, dressed in deck shoes and a light oilskin. When he saw Jo, he stopped. Sam went through to his bed-sitting room and closed the door behind him.

"I've brought the picnic," said Jo, showing the basket like a talisman. "And some wine. It's a lovely day. Are . . . are you coming?"

"Oh, Jo, I'm sorry. I forgot the trial. Why don't you come out with us?" Her big, frightened eyes annoyed him. "You won't drown," he said coldly. "We're all good sailors."

So was Denny! She clamped her teeth on the words. "I thought we'd arranged a picnic," she said. "Last week, we arranged it. You asked me."

"Jo . . ." Jem took her shoulders, kissed her shiny hair on the unalterable line where it waved back from her forehead. "You can't be afraid of the sea for the rest of your life. It's nonsensical."

I can. Please, Jem, come with me. "You did promise me first," she said. "I trusted you to keep your word."

Jem sighed. "I know. It was my fault for forgetting. But I really do want to see how this boat performs, Jo. It's my livelihood, my work."

Jo had no words. You promised. You know how I fear the sea, and the thought of losing you to its greed. Am I selfish, am I? Unreasonable, perverse. Hurt, too. "It's up to you," she said, lowering her head so that he shouldn't say, "Don't put on that pleading look."

"Well, I'd like to go. I'd like to go on our picnic too, but we could do that tomorrow. Lovely woman, look at me. You mustn't get so worried, kitten."

"I'm not worried, I'm bloody mad!" snapped Jo, her mouth square. "This is the first time you've broken your word, but I can see it might be the thin end of the wedge. Go on your trial, but don't expect me to hang about until tomorrow, waiting on your pleasure."

"All right!" shouted Jem, and marched out through the open doors.

Steve appeared, almost as if from his fountain, ghostly. Jo looked at him bleakly. "Was that me or was it him?" she said.

"Bit of both. You are touchy about boats and sailing."

"Wouldn't you be, brother?"

"I don't know. Yes, perhaps. But that presents Jem with a challenge, you see. He wants you whole, doesn't care for the idea that he might be loving an emotional cripple."

Jo nodded silently, swallowing a corrosive draft of tears. "Then he should have come when I was whole," she said grayly. "I cannot change what life has made of me."

"But you can refuse to dwell upon it."

"Dammit, it dwells upon, within, me. Should I cut my arm off, could I?"

" 'Let the Past bury its dead! Act—act in the living Present!' Jo, you will never be happy unless you can."

"I know, I know." Jo flung her arms around her brother and rested her head against his chest, solid through his shirt. His heart beat evenly and slowly, a comfort. His chin rubbed upon her hair. She said, "What should I do, Steve? I'm afraid I'm not brave enough to go to sea with you, or Jem. Not yet awhile."

Steve gave her a hug. "Promises are promises," he said. "Even for our diamond Jem. Go and sit in the kitchen." He sauntered out onto the pier.

Jo was sipping the inevitable tea when the door opened and Jem's face, all smiles, said, "Come on, then, tea-baby. I'm ready to go."

"Where?"

"Picnic, isn't it?" said Jem encouragingly.

"Yes. Yes, of course!"

Steve lounged against the sunlit wall. "How did you do it?" Jo murmured to him as Jem unlocked the car.

"I lied." Her brother grinned. "I said Sam had postponed the trial till tomorrow."

"He'll be mad."

"Mmm. But not at you. Have a nice day."

Jo joined Jem in the car. She toyed with the notion of asking why he had changed his mind, just for devilment, but a little wisdom blew in from the hills of experience and put a lock on her tongue.

They walked beside a river that day, a river which used to cough with salmon years ago but is now degraded, too brown, too muddy. The warm strong wind sleeked back their hair, polished their faces, all along the unbroken green wall that keeps the river checked. Not much of life was there, no animal, a few birds, low-steering pigeons, one or two swallows not making a summer. But for the buttercups and daisies and a few manifestations of the human race, it was abandoned. "It's very flat," said Jem. "Very verdant." This place was clean and green and little occupied for years upon years, but now the strange invader had come. He had built a nuclear anachronism, had bought the people and sent them away, had planted a pile and two pretty space-age towers, had protected it with fences and alien machines and men in white coveralls, and "They don't seem to be of my race and yours," said Jo. The invader gave warmth and light from his tall towers, like a benevolent squire whose face is never seen; and his minions worshiped his symbol—the mighty pay packet.

The place cast no shadow, and at its foot stood an empty, desolate house once called, they judged from the map, Salmon Lodge. It was placed at an angle to the river, at an angle to the fields around it, seeming to deny the natural symmetry of land and water. A fair, square stone house, it used to be, and the walls were still sound, but the colors had gone the way of the occupiers, and were faded, peeled, weather-drained. The ceilings showed their bones through great sores in the plaster, and "Elvis" and "Led Zeppelin" had been scratched above the fireplace, and the stairs looked too dry and frail for any but a child's weight. Under the stairs they found a nest, vacated. "Who were the tenants of Salmon Lodge?" said Jo. "Did they live on the fishing alone?" And live on the salmon they did, for Jo and Jem found a rusty horse sled in an outhouse and shared a picture of the patient dobbin squelching through the brown river mud with piles of the cone-shaped willow "putchers" behind him. And him sinking between the shafts while the traps were laid so craftily across the river. To Jo, the life that must have been was very real; she could see the faces and figures: a man in navy clothes and big boots, a lean, strong man; a plain, shadowy woman, and children who knew the river and the wild things before they knew how to speak.

They passed around the power station with speculations on their lips. What was *that* for, what did *they* do, whereabouts in all that was *it*? The reservoir and danger signs and navigation warnings and silt pits, the evidences of man bending nature to his will. "It seems very us-and-them," said Jo. "The sort of feeling wars are made of." There were big wheels turning, lengths of floating pipe whose use they guessed at, probably wrongly. They passed by, of necessity on the other side, a little scared perhaps, eager to pretend the world was as it used to be. And as if to give them just the required evidence, they came upon a man fishing, elbows on the wall and his line idling on its float. Behind him, seated on a folding chair, his wife knitted a brown-and-yellow sweater. They did not look up as Jo and Jem passed.

"I would love to photograph that," said Jem softly. They stared back over their shoulders. The menacing bulk of man's most modern and complex achievement, product of genius and great technological application, and there, seated at its gate, insignificant in size only, a lady knitting a sweater.

"It gives me great hope," said Jo.

It was a day of broken houses. Behind the river wall was a large, formerly sound mobile home, huddling beneath birch trees. They nosed, found the windows stoned, the interior ragged. Some lonely man was using it; there was one old shoe on the rough bed, and magazines and a lot of mess. He was out at the time, "In one shoe?" said Jem. Or maybe, Jo thought, he was dead or drunk and concealed on the floor. They did not go in. Despite the flapping door and the windblown scraps of curtain through the holed panes, it was a private place, a temple to a loser.

In the afternoon, a little foot-weary, they broke their journey in the lee of the wall to eat cheese sandwiches and ham buns and celery and tomatoes, and to drink the cool white wine. Jo had brought two thin glasses, carefully wrapped in tissue. They watched the cars on a curving bridge downriver and heard a train echoing north on the distant bank.

"I'm sorry about this morning, Yasmin," said Jem.

"You're here," said Jo.

He inspected her pale, freckled face, catching all the white light of the sun. "You don't look like a healthy, outdoor sort of girl at all," he said. "But I like your oppositeness. You are bony, marbly, different from me. Great sexy barn, you are." Her curls were sweat-damp in his hands and he could feel her laughter. "Jo. Little leaf," he said.

"Someone might come along," said Jo. "Might see us."

"No. There's not a soul in sight."

"The fisherman—"

"Is fishing, two miles downstream." Her mouth was slippery, uncertain, then sure. She ran her tongue against his teeth.

"What does it feel like to be inside of your mouth?" she said. "Let me find out how it is to be you."

Then: "Jo, why do you have to wear jeans?"

"To inconvenience you. We may have passed the agreeing-to-wait-until-we-know-each-other-better stage, but I'm still no pushover."

"Oh, you are. A glass of wine and you're anybody's. Creamy girl, your skin is so soft. You must be a lady."

"Why?"

"We always said at school that only ladies had soft skin. Silly thing to stick in the mind so long." He pinched the back of her hand between finger and thumb. "Thin, like parchment. I love you, Jo."

"Are you sure no one can see?" Jo stretched, golden, eager, a half longing to be whole.

Jem raised up, looked around. "A cow."

The grass tickled and scratched and was forgotten. The cow, and the crooning of the low pigeons, and the swallows swallowing slow sleepy midges, all were forgotten in the hopeless abandon of sunshine bodies that were hard and fluid as gold in a mold.

As they returned to the car, starlings were gathering for the mass roost of the night, swirling cacophonously against a mist pink sky. Jem said, "My daughter says they look like tea leaves."

"They do," said Jo. "Children are nice like that. Fresh."

"Like you are. Yasmin, I'd like to spend my life with you."

Side by side they went, and Jo was silent. A great bell swung joyfully in her soul, but the old fear tempered its wildness. Lightly she said, and lightly stepping, too, happiness in her heels, "If that is what you want, then come to me free, Jem. I will wait, but I can't become involved in all that . . ."

"Sordid stuff?"

"No. The people I don't know, the sympathy, the pain."

"They are still away," said Jem. "When they are back I shall write."

Jo allowed her hand to trail against his. Already she knew that, feeling her touch, he would take her hand and squeeze it, warm and dry and sure.

CHAPTER
TWENTY-ONE

Summer splurged on, hurried on, bullied on. The end of season became very busy. The oil scare was waning, the beaches had been bulldozed to render the slick out of sight if not out of mind. The weather blistered into an Indian summer whose like had not been known in years. The town sagged under its weight. Paint peeled, dust and litter collected too rapidly for the Council operatives to keep pace in clearing it, the leaves of the trees were dark old green, ravaged by insects, dry as paper. Old Sam and Steve, out upon the sea, fishing and lazing in off-duty hours, became tanned and weathered, sun-bleached and hard, like the wooden piles of Nash Pier. Mick the Artist extended his season, got a commission from the owner of a Nicholson 38 for a boat portrait, lined his pockets and bought some new brushes. Irish Steve went to sleep in a Guinness-induced stupor on a bench outside the Albion Hotel and had to be treated in Sandcliff General for heat-stroke. One doctor commented that he had rarely seen a man in such fine fettle considering that his liver had the consistency of a brick.

Jo still caught her morning bus to work, but her mind was always tuned to Jem. He was a radio station constantly murmuring in her ear, and all the world but he and she had taken a pace back. She saw the forget-me-nots under the roller return to the earth, and the grass become tawny and coarse for lack of rain, and she thought: Jem will be phoning me today at one o'clock. She talked to the old wrinkled man with the blue lunchbox, just so that in passing she could say, "Jem, he's my boyfriend . . ." Jo, who had never been particularly chic, or conscious of prevailing fashion, saw herself through Jem's eyes and bought new clothes, polished her nails, wore a little lipstick and mascara. She executed nothing without Jem at its core. He was her first thought on waking, if he had not already walked through her dreams, and he dogged her days, filling them with smiles. Even when they disagreed, and disagree they did, for both were strong in their ways and accustomed to independence, Jo talked to Fred the Red as if he were Jem, rationalizing the problem, so that when they met again her frustration was no more than a limp, wrung-out rag.

The students from the Polytechnic had gone away, except for those who live in Penquay, but Ossie Bertram and Steve Wilder kept the Committee on Pollution alive, spending their lunch breaks in the Anchor to discuss policy, tramping the beaches and cliffs as patrolling vigilantes, counting birds, noting absences and presences in the marine ecosystem, writing concise and accurate reports which were carefully filed for future use. Both wore "Save the Whale" T-shirts.

"We haven't actually done anything since the demonstration," said Steve. "I don't want to lose the interest we generated. That's one of Jem's words. What do you think?"

"Of generated? Management vocabulary. There's not a lot of it in here." Ossie's gesture encompassed the public bar of the Anchor.

"When are we going to get the written support of all the clubs and institutions that promised to help us?"

"Ah. The deadline is October first. Then we shall make our representation to the Department of Trade." Ossie's attempt at encouragement rang empty on the ear. He pulled his beard nervously, risking depilation.

"How many?" said Steve, with the weight of foreknowledge heavy in his chest.

"About a quarter so far. Steve, don't worry. Not yet anyway. It's still summer, holiday time, all that. These organizations will be back in full cry come the end of September, then we shall see some results."

" 'You may seek it with thimbles—and seek it with care;
You may hunt it with forks and hope; You may threaten
its life with a railway-share; You may charm it with smiles
and soap,' " quoted Steve.

"Okay, poet," said Ossie. "Is it a Snark or a Boojum?"

"That we have yet to discover. They were one and the
same anyway. Ossie, my saintly buddy, this campaign has
become a matter of personal pride and proof to me, and I
can't say I like the trend."

"How so?"

"We are all quite nicely set in our ways, aren't we? Not
only in the habitual things that we do, but in our attitudes
and thoughts. We are content with our morals and our
values, our inner lives, and we quest only for knowledge or
action that will accord with those values. What is more,
we are a small and close community who generally accept
each other, indeed have accepted each other for so long
that our face values are not questioned. Follow?"

Ossie nodded slowly, foraging in his beard. "True
enough," he said. "Does it pose a problem?"

Steve chuckled. "I don't know. It would if it exemplified
stagnancy, but not if it means harmony and understanding. There has come a stranger in our midst, a cuckoo,
sowing seeds of doubt."

"Who?"

"Jem Merriman. Now, I could adopt the provincial cold-
shoulder attitude and pretend to myself that he is alien, or
plain nonexistent, but because he is a clever man, and
likable, I'm loath to do that. Yet he has come here, to a
space in a jigsaw puzzle that is not his shape, and he chips
and splits and cuts like a diamond, and reveals ourselves to
ourselves. His views and mine about pollution, and other
things too, are totally opposed. But he has forced me to
see with his eyes. . . ." Steve drank his beer in slow, cool
mouthfuls, savoring the malt and hops and gas bubbles.

"It sounds as if he played upon your reasonable doubts,"
offered Ossie. "Does it matter that much to you?"

"Dammit, yes. That's why this campaign must succeed.
To fail would prove him right and abnegate the very purpose of my existence. So, he must be wrong."

Ossie laughed softly. "We all come down to it, poet. There is no interest that is not self-interest. Yeah?"

"Yeah."

If Jem had had any recollection of the incident which caused such an impact upon Steve's inquiring mind, he would have been amazed at the consequences. But the men had shared their apartment in harmony since, and the demonstration had passed beneath the surface of their daily pond, and as far as Jem knew, or looked, all was bliss. Jo, his friends, and his work filled his life to the brim. Only a reflection of regret flickered in quiet moments, as he woke, just before he slept. He wanted to see his daughter.

He wrote to Annette, but the reply was so long in coming that when it did, Susan was already back at school and could not be released. He screwed up her letter and threw it at the wall.

Jem took his unrequited irritation out on Jo that evening. He collected her from work, and was unexpectedly moved by the sight of her face. She smiled, as always, kissed him, said, "How was your day?" and he held her very tightly, so that she sensed a discord and tensed with sympathetic concern.

"Fine," he said. "Would you like a drink?"

"It's a little early," said Jo.

"All right. What then?" And his voice was flat, full of squares and corners of impatience.

"No, we'll have a drink. That's okay."

"I thought that place down in the docks."

"That's nice. Or the Bell in Marshgrove Street."

"You don't sound very enthusiastic about either."

"Jem, I'd love to do anything you'd like to do."

"But what would you like? Every decision I make, you always have an alternative."

Jo hesitated between anger and pain. Patiently she smiled and said, "Let's go to the place in the docks."

"All right."

Just like Sam, thought Jo. A last-word merchant.

In the evening they sat, outside the lilac-painted pub, in

the air bath of the evening, the dry, wispy, cuddly evening.
Jo moved her shoulders, testing for the underlying chill so
often present in treacherous September, but it had been
trodden flat by the hot foot of the day. "It's nice here," she
said, relaxing against the unyielding wooden seat. "Quieter
than the country, except for that crane."

Across the dock, a crane with a free-swinging grab dis-
emboweled the *Harry Brown*, a sand-and-gravel tramp.
Already a brown round mound lay on the wharf beside the
ship. The crane driver was an old hand, expert, splendid.
The machine could have been alive, balanced and con-
trolled as an athlete. The grab swung in a neat, fast arc,
jaws opening just as it passed over the heap, not pausing
as the sand pancaked down, on around the circle, the
movement stopping dead with a quick backward flick of
the jib as the grab aligned with the ship's hold. Wires
protested metallically as the crane dipped for another
mouthful. They watched for a long time in silence and
pleasure.

"Good, isn't he?" Jo said.

Jem nodded. With the edge of a coin he had etched in
the dry blue paint of the table, "Yasmin and Jem," with a
heart and an arrow. He felt too old for that sort of thing,
which made it fun. He now played with his pint mug,
turning it, watching the sun break through the beer onto
the rough tabletop, making fingerprints on the surface. He
studied his hands. They were very brown. A woman
strolled by, swinging a toddler from one hand and an
empty glass from the other.

"What enormous tits," remarked Jem quietly.

They were. Two large unbaked loaves. "You're not a tit
man," Jo reminded him. He rarely commented upon other
women.

"Mmm. But they're something of a landmark in the
mammary field, aren't they?"

Now Jem held the key. They knew the delicate balance
of insecurity, his and hers, and like a balance, the slightest
extra weight on either side set the pans swinging inordi-
nately, undamped by reason. Jo saw their key, passed or
taken from hand to hand, as a big old-fashioned brass
thing with three fancy interlocking circles at the top. They
knew the unspoken game, but knowing did not stop the

action, and since the first mention its existence had been unacknowledged.

"I saw Colin Whale today," Jo said without expression. Jem gazed away from her. "He called in at work." Now Jo held the key. It could come to a fight later on.

"What did he want?" Jem sounded bored.

"I couldn't figure it out. He has such a glib tongue that he confuses himself sometimes. I didn't have much time. I think it was money. He's out of work, as usual."

"Did you give him any?" Jem's eyes were blue or gray, hard or soft, now bright blue. In temper they waxed as the blood drained, and became all blue, even the whites.

"Don't be silly," said Jo.

There was a long, tight quiet, both of them pretending that the air was unruffled, that tension did not exist. Jo hummed a bit of a pop tune she had heard. It had been in her head all day. "Want a cigarette?" Jem asked lightly. She took one.

"I found it embarrassing," Jo consoled. "Vic Allson was there, and I could hear him sighing and puffing to remind me not to waste time. I know Colin's a parasite, but I feel sorry for him. He tries too hard at everything."

She did not know what was in Jem's head. He said nothing, and his expression did not waver. It was always difficult to understand. Things of great importance to one have little significance to another. She knew he was unhappy, frayed, but it could have had many sources. That she had lent, or not lent money to Colin, that she was sorry for him, that Jem was not thinking of her at all, but of Sue, or Annette . . . She could not ask because she knew he would deny both his misery and his mood. It was a shame that Jem admitted of no weakness, for women like a flaw or two with which to sympathize. Jo thought he would visualize himself as a solid length of wood, fine, tight-grained, and without an interesting, invalidating knot in all its smooth surface.

She studied her love from the sides of her eyes. Might he break, with the tugging of a love for a child on one side, and the grasping hand of a lonely, needing, insecure woman on the other?

The sky lowered itself among the cranes of St. Jude's, and their shadows lengthened and lay like black scarves

right across to the wall of the Mexico Well. The blue-
bloomed tables grew luminous, their hands and faces
glowed redly, and in the corners that were out of the sun
the air absorbed light like black holes. Even in the night
there is not such darkness. The crane driver had stopped
rotating and the machine stood idle, its jaw slack. The
yellow paint of it caught the horizontal rays and the crane
enlarged as if it inhaled. Later, it sighed back to gray and
stood dead in the dusk. Jo shivered.

"You're not cold, are you?" Jem sounded impatient.

"A little. It creeps up round your ankles from the water
when the sun goes down."

"I had a letter from Annette today," Jem said. "Sue
can't come down because of school. Maybe Christmas, she
said."

Jo tried to read him, but his cover was good. "I'm so
sorry," she said shyly. "I would have loved to meet her."

There was an inch of beer left in Jem's glass. The key
lay on the table between them, and both their minds
stretched toward it. Jem took his time to drain the glass,
and Jo shrugged her jacket around her shoulders. "I think
I'll have another drink," Jem said pleasantly. "Would you
like one?"

"You haven't eaten yet," said Jo easily. "How about
dinner at my place, and down to the Anchor later on?"

"I'll just have one now, Yasmin," he said. As he crossed
the uneven, cobbled yard, Jo could have sworn she saw
him put the key in his pocket.

THREE

CHAPTER
TWENTY-TWO

In mid-October the weather, teetering, tumbled over the brink of autumn into an early winter, warmish, wettish, dullish. Life continued gently. For some old and sick ones it stopped, for tiny pink new ones it began, but mostly it went on, for the happy, the sad, the mean, and the open-hearted, the sober, the drunk, the givers, and the takers. Leaves fell from the trees and were dusted like gold across the town. The harbor was denuded of boats, the pontoons like stems devoid of bright flowers. Nash Marine and Lawder's Chandlery stacked the speedboats inside, took down the awnings and cheerful pennants, brought in the baskets of water wings and denim caps and rubber balls and waterproof torches and flippers and yellow sea boots. The kiosk closed, boarded and boring, and posters were affixed to the shutters advertising the Little Theater's program and the Odeon's coming attractions. The buses ran at half frequency. Penquay Rovers were on their annual muddy descent to the bottom of the table. Half Moon Bay absorbed the trash of the summer and settled smooth under the tides and the rain. A relieved monotony pervaded, and townsfolk were pleased to be able to shop without queues or crowds, to eat and drink quietly and comfortably in the restaurants, to live in their own houses without guests and breakfast gongs and damp towels. Redecorating started, and plans for Christmas.

The building stocks were erected at Antlercraft for the new schooner's hull, and the mold loft once again came into its original use, the transferal of design onto material.

Old Sam had not enjoyed himself so much in years. Tables of offsets floated frequently from his pockets, line drawings were pinned everywhere, talk was of waterlines and buttocks. The skeleton hull was firm, without twist, "Out of wind," said Sam approvingly, and the new boat grew in the gloom of the big shed, a nautical flower blossoming more beautifully in the flesh than on Jem's drawing board. Sam is never one for overt praise, nor adulation of any sort, but he added a substantial bonus to Jem's fee, and offered to play chess with him as often as he wished.

Jem flew to Jo almost every evening, and enjoyed full days of keeping up with requests for plans, commuting between the pier and the only printing business in town that has a dye line. The handful of letters that Stotty placed on his desk each day were always business, so it was with no sense of foreboding or even particular interest that he slit open a blue envelope addressed in type to "J. Merriman, Esq., B.S., MRINA."

The letter was from Annette. Jem stared at it bleakly. He read it, reread it, and still grappled for understanding. The room receded, leaving him homeless as if he stood, like long ago, on the pier wall. And the past came in, and responsibility, and Susan, and Annette's lovely face. Her letter was hysterical, broken, dreadfully unhappy. Jo became creeping moor mist in his mind. The life in Port Penquay became insubstantial, a cursory spasm, as if he had left London only yesterday.

Jem lit a cigarette. Already one burned in the ashtray. As he put down the lighter, it slid across a slip of paper and revealed the corner of a photograph. Jo, laughing, pulling like hell on a fishing rod, reeling in a big pout. God, he'd been so happy that day. My love. My only love . . .

The letter in his fingers burned them. He read the smooth large words again. And again. ". . . do anything to have you back . . . Susan misses you . . . that awful unstable life . . . need you . . . miss you, realize how wrong . . . start again . . . we could have a new life . . . please . . . please . . ."

Jem groaned aloud. He tried to harden his heart, against one, against the other, but it was a cruel attempt, and a cruel blow for a man of his ilk. Jem needed to control, to be in control at all times, of all destinies related to him. He

needed maps and precision and places for this and loca-
tions for that. He needed not only to know where he was,
but by what process he had arrived and by what route and
method he should leave.

He sat at his desk and felt his head pound and his guts
contort; and the pedestal upon which he, with the approval of his loved ones, had placed himself, turned to
mud beneath his feet.

Steve climbed up to the landing; Jem recognized his
tread; they were each of them different. He carried a mug
of coffee.

"Thanks." Jem spun his chair and flipped the letter into
a pile of other correspondence. "How's the work coming?"

"Good." Steve nodded. "One thing I thought worthy of
mention. Are you absolutely sure that those masts will be
safe unstayed? They're going to whip about a hell of a
lot."

"They're aluminum and they'll take it. The manufac-
turers assure me they've been very thoroughly tested. Anyway, we've time enough before we come to that."

Steve hesitated. "Are you feeling rough, Jem? You look
a little gray."

"I'm okay. See you later, um?"

When Steve left, Jem yearned after his fading footfalls.
A man to trust, who would give good advice and would
not mind if one ignored it. He stood, but then he sat. Jo's
brother, and what would he think, what would they all
think? What was to be done?"

Oblivious, Jo sat in her office. Afterward she said, "I
should have sensed a black thing coming, it must have
been so huge. But then, I didn't know about Denny either
. . ." Fred monopolized the gas fire, edging his nose to the
rose-pink clay filigree columns. Jo gazed happily out of
the window at the heavy sky. A few roses still trailed
the garden wall, but the hollyhocks had collapsed and the
grass was its rich winter green, quenched after the long
summer thirst. She thought of Jem for the thousandth
time that day. She stretched her arms and wriggled her
fingers and pressed her knees together. Things were so
good with him. He listened to her silly hopes, spoke words
to her that no man had ever spoken, gave her pearls of

attention, diamonds of compliments, all in the warm solid setting of gold that wrapped her about and whose name was love.

She tried to draw his face on the shorthand pad, but it wasn't very good, so she drew his naked form, viewed from behind for propriety's sake, and was pleased.

"Where shall we go tonight, puss-cat?" she said. The animal twitched an ear. "I'm going to cook a beautiful dinner, boeuf bourguignon, and I have a bottle of Nuits St. Georges '73 that cost me a fortune, and then we shall go out, and then we shall come home . . ."

Jo's natural wariness of future planning had sublimated into a vapor of pallid nervousness that was dispersed in the breeze of Jem's presence. "I have written to my solicitor," he had told her. "He says I have ample grounds for divorce. The only complicated issue is the division of property, but it will be dealt with."

"Have you told him to proceed?"

"I'm writing tomorrow."

Jo started to sing, taking care over the words of the last verse of a recorded song she had bought for Jem.

Now I'm looking at new spring rooms
In the future of your smile,
Starting over
With another green bud,
Imagine summer for a little while

He had said, "I borrowed Steve's record player. It's a nice tune."

"Do you like the words?"

"I don't really listen to words."

And Jo had laughed. She was still singing when the phone rang. "Allson's. Can I help you?"

"Hello, Jo."

"Jem! It's lovely to hear your voice."

"How are you, Yasmin?"

"Pining. Longing to see you. I have a lovely dinner planned. How are you, darling?"

"Uh, fine . . . Jo, I think I'll have to miss dinner tonight."

Cold crab pincers fastened on the nape of Jo's neck. Not what he said, how he said it. "Why, darling?"

"I've had a letter from Annette. She and Arthur have quarreled and split, and she's back at our house."

Our house. Our house. Carefully: "What does that mean, Jem?"

He sounded very tired. "She wants me to go back. She needs me and so does Sue. By her letter I'd say she's on the verge of a breakdown. They are my wife and daughter, Jo."

Oh, God . . . oh, no, God . . . no, God. I don't believe, but please, God, no. "What do you think you should do, Jem?"

"Oh, Jo, I just don't know. I want to pummel it out, that's why I thought I'd like to be alone tonight."

"Oh, Jem, Jem. I love you. I want to see you."

"I love you, Jo. You'll never know how much. I'll come over later, about ten. Will that do?"

"Why not earlier? We could talk."

"No. About ten." There was a silence that not even the wind rubbing the corners from the old building could blow away. "Bye-Bye, Jo."

He came at ten minutes after ten. Jo had dressed in a long wrapover skirt and thin shirt and wore nothing beneath. She had smoked seven cigarettes and drunk half of the Nuits St. Georges. Her color was high. She glowed, falsely healthy. Her face was perfect. She gave Jem a warm and loving smile as he came in, and he kissed her and held her so hard it scared her.

"I'm sorry about all this, Jo." He sagged into a chair. "It's got me very confused."

"Have a glass of wine." Jo poured with a shaking hand. Their eyes met as she gave him the slender glass. Such close contact, eyes. We do not gaze into the eyes of strangers, nor even of friends. "May I see the letter?" she asked.

It was a pathetic, blackmailing letter, the sort of letter Jo could have written but would never have been craven enough to send. Couldn't he see it for what it was? Carefully, always carefully, she said, "Doesn't it sound as if she's using you as a last resort, Jem? She knows you have a strong sense of responsibility, and that you want to see Susan."

"Yes," said Jem. "That's true."

"But she has not said she is sorry, or that she loves you, or that she would not leave you again if this Phillips wanted her back."

"No. But Annette is loyal. She wouldn't flit from one man to another."

Wouldn't she? "Jem, do you love Annette?"

"No. I think that stopped long ago, before she left me. But love isn't everything, Jo. There are duty and loyalty and friendship, too."

"But you love me?"

"I do."

"And you have duty and loyalty and friendship for me?"

Jem sighed and lit another cigarette in a long day of cigarettes. "Yes, yes," he said, irritable. "But not like for them. You should understand that."

"Should I?" Jo was mystified. She turned to the table for the wine bottle, tripped on her flowing skirt, and measured her length on the hearth rug.

Jem, with a relieved downhill laugh, pulled her to her knees and said, "You clumsy, lovely, silly cow." Then he kissed her, and his problems dissolved and he wanted just to laugh and be free and have Jo; and he took the dive from the mountaintop and succumbed to the fall and let the world go to hell on a bicycle.

Much later, Jo said, "What will you do, Jem?"

He replied, "You must not worry, Yasmin. Annette is nothing compared with you. I shall write back firmly, regardless of what anyone thinks of me. I love you, Jo. I promise."

And as she dropped into the pool of sleep, Jo thought: So it pays not to give in too easily, and it's worthwhile to prevent tears and to look good and to be sensible and to laugh. But, God, it's hard, this thinking like a winner. Exhausted, she slept.

The following day was shot like silk with the dye of sadness for Jo, as Jem could not see her in the evening. All the lads were going to a stag party for Alan Jones. "If you must, you must," said Jo. "Don't get too drunk. They always overdo it."

"I won't," promised Jem. "I'll miss you. See you on the day after, without fail."

So Jo washed her hair and passed a suspended evening baby-sitting for Peggy and watching her television, and scarce a ripple ran across the surface of her trust. Of course Jem would be upset by such a letter, he was only human; but he had promised, had decided, and that was that. Belief like a forced hothouse plant quelled her fears, yet before she went to bed she took Denny's photograph from a drawer where she had hidden it from Jem's eyes, and examined it closely.

The face was as blank as new paper.

There is a woman who passes along Gypsy Lane almost every evening, past the cottages and small houses with lights in their windows, and she looks into those private-life windows as an outsider, and she is angry. She is small and dark and black of hair and of demeanor, and she is angry. She is frustrated beyond tolerance. All along the road she comes, short angry steps, berating in a voice that is a line of sharp black angled fence posts. An auctioneer of venom, and she points a finger of accusation at each front door and flays each private life with words that might be deadly if one could understand them. But her tongue is as fast and angry as her feet, an incoherence of fury.

Steve and Jem, walking to the club for the stag party, passed by on the other side, and the woman, stopping, waved a fist at their embarrassment. "They call her Mad Mary," said Steve. "She's just a little over the edge, but sometimes she's quiet. I often wonder how she is at home."

"Strange, I never think of people like that having homes."

"Yes, a Spartan little house where every speck of dust is murdered on sight. She has a son—he must be about twelve years old now."

"Good God!"

"She wasn't always angry. Her husband left her, that's all. It takes less with some than others."

Mad Mary's voice dwindled like perspective, but to a wavering Jem, both her words and Steve's rang like a siren through his temples. "Is there a telephone at the club that I could use?" he said.

Steve nodded.

CHAPTER
TWENTY-THREE

Peggy's voice came up the stairs as Jo was changing from dilapidated pink slippers into new boots, leather and luxurious. She had intended to parade in front of the mirror to appreciate her own good taste. "What is it?" she yelled back shortly.

"Someone to see you."

Jo went to the head of the stairs. The electric bulb had failed in the hallway, and neither Jo nor Peggy could remember to buy a new one, but there was enough light from the street to reveal the familiar figure. "Jem, what are you doing down there? Come on up. . . ." She ran down to meet him. "Why are you . . . ?"

He said it clearly and fearfully to her face, but his eyes rat-cornering away. "I'm sorry, Jo, I have to go. I can't stay. I've had a couple of drinks for courage, but I'm not drunk. I'm sorry, Jo, I have to go back. I rang Annette, and she really is ill."

She saw him clearly and fearfully, a disheveled small man, yellow with worry. His face was anguish-lined and his hair knotted from walking in the wind. Jo saw him and felt nothing but the icy drench of shock. "You can't," she said. "You can't. You promised." Then an anger that was volcanic. "Wait here!" she stormed. "I'll . . . I'll get my coat."

She scrabbled at the coat hooks with hands that were cold, sweat-cold and shaking, and no thoughts in her head. The loop broke on a jacket as she tore it down. Jem was standing as she had left him, head down with his hands at his sides. "Walk with me," Jo said. "Please walk with me."

They walked along a road that had no location, an unknown, unfriendly road. "What happened?" said Jo. "What happened? You were all set to say no—you promised, Jem, you promised!" All was said with downcast head, no eyes, no touch, no sweet contact. She knew that if she brushed his hand with her own, he would not take it, warm and dry and safe.

"She's on her own," said Jem, flat, rehearsed. "What if Susan is ill, what if Annette has a nervous breakdown. She's so distraught because he left her. Jo, I can't ignore the responsibility."

"And what about me?" It was not indignant, or selfish. It was the pan pipes on the lonely wind. "You shouldn't have told me you'd stay. You shouldn't have started if you won't finish. Damn you! Damn you to hell! If I have to survive alone, why can't Annette? Oh, you bastard! You weak-minded bastard!" And with no warning she turned and hit him, eager to feel the pain of her hand against his face, longing to hurt and rip and tear and bruise and maim. But he fended her blows with blind hands and he said, "Go on, I deserve it." So she stopped and the killer urge stepped fast aside as contempt trod its heels. "I wouldn't give you the satisfaction," she panted. "Find your own punishment."

But he stood, and the wind tugged his hair and the first raindrops, fat as cats, fell through the early street-lamp yellow. Still, his eyes were hiding. Jo put her arms around him and hugged him tightly. "I'm sorry," she said, "I shouldn't have given way to my temper. I love you." Jem said nothing, nor did he move, and his skin was cold.

"It's all right," he said, pulling away.

Jo walked off, fast and straight, not caring if he came along, but he came along. "How can you do this to me?" she said. "When you know how it's been before. Jem, you can't mean it, you can't."

"I can't stay," he said. "I love you, Jo, but I can't stay."

The rain fell steadily now, and Jo found that she was walking up out of the town toward the High Moor and its dangerous fears and deep blackness. That is where I'll go, she thought. I'll go up to the moor and walk and walk until I can't walk, and then I'll fall and nothing will matter. As she thought coherently, in the turmoil below, her voice was raging. "Go away from me," she said. "I don't want you."

"Jo, where are you going?"

"I don't know. Leave me alone. You want to go, so go. Now!" She began to run, and Jo had been a runner, for school, for Penquay Athletic Club, for her life. She ran away and kept running, and when she'd run half a mile she forced her lungs to run her the rest of the mile. It was terrible, running through the rain along the empty road that had no houses now, just the occasional lamp, and terror chased her heels, but she could not get away. It ran beside her and needed no oxygen. Trembling, she slowed to a walk. As she walked, she repeated aloud, over and over, like an incantation, "I don't want you, go away. I don't want you, go away."

At the junction of St. Philip's Road and the arterial road south, she turned to look back before she crossed over to the narrow track that is Moor Lane, and Jem was behind her like a shadow. Ignoring him, she moved toward the moor, stumbling on the black, uneven surface. No lights now, no moon, no stars. All the lights all over the world had gone out.

Jem caught up, breathing fast but trying to hide it, wanting to impress, even now. They strode along, Jo with her hands bunched wet in her pockets and her head low against the beating of the rain and the bitter beating of betrayal. Jem cupped his hands to light a cigarette, and Jo saw how wet his hair was, and how gray his face, even in the soft flicker of flame. "Where are you going?" he said.

"I don't know. How can I go back and face them all? They will ask me why I failed. Jem, how could you . . . ?" Tears were very near but would not run out to join the rain streaks. She felt her mascara running down her cheeks, and it said "waterproof" on the tube.

"You can't just wander out here. You'll . . . you'll do something silly."

"Go away. You've made me no concern of yours. 'You can come under my coat'—huh!"

"I know. I'm sorry, Jo. I'm not strong enough. You're too good for me."

Jo stopped, tripping. The night was hollow and roaring and mat as a blanket. "How bloody nauseatingly noble!" she wailed. "Oh, Jem, go away. You're not my Jem anymore. . . ."

He held her then, but all she felt was the sodden coldness of his jacket and the water running from his hair, colder than her face. "You mustn't stay out here alone," he said. "Come back with me, Jo."

"No!"

The wind cried across the High Moor, slinging rain like small sharp stones. No cars moved along the far highway. Nothing lived upon the earth but two warped and tortured people surrounded by the numb halo of their own little hell. "Come back to town," urged Jem, shivering as his blood slowed. "You'll catch pneumonia."

Jo collapsed inside. Her light flickered and dimmed, and the sooty trails of incomplete thoughts, unfinished hopes, smothered wishes, ran from her eyes and down her cheeks. Wordlessly she pulled away and turned back the way they had come. Denny fluttered on the horizon like sheet lightning, but very far away and soundless. In the past few months he had faded as a red rose fades, never to return. Jo was vaguely aware of wetness and discomfort, but she was not cold in a physical way. At the top of Penquay Road where it turns into St. Peter's Road, she stopped in the shelter of a tree that rustled in the rain and dropped bombs of water as the wind moved through it.

"Please, Jem," she said quietly. "Tell me why. Tell me if you have the right reasons."

He looked at her but could see only the tangled outline of her hair that he knew was red, and the gleam of streetlight reflected in her eyes that were big and a little on the diagonal. "I think I'm doing the right thing," he said firmly. "I've made my decision, Jo."

A long and animal sound came from her, but she cut it off and whispered, "Kiss me, then. Last time. Then go away."

Jem kissed her, but it was the kiss of Judas and they both knew it. Never was a kiss so devoid of all its name implies. "Come on." He sighed. "I'll take you home."

"Oh, no," said Jo. "Good-bye, Jem." She disappeared into the rain, and her figure was bent and hurrying and aimless. Later, she sat in the doorway of St. Peter's Church and smoked a cigarette. She did not know the time, but no one walked in the street, not even a drunk or a cat or a burglar. Or a cat burglar. She sat until the stone froze the bones of her pelvis and the rain ran in streams from her shoes, and she sat some more, and then she realized that Jem would not come and that she must go home.

The white car was outside 26 Dundee Road under the streetlamp. She wanted to run toward it; then she wanted to run away. Jem was at the door, about to ring the bell. She stared at him, white with black streaks on her face. "Have you come back?" she said.

He hiccuped and shook his head. His eyes were red, red and blue around the rims. "I'm sorry," he said. "I wanted to be sure you got home."

Jo began to cry, an awful pained bellow, pulling her lungs apart. "Go!" she said on an indrawn breath. "Leave me alone."

Jem backed toward the car and stood within its protection, staring at her. "What can I do?" he said softly. "I've lost my best friend."

"You'll have to be brave," choked Jo. "Like I'll have to be." She opened the door and went straight in without looking back. The door slammed. On the pavement outside lay a golden key bespattered with mud, and Jem saw it, but he left it lying there.

CHAPTER
TWENTY-FOUR

Jo lay in bed shivering. Her wet clothes, staining the pale carpet, lay where she must have left them, but staring at them, she could not recall undressing. Her arms, outside the bedclothes, were covered by the sleeves of her thick blue robe. Turning her head to the right, she saw that the framed photograph lay facedown on the stool.

Empty, all empty.

She breathed shallowly and went on shivering. Have I got a cold or pneumonia? Perhaps I will be ill. No reaction. Passing thoughts ran across her mind, water on wax. No reaction. No interplay. No thought.

Jo fell asleep and dreamed that Jem's head rested close by hers on the pillow, and it was a good sweet feeling. He spoke, but try as she might, she could not hear, could make no sense of the words. She fought like a gladiator to hold on, to decipher, but he had gone, like Denny had always gone. Like she knew he always would.

She woke later—it must have been afternoon, gray dim light—to a knock on the apartment door. She gave no answer. Seconds passed and Peggy called, "Jo? Are you there?"

Jo listened. Her heart rattled under her ribs, and still she shivered. Her eyes were wide and expressionless.

"Jo?" The voice was clearer, sliced by the closing of the living-room door. "Are you in?" A knock at the bedroom door, then Peggy came into the gray afternoon room. "Jo! What is it, are you poorly?"

Jo shook her head slowly. "Jem's gone." The words were hooked and shredded on the barbs of desolation.

"Oh, my dear . . ." Peggy came to the bed and put both arms around the shaking woman.

"I got wet," said Jo.

Peggy held on, and for a long time no words passed. Finally she said, "I'll get you some soup."

Jo did not hear. Once more she retired into sleep.

She woke again to a blackened room, curtains drawn, just a narrow column of light standing in the doorway. Movement in her apartment, and a meow—Oedipus, so different from Fred, all long fluff and passion, rubbing against her face with a wet nose and ecstatic teeth. She stroked him absently, and he collapsed lovingly onto her chest. "Peg?" said Jo.

The column widened. "Mind your eyes," said Peg, and the soft yellow shaded light came on. "Oh, Oedipus, you fool!" The cat smiled through a hypnosis of purrs. "Let Jo sit up and eat her supper."

"Thank you," said Jo. "This is good of you, Peg. I'm all right now, you needn't worry."

Peg looked quizzical, but little Joanna was alone downstairs and her attention was necessarily divided. "Go back to sleep after you've eaten," she said. "I'll get the tray tomorrow. Are you sure you're . . . ?"

"Sure. Leave Oedipus. He's warm."

As if drugged, Jo slept, deep in a dark sea, occasionally rising almost to the surface, only to feel the sear of pain, to see a face, two faces, three, waxing and waning and turning away. So down she sank, hunting for a cave of refuge, alone, and no song except empty, empty.

She slept for twenty hours, and in the early evening woke and felt refreshed until, in only seconds, the foul breath of memory soured the air. She gagged upon it. The bed was cold, rumpled, miserable, so she got up, dressed in clean clothes, put the damp ones in the laundry basket. She wasn't going to get pneumonia after all.

It was cold in the kitchen, but Jo sat there at the little table by the window. "Denny," she whispered. "Are you anywhere? Is there nothing I can do?" Tears rose and were strong solutions of pain, having a rusty taste. And there was Denny, across the table. She had told him that her mother had an inoperable cancer, and his hand had sought hers, and the whites of his eyes had veined with red, and the lids had gone puffy, and he had blinked and blinked. Across time and across the kitchen table Jo stretched out her hand to his and wished the lost wish of all those who are too late. As her hand hovered, untaken, she saw another face of Denny, smiling, kissing her cheek, and saying, "See you later."

He left, and could not be recalled. Mum's face, then, and what she would have said, lively, in her way: "He'll come back. Love conquers all." But Jo could not dare. She sat at that table for a long, long time, searching through her heart's reasons, cataloging as if for a sale. "It's dark," she said. "I'm afraid of nothing. Eternal silence could be no worse than this." A shadow figure who was like Denny yet not like him called her name, but when she looked, it was Jem with another woman in his arms. "You were my chance for loving again," she said, as the couple whirled on some dark and cozy dance floor of imagination. "You fooled me, Jem, and I had really begun to trust you. Never mind . . . I shall miss your pictures, all of you. I think I'm right now, but I don't think I can face it."

She was quiet. Truth brought a certain stillness, so that she thought of "Be still . . ." and the morning when it had echoed through a dream. Religion had never bolted her life together, never formed a vital step in any ladder, but now she knew some of the comfort coined by the believer; the passing of an ache to a broader, infinitely more capable back.

She decided to make some tea, and while waiting for the kettle to boil, she went to the bathroom and searched through the cupboard below the hand basin. Flakes of white paint fell to the floor, and inside, the walls were black with mold. "I must scrub that out," she said. But no, it doesn't matter at all. As she took out the bottle of pills a dry humming sound escaped her lips, but she did not notice.

There was a knock on the door of the kitchen. Jo dithered in silence. At last she called, "Come in!"

It was Roger Payne. "Hello!" he said brightly, hovering in the doorway. "I've come to ask a favor."

Jo absorbed the details of his dress as if he were a stranger. The narrow greasy tie, the wool pullover, with a hole right in the center of the front, pipe-cleaner pants, neatly pressed, the toothpaste-tube shoulders not fitting the sports jacket. She gazed at him dumbly.

"It's not that much of a favor," he added with a grin. Something about the angles of her worried him. She was out of true, mentally asymmetrical.

"Come in. Have a cup of tea." Jo seemed to have woken up. While she found a cup and saucer, Roger seated himself at the table and pushed his glasses up the bridge of his nose with his middle finger. Then he noticed the small brown bottle of pills. Ants of apprehension scurried across his shoulder blades. He knew that Jem had gone, else he would not have asked his favor of Jo, but he did not want to speculate. She must have a headache, he surmised. "I thought you might be out," he said, watching her small, slim hands lift the teapot. The tea came out very brown, just as he liked it, and Jo piled in three sugars without asking.

"No," she said.

"I thought of you because I know you watch *Connections*. Our television's broken. A cloud of blue smoke came from the back and the picture disappeared. Elsie is at her cookery class and the lads will be at the club, so I came to ask a favor. Were you going out?"

"No." I'm coming to you, Denny. I wonder what I shall say after all this time, or has your soul blown away on the cold wind through the garden? She shivered as the black cold wind wrapped her mind around. There will be nothing, said a low, uncompromising voice. No rationalization here, nothing but the deep, deep sea of oblivion. Too old to be Hamlet, she thought. I am not scared of possibilities. She found herself gazing at the bottle of pills; it seemed to have grown, and she glanced at the plain and friendly face across the table. Roger had been gazing too, and as Jo caught his perceptive little eyes, she knew he knew.

"May I watch it?" Roger leaned back, holding his cup with his little finger stuck out.

"Yes, of course. It starts at ten past, I think." She avoided looking at him, offering a cigarette with her eyes on her fingers. Years ago, long back in the pretty, hopeful past when green things grew in lawn-roller shade, that was her focal point. "Jem has gone back to London," she said, flat, flat.

Roger sensed the weakening of defense and looked with pity upon the bent head with its untidy red curls. Not beautiful, his aesthetic mind commented, but nice . . . nice. This little human combination should not be wasted, not so easily, not when it had come through fire. "May I be personal and ask why?" he said.

Jo stubbed out her cigarette heavily. "Partly to be loyal, I think. Partly because my insecurity undermined him, strained our relationship. I don't understand." Her eyes were wells of unknown secrets. "I wish I'd done it right . . . but it's too late now."

Roger's face betrayed nothing of his scratching-hen mind. Outside the window the last confetti of orange blossoms leaped from an old sweet shrub, and the wind sneaked through the window frame, raising gooseflesh on his thighs. He rubbed his hands over them slowly. Roger rarely speaks in haste; particularly now, when his words might control a life, there was need of great care. It could be that he was born for these moments, never again to hold the destiny of another in his hands. And here it was, life's pinnacle, thrust upon him all unprepared.

You bloody idiot, he told himself, you've been watching too much TV. You'll be grabbing her by the elbows and begging her not to do it next. "We all know how Jem felt . . . feels about you, Jo," he said, staring purposely at the pill bottle. "I think he'll come back. Don't give up."

Jo sighed through her nose, screwing her mouth sideways. "How I long to believe, Rog. But they don't, do they, these married men? Would you?"

Roger helped himself to more tea. By now it was tannin-black, cool, and metallic. It annoyed him. He picked up the brown bottle casually and rattled it in a rumba rhythm, watching for reaction. "I believe that a good marriage that has merely gone on the rocks for a while might be revitalized," he said.

"So?" said Jo softly. She stared at the blossom petals accumulating in the window-frame corners and hiccuped.

"I believe that loyalty without love is not strong enough." He stopped swinging the bottle. "Give him time to find out. Did he want to go back, or did she ask him?"

"She asked him. The other man let her down."

"There you are, then, he'll be back." Roger crossed his fingers under the table.

Jo blurted, "Roger, I've lost all the people I'm ever going to lose. I dare not hope again."

Roger sighed, waving the bottle of pills gently. "Were you going to do something silly?" he asked sternly.

Jo felt ashamed, even in anguish. "I'll do what I damn well please," she said. "Besides, I have a headache."

"Jo, you're obviously very depressed and it's hard to see things straight. Why don't you go to a doctor?"

"He'd feed me drugs, wouldn't he? I've had enough Valium. That and a bottle of wine were all that could make me sleep once upon a time. All I want is a little peace, away from my mind."

Her quiet wistfulness worried Roger more than tears would have done. He was missing the program he had come to see, and he struggled on the twin horns of a dilemma composed of shallow self-interest and deep but time-consuming concern. "Come and watch *Connections* with me," he said, taking the brown pill bottle from the table. "Bring us both a beer, eh?" He wandered into the living room.

Jo heard the armchair creak and spurts of noise from the television set. "I'll be there in a moment," she called.

Leaning against the door of her bedroom, the pale green, private, once-shared bedroom, she looked across at the photograph propped again beside the bed, across the time between life and death, and Denny smiled a compassionate paper smile.

"I love Jem," she said boldly. "I want him, his arms, his face. I miss him as if he were dead too, but worse . . . Den, I can never erase you from my horizon, you were my paradise island where I learned loving. Give me hope, Denny. Tell me old Roger is right."

She went to the cross-framed window, looked across the old town houses, up to the dusking sky, hoping for a shooting star. There were none, just the steady flawless constellations, and below the yellow windows of early evening families. As she turned into the room, and maybe the contrast played tricks with her eyes, she saw Denny nod once, minutely. It was the last time he spoke to her.

Later, she went to watch television with Roger.

CHAPTER
TWENTY-FIVE

For more than a week Jo avoided her friends. Somewhere in the whirlpool of her mind was a twisted fear of them. Almost, she could blame them for their interfering engineering, but the blade of truth was too sharp and she knew them not to be culpable. "They will pity me," she told the goldfish. "Assess my every nook and cranny. Much too kind, and I would cry. Poor Steve, I should have let him come."

"She wouldn't let me go to her," said Steve. The club was quiet, the mood somber. "And I think she is right. My God, how obnoxious are so-called friends who use the excuse to tamper." Trix crawled into his lap, whimpering. He tickled the velvet patch under her chin, his brown eyes as limpid as the dog's.

"We didn't," said Jacko. "Jem said himself that no one would have made him, and I believe that."

"Balls," said Steve shortly. "We gave him home, job, friendship. He might think it was all his own doing, but no man is an island, not even our strong-faced Jem. If you live, you are influenced, period. We pointed him at Jo."

"But he could have ignored us," pleaded Ivor. He was very distraught, and the hand that held the martini glass shook. "He could have refused to be interested."

"He did at first," said Steve. "But Jo was there because we placed her there, and he was lonely."

Jacko's eyes were full of Amy, white in the water, green in the sea shadows. "Are you sure she's all right?" he

begged of Steve. "If anythin' happens to that little girl, I'll
. . . I'll kill him."

"Roger said she seemed to have made up her mind to
. . . exist," said Steve.

"Ring her again," said Sam. He felt very old, very useless, guilty yet bored with upheaval, and like Lear, angry
that no outpouring of love and need had come from Jo,
best-loved. But he said, "Ring her again. Take her out of
herself, bring her to us. I don't know what that young fool
thinks he's doing, I'm sure. All so bloody noble and so
bloody wasteful. I was in the navy with a bloke like him,
forever sacrificing friends on the altar of his conscience.
Damn the consequences to others as long as he felt good
with himself. Pah!"

Steve had heard the story of the stolen rum before. He
said, "What arrangements did he make with you, Sam,
before he left?"

"None. Said how sorry he was, all that, tried to explain,
but I told him it was his own life and none o' my business.
He left two months' rent and his address."

"Bastard!" said Jacko.

"No, no," said Steve. " 'What's done we partly may
compute, But know not what's resisted.' "

"Aye," said Sam. "Bring her to us, lad."

"I'll come for a walk with you," said Jo. "Just you
alone."

The day was full of elbows of wind. Jo and Steve wound
up Fort Hill, blasted by cars that raced down the narrow
road, nudged this way and that. Jo's blood ran fast with
exercise and wind friction, making a red spot in each
cheek. She had not altered, but her eyes were heavy.

"Don't stare at me," she said, soft in the roaring of the
copper beeches, now green at season's end, going brown.
"I had a glass of whiskey before I came out."

"Good for you."

"I've taken some holiday due to me."

"Good, have a rest, but don't brood alone, eh?"

"I shall if I want to. What's wrong with grief? But it is a
lonesome thing, and not to be displayed."

They took the path that leads away from the old place

of loving among the spruces, and down to the spot where Jo, in some past life, had searched the sea for a yellow catamaran. Steve said, "I heard once that in Turkey women wear headscarves of particular colors and embroidered patterns to indicate their mood. Paprika means bitterness—that's the only one I remember. Perhaps it is good that feelings are displayed, to give the others a guide."

Jo smiled. "I have paprika hair," she said. As they moved along the cliffs away from Penquay, she added, "Did he say anything to you, Stevie?"

"He was torn, thin with stretching."

"I know. But he told me he was not going. Then he went."

"He asked me to try to explain. His first loyalty is to his family, that is his conscience's dictum, the way he was raised and taught and disciplined. He felt his wife and daughter needed him."

"More than me? Fuck it, more than me?"

"Ssh. I didn't say I agreed. I tried to tell him, but he was too far away. The pulling in two directions almost bored him. He began to care for nothing, and when he drove away he spun the car on the roundabout and just missed a bus." Steve's kind heart hurt in him to speak the truth and watch its impact. "He told me he loves you still, through all the dark ages . . . that is what he said."

"I've talked with Peggy," said Jo, "and she is so much more philosophical than me. Little Jo's father left her, flat broke and pregnant, but still she trusts the world. Do I overreact, brother? Is the situation as desperate as I think?"

"You are you and Peg is Peg. The ability to suffer is only as deep as the ability to love. But Jem has suffered, and must have known. Sam would like to see you, and Ivor, and Jacko."

"Later."

"Okay." Steve breathed deeply. "Doesn't the air blow your face clean? I feel like a whippet, sleek and my ears flat to my skull. Doesn't this beauty and quiet color help?"

Jo's eyes were blank and with a flat glaze of hatred as she looked up at him. "It is nothing," she said. "Nothing at all to me. I hate the murderous bloody sea and the thoughtless wind. It's like the back of a giant hand sweeping away little lives. When there is no one to love me, I can see nothing at all."

Steve fidgeted. His love of nature was suddenly a burdensome thing, a great sack of affection collapsing like a parachute about his shoulders. "I love you," he said. "I don't know how to help."

"There is no help," said Jo. "Remember the poem you recited at my birthday party, 'Since there's no help.' I read it yesterday. I didn't cry. It was a relief, I gave in to it. The trouble is that he has shut out Denny. I used to find comfort there, but it's as if he's taken all the love that ever was . . . and hidden it and locked me up alone so that I can't search and can't find. It was mean of him to take Denny too."

They tramped along, single file, and far below in the oblivion of the sea, two cormorants dived for fish.

"Jem did not want with his heart to go," said Steve, the words flowing over his shoulder. "That is important."

Jo said, "I want a man's body in my bed. His body. Not yours, or anyone else's. His."

"It's a long time since we shared a bed," said Steve. "Over twenty years, kid sister."

"Am I undesirable, is that what he thinks?" Jo grabbed her brother's arm and turned him around, and in a madness spawned in rejection kissed him full and passionately on the mouth.

Steve backed in shock, pinning her arms to her sides; then his eyes softened, brimmed with pity. "Crazy Jo," he said gently, hugging her like a child, turning her so that his back was to the slick wind. "I have never been as lonely as you. Crazy Jo. I have felt some strange sensations in my life, but never one so strange as this."

"I'm sorry," Jo mumbled. "I don't know . . . God, I'm crazy, I must be."

"You are sick with grieving," said Steve. "But you will be answered."

" 'I shall be answered . . .' " said Jo.

CHAPTER
TWENTY-SIX

Guilt is a sticky thing, obvious as flypaper to those not trapped in it, and best avoided. Sam said little except abrupt orders to his cowering lads, and he and Steve saw the guilt in each other's eyes across the breakfast table every morning. They ate in silence and went about their work with the quiet diligence of Trappist monks.

Friends at the club refrained from conversation, and there was pity in their eyes, and reproof. The men from Antlercraft huddled together under a banner of shared peccancy that they could not discuss, even among themselves. A monotony of low-grade sin hung about them that was as self-indulgent as an excess of cream cakes. But nothing lasts forever, and nature, as is her wont, overcame the tedium with swift, if unjust, reparation.

So it was then that Steve, rolling from bed, rubbing out the sleep wrinkles from his face, noticed something amiss. His idling mind could not pinpoint it. The window, maybe, cracked at last. But no, the glass was intact, the putty undisturbed. "Trix!" he called, and heard an answering yip from the landing. He checked the clock, shook it, held it to his ear. It showed proper getting-up time, and it was Monday, wasn't it? He counted the days in his head and on his fingers, then checked that all the electrical switches were on or off, as normal.

He was at the kitchen door before the truth assailed him. Nothing else assailed him, that was the trouble. There was no smell of good frying bacon, no bubbling of eggs, no kitchen noises, pan clatters, kettle boilings. The rod of disaster smote his guilt-thick head. "Sam?" The kitchen was cold, neat, left exactly as last night, just one empty cocoa cup under the tap.

"Sam?" Steve tapped on the bed-sitting-room door. "Sam?" Unanswered, he entered the musty, dim room. Sam lay in bed groaning softly, his knees drawn up to his chin. Steve pulled back the curtains, and the daylight revealed a frighteningly old man, white-faced, sweating, frail. His huddled form under the army blankets was no larger than a child's.

"Sam, what is it? Have you a pain?" Steve soothed the contorted hot forehead.

"Christ, my belly," Sam moaned. "Get me some bicarb, Steve."

Steve's medical knowledge was not great, but in the dust of his recall lay a suspicion that bicarbonate of soda was not good for ulcers and such. "Where does it hurt?" he said.

"Me belly, for Chrissake! Get me some stuff."

"It could be your appendix."

"Haven't got one," snapped Sam. "Get me a cup of tea, then."

Steve made a harassed pot, forgetting to put the tea in, trying to fit the lid of the caddy onto the kettle. Old Sam's white face floated before his eyes. When he returned with the steaming cup, it was even whiter. Before he could drink the tea, Sam was sick, and had to be half-carried to the bathroom. By the time Steve got him back to bed, the pain was worse. "My head's spinning," Sam mumbled. "Christ, I feel bad."

"I'm going to call Dr. Barrett," said Steve, and realized how ill Sam must be when he did not offer objection. Sam's attitude to doctors can best be described as that of a mouse in a roomful of cats.

Barrett arrived in less than fifteen minutes, a large tweedy man, solid as a side of beef. His cheerful bulk filled the room, exuding competence. He bent over Sam, probing gently the age-emaciated abdomen. "What did you eat last night?" he asked.

"Crab. Fresh. Cooked it myself the day before. Tasted all right." Sam doubled with pain.

"Easy, old chap. I'll give you something to stop that.

But I'd like to have a look at you in hospital, just observation, all right?"

"No!" Sam's vehemence was pale but stinging. "You're not getting me into bloody hospital just for a bellyache." His breath caught and he panted like an exhausted dog.

The doctor frowned at Steve. "Can I have a word?" he said. Outside in the workshop he went on, "This may be simple food poisoning, or it may be worse. He's getting dehydrated already, and he's not a young man. Could you persuade him? Hopefully it will only mean a day or two in Sandcliff General."

Steve assessed the seriousness of Dr. Barrett's expression and felt a deep fear for Sam. "I'll persuade him," he said. "even if I have to hit him over the head."

He damn near had to. "Do you want to die?" he shouted finally.

And Old Sam must have been feeling sick, because he believed. "All right," he groaned. "All right."

The lads arrived for work just ahead of the ambulance. Jacko's eyes fretted and protruded. Ivor comforted old Sam, and Sam said, "Don't bloody fuss over me!" An injection had taken the edge from the pain, but left enough of its nagging bulk to squeeze out a weak tantrum.

"What's wrong?" demanded Jacko.

Steve said, "The doctor thinks he may have food poisoning."

"But hospital?" Jacko watched the stocky ambulance drivers manipulate the stretcher with easy flippancy. Sam's narrow form, well-blanketed, disappeared into the white vehicle.

"Only for observation. He's not young, Jacko."

"No, I guess not. I never thought of him as old, you know."

Jacko and Ivor watched the ambulance go rapidly away, blue light turning, with expressions of great solemnity. "Someone ought to tell Jo," said Ivor.

Two days later Sam was very ill. Jo went into the small isolation ward, carrying two paperbacks—a novel and a treatise on home wine making, the latter because Sam's previous efforts had been offered to the harbor gods as undrinkable by mere mortals. She was shocked at the old man's condition, more so because of the all too familiar smells of antiseptic and polish, the sights of thick white pillows and of drips and charts and bed apparatus, of nurses precise and squeaky-shoed, efficient in all the inefficiency of sickness. Sam lay in a high bed, alone in the ward.

Jo stood over him, watching the closed yellow eyelids, the baggy mouth ajar, and the top lip caved inward. His left hand, taped to a block, was stained with bruises where they had tried to find a vein for the drip. Sam's thin gray hair was rumpled, old cobwebs on the pillow.

Jo had been skeptical when Stotty had phoned, suspecting a ploy, unwilling to be drawn. She talked on the telephone and stared out of her window at the distant boat yard and wondered whether Sam was actually sitting beside Stotty, telling her what to say. "Is he really ill?" said Jo. "I mean, seriously."

"He's been taken to Sandcliff General. Is that serious enough?"

"You're sure?"

"Of course I'm sure! What the bloody hell, Jo?"

"I'm sorry. Thanks for letting me know. When is visiting time?"

"All day until nine P.M. except for mealtimes," said Stotty sharply. "I presume you'll go."

"Yes. I'll go."

In her head she could see the little ward, Sandcliff General Ward 3, and her mother, yellow and smelling of death. Her loathing of hospitals was almost as great as Sam's, yet they had done all humanly possible to save, to relieve. Terminal ward. Jo sagged against the window frame. Doesn't matter, doesn't matter . . . but that old song was long gone, ratted cowardly away at the first breath of a charming man's love-war cry.

Depression has a physical manifestation too. Jo had been finding it difficult to move quickly, to blink, to lift even a book, to cry, and to taste. It was only with a determined effort that she pushed away from the window and walked like an old dog to the living room. She stared at the door handle for a long time before she turned it, and her head was empty, empty. "I tell you, friend, all the blue sky!" she said. "What shall I do? I don't care.

Fish-face, are you there? I'm so altered that I don't care, not even about Sam. Isn't that awful? God, that's awful."

She sat down in the older of the old armchairs, the one she had repaired so you didn't notice, almost.

It took two days to glean and scrape and inhale and ingest enough energy from the air around her, to make the trip by bus to Sandcliff General. As she stood beside Sam, the weak hydraulics failed and her fiber folded and tears ran from her eyes and dripped from her chin. "If you cry on your back, you get tears in your ears," Denny had once said, apropos of nothing.

A nurse gave her a Kleenex. "Don't get upset," she said quietly. "He'll be all right, don't worry." She gave Jo a chair, a plastic, stackable, hospital chair. Jo hated the discomfort of hospital chairs. Cold, and shaped so that you either slid to the back or stopped your blood supply by perching on the edge. She perched.

Watching Sam, she felt the rise of panic, the surge of adrenaline, the constriction of the guts. You must not die, she said inside. If you die, so will I die. I have enough strength left for you, old man, but if you die, my bravery will go. It's a little false already, like alcohol, strong but quick to evaporate. Sam, don't you dare die.

He woke and saw her. His rimey lips moved, the furred tongue tried to freshen them. "Hello, love," he said in a discolored voice.

"Hello, Sam. How are you?" Silly question, but what else?

"Not so bad, lassie. Are you all right?"

"Yes. Don't worry for me." She saw that his eyes were the eyes of old men, leaking, bleared, mucus in the corners. "I brought you a couple of books, but . . ."

"Put them on the locker. I'll read them later when I perk up a bit. They keep giving me stuff that makes me dopey."

"Do they know what's wrong with you? Or are you here under false pretenses?" Her smile was the best, and good enough. Her fists bunched. You'll live, Sam, dammit.

"Pain in the belly," said Sam, with some of the old asperity. "They're blaming the crab I had for supper."

"Who did it come from, Sam?"

"Alan Jones. You know he has a few pots round the

Spit, there. Brought a whole basketful of live ones into the club to sell." Sam's face flushed unhealthily. He breathed fast and irregularly.

But Jo felt she had to persist. "Who else bought them?" she asked gently.

"Dunno. Can't remember who was . . . Alex, I think, and the commodore, he'll go for anything cheap . . . Dunno of anyone . . ." Sam closed his eyes and rambled along the corridors of his past. He said, "Where's the bloody soap?" and later, "MacGillycuddy's Reeks . . ."

Fearfully Jo stroked his hand. Come back, old man, you must not leave me here alone in this barren place. "Sam," she said urgently. "Sam!" But he merely mumbled and twisted and frowned. Jo sat awhile, stroking the knotty string hand, willing him to return, but his journey could have been to the stars.

Leaving, her feet were slow and her head was down in thought and the circulating adrenaline made her fingers dance in her pockets. She longed for a cigarette and headed for the nearest exit. Steve entered as she left.

"Jo! I wondered when you'd come."

"So did I. Steve, he seems very ill. He must not die. Do they know what is wrong with him? Do they? Are they doing enough—?"

"I've asked to see Dr. Blair, the man in charge of Sam's case. Come with me."

They had to wait for ten minutes outside Dr. Blair's office. "I hate these bloody chairs," said Jo. "They give me backache." She knitted her dancing fingers, forcing them still.

At last they were called in. "Sit, do sit." Dr. Blair shoe-horned them into chairs with the quiet persuasion of his professional intonation. "Now, I've asked you to see me because you may be able to help me with this case of Mr. Antler." His white coat creaked as he leaned across the desk. His eyes were encouragingly blue, with flecks of green concern.

"Anything," said Steve, and Jo nodded.

"Good. Now, do you know anything of the history of the crab that Mr. Antler says he had for his supper on the day before he fell ill?"

"He bought it live from a local fisherman," said Jo. "He's done so before."

Steve . . . tingled, thought Jo. She felt the electric shock of his tension, glanced quickly at his face, saw his jaw in the process of setting. "Was it contaminated?" he said coldly. "Well, was it?"

"Uh, we rather think it was." The doctor shook his head. "But it's a very unusual thing."

"Is it?" said Steve harshly. "With all the effluent of every sort that is floating around in our local ocean, would it be so unusual for some poor inoffensive old man to contract a disease from it?"

Jo gripped Steve's arm firmly. "What has he got?" she asked. "Will he recover?"

Dr. Blair played churches with his fingers, made a steeple, turned it inside out to see all the people. He was embarrassed, thought Jo. Finally he said, "We have to run more precise bacteriological tests, we've only just received the remains of the crab, but, believe it or not, Mr. Antler has the symptoms of cholera."

"What!" Steve's word was a whiplash. "How? We don't have cholera in this country."

The doctor nodded agreement. "Very rarely," he said. "Thanks to our clean water supplies. Most often it is contracted by people who have been abroad to an endemic area. It is spread in water or food contaminated by sewage, that sewage itself bearing the vibrio cholera."

Steve said, "Do you mean that Sam ate food, presumably the crab, that had been contaminated by cholerabearing sewage?" There were beads of sweat on his upper lip.

Dr. Blair disentangled his congregation. "We can't be sure of that. Recent research hasn't shown much of a tie-up between the consumption of fish feeding in polluted waters with incidences of the disease. But the crab could have come into contact with dirty water after it was cooked, or the water supply could be contaminated, or an associate of Mr. Antler could have the disease, though that is highly unlikely. We have checked already with the Environmental Health people, and they assure us that the domestic water supply is sterile, and so far there has been no other case resembling Mr. Antler's." He shrugged. "It's a bit of a mystery at the moment, though contamination of the crab looks like the best choice, in which case either Mr. Antler did not cook it sufficiently or he somehow polluted it after it was cooked."

"You're blaming him?" Steve exploded from his chair. "What business has sewage to be where it could infect the food that innocent people have to eat!"

"Indeed." Dr. Blair seemed undisturbed. "But before we jump any guns, let us get the full bacteriological picture, shall we?"

"Will he get better?" said Jo quietly. She watched every movement of the doctor's lips as he breathed in, held it, exhaled.

"I'll be frank. The prognosis is only fair. Mr. Antler is a tough old man, but he *is* old, and there's not a lot to him. We are doing, and shall continue to do, our utmost. . . . At least I can tell you this. The last person to die on United Kingdom soil of cholera did so back in 1909, so we have a working chance."

Hand in hand, Jo and Steve left the hospital, blank-faced, stunned. They walked to the car park in silence. As they reached the Transit, Sam's Transit, Jo said, "He must not die, Steve. If he does, all is lost with me."

"He won't if I have anything to do with it."

"It's always a comfort, your resolution. My good brother. Gardener to broken roses, you." She paused, did not notice her brother's pain. "I wonder whether that's why no one else got it. Lots of people bought Alan's crabs."

"Whose?"

"Alan Jones's. He drops a few pots round the Spit, you know that. Sam had one of his."

"Oh, my Christ!" Steve stopped struggling with the van's door lock. "The Spit. Sewage. Jo, do you remember back in summer that someone complained of sewage in the sea off the Spit?"

"Vaguely."

"Sewage that is dumped in the sea doesn't need to be treated. My God, if that complaint is still lying in some lazy sod's in tray at the Town Hall, if they plead lack of money or time, if they have caused dear old Sam all this suffering, I'll raise such havoc that it will be heard all over this country! I swear it, Jo. No one cares that pollution kills fish and birds and animals, but there will be a public outcry against the pain and distress of a human being."

"I don't care," said Jo. "As long as he does not die. Steve, don't try to make capital out of his illness, it would be typical of fate to lend the left hand. I'd rather you were wrong than he was dead. I'd rather the whole bloody world polluted than a world without Sam."

"Don't worry." Steve yanked the door back viciously. "Nothing I am about to do will adversely affect Sam."

They climbed in. Jo knew from Steve's expression that he was not to be moved. She had seen it often, knew it well—the overbright stare with an intensity that was eye-watering, like looking at the sun, the rectangular indentation just under the lower lip. He had worn that look prior to setting out to swim to Sandholm as a boy of fourteen, and was still wearing it when they had had to haul him out, blue and exhausted, two miles short.

It doesn't matter. She grabbed for the old song. Nothing matters except Sam and me.

CHAPTER
TWENTY-SEVEN

Steve Wilder has the compelling aspect of an Old Testament prophet when roused. His mobile face stiffened as he drove from Jo's house to the Town Hall, was a white mask with burning red eyes when he arrived and parked illegally in the private zone, and had become so severe by the time he entered the building that the commissioner jumped to attention with unaccustomed alacrity.

"You'll want the District Engineer's Office," he said. "Second floor, to the right of the lifts."

"Thank you," said Steve curtly, and bounded up the stairs.

"Do you deal with the sewage outfall at Port Penquay Spit?" he demanded of the first man he saw in the small be-desked office.

"Uh, it would be within our jurisdiction, yes." The Assistant Engineer pushed back from his desk on a revolving chair and began to rotate this way and that, nervously.

"And has any action been taken upon a complaint lodged back in the summer about excrement in the sea off Half Moon Bay?"

"Uh, I should think so, if it was serious. I'll check." Gratefully, he shot away to a multistory block of filing cabinets.

Steve prowled a three-foot square. His nostrils hurt but he could not relax the anger in them. Mad Mary had nothing on him at that moment. The engineer came back.

"Yes, Mr. . . . uh, we did receive the complaint. The outfall at Port Penquay Spit is planned to be scrapped as part of a new sewage-treatment project involving the whole area. It should begin in six months or so."

"Six months!" Steve grew inches taller. "That is untreated sewage, just floating around in the sea!"

The engineer sat at his desk again. "We've had no complaint of any effluent coming ashore," he said. "And the waste is of a nature to decompose very rapidly. It is not an uncommon practice."

"Is it usual for old men to contract cholera from it?"

The man behind the desk gobbled, swallowed, tried to pacify. "Have you some experience directly relating to us?"

Steve laid about him with the wrathful eloquence of a preacher. His voice brought the total office presence of five together. They wilted before his elegant fluency of rage, and burned under acid, nonidle threats that sprayed their imaginations and stuck like napalm. They were hypnotized by his articulate, rapid sentences, regarding him wide-eyed and fixed, rabbits before the snake. He laid sins at doors like an overenthusiastic milkman. Lawsuits pimpled the smoothness of his speaking, and media, and the possible death of an innocent old man, victim to lack of care. Trouble with a capital T impinged upon the tranquil routine of the office, and when Steve had gone, a silence grew as in the aftermath of a hurricane.

Someone chuckled self-consciously. "Cholera?" said another. "I don't believe it." And, "There are some nuts about, but why should they all come here?" And someone else said, "It could be scare-mongering, but better tell Big Ears, just in case."

Big Ears, otherwise Mr. Cambridge, District Engineer, was told. Delicately and without exaggeration. "See to it," he told his Assistant Engineer. "I have enough problems."

Steve was telling the editor of the Sandcliff and Penquay *Gazette*, a man who bears circulation in mind as a preacher bears God. A plump man, Mr. Ewell, fond of Latin interspersions and model railways. A reproduction of the Flying Scot in one-sixteenth scale adorns his desk where most people have their telephones. The telephone is on the floor.

"Suspected cholera?" he mused. "Any idea where he got

it from? It's a newsworthy subject *per se*, but it would be more valuable if we could trace its origin."

Steve told the whole story. "I can't prove that Sam actually caught it from contaminated crab," he said. "The lab has a sample of what was left, and they're working on it now, but the circumstantial evidence is strong. Mark my words, it's that damned sewage pollution."

"May I quote you?" The editor gleamed.

"You may."

"Then the *onus probandi* does not rest with us. We will merely quote your opinion. Press day on Friday. Have you a photograph of the old chap?"

On Friday old Sam took a turn for the worse, the *Gazette* came out with a better headline than it had worn in many a long year, and the balloon went up. In the boredom of off-season, Port Penquay's inhabitants are ever ready to enliven the days with a bit of gossip, a fruity tale, more often than not of the carnal variety, or about a crime, or a prejudicial rumor about the Polytechnic students; but Friday's *Gazette* took them by the ears and shook them from malicious apathy into concern for personal safety.

"PENQUAY MAN WITH SUSPECTED CHOLERA," announced the weekly. "DISTRICT ENGINEER ACCUSED." Those who read further discovered that Samuel Antler, seventy-seven, respected shipwright of Port Penquay, was lying close to death in Sandcliff General. His godson, Stephen Wilder, thirty-four, also of Port Penquay, had insisted that, in his opinion, the disease had been contracted from shellfish contaminated by sewage in the Half Moon Bay area. There were two more columns detailing Steve's actions and opinions of the District Engineer's office, his previous antipollution campaign, and his concern lest anyone else should become ill via the same source. If there were any in Penquay who had missed Steve's name in former capacities, they sure as eggs knew it now.

In the same issue, the Town Hall's reaction was printed. It was cool and explicit, stating that the Council, having received a bulletin from Sandcliff General Hospital, were of the opinion that, most unfortunate though Mr. Antler had been, responsibility must rest with him in that he had improperly processed his shellfish before consumption. Also that the sewage outfall at the Spit, soon to be made redundant, did not constitute and had not at any time constituted a health hazard. There were such systems in use elsewhere in the country, meeting all the requirements laid down in Statute . . . et cetera, et cetera. They added that the Environmental Health officer had been called in to assess any possible risk to public hygiene and safety.

Mr. Ewell printed it in full, but this did not prevent a group of students picketing the Town Hall with placards denouncing all local government as blackhearted feeders upon human suffering, nor did it stem a spate of indignant letters from the public, complaining about everything from ratable values to doggy toilets in local parks.

Ossie Bertram laid aside his paper and laughed glee-fully, evilly, slapping his thin thighs. "You've got 'em this time, my old lad," he told Steve. The Anchor was Saturday-morning quiet, the cool sun breaking through the leaded panes to highlight sticky, ring-marked tables. "You've got 'em. Since this broke, we've had more response to our standing committee than in the past two months. The fish-ermen's coop have given us their written support, the Penquay Institute, the Sandcliff OAP's Clubs, the Boys' Club, the Workingmen's Club, and plenty more. Good for you, poet."

Steve should have been pleased. Any other time he would have been over the moon, buying drinks for the whole pub, but Sam dragged at him. "I'd rather that poor old man was walking about fit and healthy than any of this," he said, taking up the paper and throwing it down again.

"Come on, Steve. He'll be all right. It's an ill wind."

"He was worse last night, Ossie. He's like a wafer. And I'm scared for Jo. I get this purple-black feeling that if he dies, so will she." He shivered. "If he lives, it will be down to her too; she's putting everything out to him, hanging on so hard you can feel the determination round her. But if the line breaks . . . I don't know."

"Don't give in," warned Ossie in his student-bullying voice. "Don't you give up this struggle, Stevie boy. You're the one with the guts to speak your mind, and the truth. You don't know how many of us in this town regard you as a leading light against the clouds of oppression."

"Balls. Ossie, I don't want to lead. It's not an abdication of responsibility, but if people rely upon me, they don't rely upon themselves. To stem pollution, even locally, each one of us must feel equally responsible for our environment. This publicity came about almost by accident. I was good and mad and I did not care who knew it, and nowhere in my head was there an ulterior motive."

"No?"

"No, Ossie. But I don't expect anyone to believe it. Now I'm going to see old Sam." He drained his pint. "If praying is your forte, pray for him, um?"

"I shall keep hoping," said Ossie.

CHAPTER
TWENTY-EIGHT

Roger Payne found Ivor and Jacko drowning their sorrows in Sam's corner, alone, unloved and unlovely, both having neglected to wash after work, a fair indication of how Ivor, in particular, was suffering. They nodded morosely.

"Jo says Sam is a little better tonight," said Roger. "But very weak and still wandering. I hope to God he gets over this."

"I can't bear to think about it," mourned Ivor. The stubble of his chin emphasized his pallor. "It's such a disgusting thing to happen. Steve is being perfectly magnificent. I wish I had his courage. How is dear Jo? Poor little soul. First Jem and now Sam. Poor Jo." He finished his second martini and pushed the empty glass toward Jacko.

"I'm not sure how Jo is," said Roger mysteriously. He kept them waiting while he cleaned his glasses. "When I left her place tonight, I saw Colin Whale hanging around outside, plainly not wanting to be recognized."

Jacko awoke from a wretched daydream. "That bloke," he muttered lethally. "What was he doing there?"

Roger shrugged. "Search me, but I could guess. I couldn't figure out if he'd been inside or not."

"You mean Jo is having him round?" Jacko's eyes fired. He throttled his empty glass like an enemy neck. "What are you hinsinuatin'?"

"Nothing, really. She didn't say, and I didn't ask. But jealousy is a strong emotion, isn't it?" There was a marked pause, bulging with hypothesis.

"But Jem wouldn't know, would he?" breathed Ivor at last. "He's hundreds of miles away."

"Not unless a little bird told him," said Roger softly.

Even Jacko's tired and vacant eye assumed a wily gleam. "How will you do it?" he said. "Steve said—"

Roger cut him off. "Never mind Steve for the moment. He's got plenty on his plate without concerning himself over . . . um, trivial matters. Would you happen to know if Jem has been informed about Sam's illness?"

Ivor fingered his chin. "Go and get a drink, Jacko," he said, and waited until Jacko, glowering, went. "It has made some of the dailies," continued Ivor. "But, as I recall, Jem rarely read newspapers. He said they were boring. Besides, if he knew, he'd surely have telephoned or written by now, wouldn't he?"

Roger grinned with all his dentures. "So it is your considered opinion that he doesn't know and should be told, right?"

"Indeed, dear thing, indeed. And if one happened to mention a few of the other little peccadilloes in passing . . . ?"

"What are you bloody smilin' at?" demanded Jacko, spilling the new drinks. "Ain't nothin' to smile at round here."

It is as natural for a man like Colin Whale to gravitate toward the easy buck as it is for water to flow downhill. It is in his blood, if such a material instinct can be said to have any basis in heredity. From the orphanage, to which he was constantly returned in the company of the local police, having gained a certain notoriety as the youngest shoplifter on their records, he naturally graduated to Borstal, where he learned a great deal about crime in all its phases, and precious little else. However, Colin always was a clever lad and discovered quite early that getting caught pays nothing, and most of his gleaned abilities, being illegal, tended him toward the ugly maw of the Law. At sixteen he sat down and had a good think. The thought of work appalled him unless—and this is not uncommon—the work was for himself and the reward considerably in excess of the effort expended.

He became a car salesman. He joined a doubtful small

business run by one man from a wooden hut on a back-street lot in Wolverhampton. The sales pitch thrilled him, came as easy to his tongue as lies had always done. He loved the turning back of odometers, the filling of crank-cases with heavy oil to disguise knocks, the greasing of nipples, the fiberglass fillings, the resprays, the occasional obliteration of engine and chassis numbers, in fact the whole caboodle of fiddling, to use his own euphemism.

He had been doing quite nicely on a percentage, when one fine day a woman, older, buxom, flashy rich, walked onto the lot looking for a little runaround for herself. Her eyes fastened upon Colin and made it obvious that they liked what they saw. He barely looked back. It was not until six months had passed, of idle, sponging luxury, his own apartment, clothes, good food and drink in exchange for sundry services, that her husband found out and Colin left town. Her husband was connected with a local gang not renowned for faith, hope, or charity.

But Colin was imbued with a taste for the good life and continued to pursue it, more circumspectly, upon his arrival in Port Penquay. Unfortunately the scope was small, and he ran through several legacies, life savings, and alimonies in a short time. He was panning for a more stable, longer-term arrangement, and for many months now, since Frances Wilder's death, his eyes had been trained upon Jo Wilder's inheritance.

And, to give him proper due, he found Jo both attractive and challenging, quite aside from her money. Very few women had actually interested him personally, and even fewer had steadily resisted his advances.

He sneaked up the stairs of number 26 in the dark and tapped on Jo's door. She let him in, surprised. It was after ten o'clock. "Jo, darling, how are you?" He eased past her, caressing her shoulder. "Are you alone, sweetie? Not involved with anyone?"

"I'm alone," said Jo. "There's no need to be sarcastic."

"Oh, darling, no. The last thing. It's just that I came earlier, and who should I see entering your front door but Roger thing, the tooth man. I didn't want to interrupt." He flopped gracefully into a chair and placed his feet elegantly on the coffee table. "I confess, I crept up the stairs like a cat to avoid old Peggy. Every time I come here, she pokes her nosy little head out of her room and watches me as if I carried the plague." He grinned disarmingly.

"She does rather look after me." Jo smiled. "She's motherly. Now, what do you want?"

"I'm cut to the quick!" Colin grabbed his beautifully white shirt front. "I come all the way up here to suburbs-ville just to offer you crumbs of comfort, and I'm spoken to like a common tradesman." He pouted affectionately. "Josephine, you should know me better."

Jo fetched a bottle of Scotch from the kitchen, some ice, and a plastic jug of water. "I know you well enough," she said. "Have a drink and cheer me up."

Colin poured, small for himself, large for Jo. She noticed but could not trouble to comment. "How is Sam?" asked Colin seriously. It had crossed his mind that if the old man died it was almost certain that Jo and her brother would inherit, but he genuinely liked and respected Sam, whose intolerance of fools was a virtue in his eyes. "Any better?"

"Yes, thank you," said Jo. "I have been willing him to get well. He has to get well, Colin. I have been sitting here for a week or more concentrating only upon that." Her face was pale, thinner, her hair tousled, a blackness around her creeping into the shadow planes of her cheek, into the eye sockets.

"Poor little Jo," said Colin. "You look all in."

"Don't . . ." she said. "Kind words will make me cry, and that's not fair."

"Poor little Jo," said Colin again.

"Don't, I told you. Now, look what you've done."

Colin came to sit beside her on the couch, offering a snowy handkerchief from his breast pocket. "Now, now," he said, stroking her hair. "It's better out than in, old darling. Tell Uncle Colin all about it."

Jo mopped her face, blew her nose, took a drink and a cigarette, which Colin lit for her. "You'd be a strange person to tell." She sniffed. "What would you know of love that is so great that it consumes, it burns, it hurts so much? Colin, you've never been a man for love." She swallowed another slug of neat whiskey. "Jem has gone away," she whispered.

"Poor kid, I heard about it. I'm afraid we men are all the same, Jo, and a woman like you is too good for us. We like the easy way, you see, the least possible trouble. Has he gone for good?"

Jo shook her head. "I don't know. But I can't just wait in this awful limbo. I can't make any plans, not one."

"Then how about you and I filling in time, sweetie? I'll take you wining and dining, make you forget. It's not right that a lovely woman should waste herself on one man."

"And who will pick up the tab?" said Jo with a hint of humor. "Good old Colin, at least you don't change. I can always rely upon your total rascality."

"But you like me, don't you?" He winked.

"Yes, Colin, I like you, warts and all."

Colin hesitated to follow up his advantage. Afterward he could not figure out why, but he poured another couple of drinks, removed his tie and shoes, and suggested some music. Jo played an Elvis Presley record that she knew he liked.

"Why did you come?" she said, sitting beside him again. "You always have an ulterior motive."

"I don't know why I bother with you." Colin was mock stung. "You're the only woman I know who constantly insults me."

"But you like it."

"Yes."

"Then why did you come?"

"I thought you'd take pity on me. I'm broke." It was not strictly true, but he felt she expected it.

Jo laughed. "Really? Is that on your honor?"

"Upon my heart, darling. Flat bust. I have a deal cooking, but I need a little to tide me over. Um?"

A cold and wicked devil entered Jo. When she stared back from the future at that spot in time, she could see it walk up behind her and whisper in her ear, "That would show him. He's doing it with someone else. His body and hers. She full, maybe of child again, full anyway, replete, running down her thighs. And him, kissing, holding, hardening for her, giving all your love away. . . ." She and the devil blended.

Jo went to the small bureau that had been her mother's,

opened the flap, and pulled out her checkbook. "How much, Colin?"

"Do you think you could manage cash, darling? About twenty?"

"Is that all you're worth?"

"Eh? Well, thirty would be better."

"Okay. Give me a moment, I'll get it."

Jo came back in ten minutes with a fold of five-pound notes in her hand. She wore nothing but a green silk negligee, a present from Jem, saved for the future they had once had. She waved the money slowly.

Colin was perplexed, but he got up and walked toward her, saurian eyes flickering between the blue notes and the pale suggestion of her body. "Wow!" he said approvingly, reaching for the money.

Jo held it away. "Not yet," she said slowly. "You're not normally paid in advance, are you?" She smiled recklessly. "Come on, Colin. You've been trying to lay me for ages. Now is your chance."

This time he did not hesitate. He carried her to the couch, kissed her mouth, her nose, her ears, released the negligee, and kissed the white skin between her breasts, but their pale roses were flat and smooth and soft. He looked up at her face, over her round chin and bean-shaped nostrils. Her brown eyes, wide open, stared at the ceiling. Colin lost his thread, his concentration. Jo stroked his back gently, like a child's. After a long, groping while, Colin said, "I can't, Jo."

Jo giggled. "Life isn't fair, is it?" she said as he moved away. "I never do anything right. Here you are, Colin old enemy, take the money and run."

"It must be the whiskey or something . . ." Colin replaced his shoes and tie as quickly as he could. "Honestly, Jo, I've always—"

"Perhaps it was me," she interrupted. "Here, take your money." She tossed the notes casually onto the carpet. Colin knew he would not be asked to repay. He counted to six as he picked them up, then, pulling his image close about him, left the apartment without another word.

Jo fingered the warm fineness of the negligee that Jem

had bought for her; then she pulled the hem up over her face and pressed it into her eyes.

"Elsie will wonder where I am," complained Roger, "She's a good girl, but she doesn't trust me."

Ivor sat back in his chair, pulling in his midriff. "Tell her you were with me," he said dryly. He laid the fountain pen down carefully beside the pad of Basildon Bond. His square black script covered two sheets, and the letter was signed with his best flourish. "There," he said. "Read it, but mind you don't put greasy thumbprints on it."

Roger rubbed his thumbs on the knees of his slacks and took the sheets up timidly. "Very good," he said finally, dropping the letter on the blotter. "Just a hint, but he'd have to be thick to miss it."

"He's not that, but will he be looking?"

"Anything more would be blatant. He'd resent it."

Ivor nodded. "I'm a terrible ditherer." He sighed. "Shall we send it?"

"Yes," said Roger firmly. "Address the envelope."

Ivor took a folded square of paper from his shirt pocket and flattened it on the table. "I sneaked a look through Stotty's address book while she was at lunch," he said. Roger watched in silence as Ivor took up his pen again, slipped an envelope from the writing case, and began. The pen nib scratched in a soft whisper across the crisp white paper. Soon it was done. Ivor took a stamp from the pocket marked "Stamps" in the writing case, licked it delicately, attached it squarely in the top-right-hand corner. "There," he said.

"I'll post it on the way home," offered Roger.

"I'll put it in a paper bag for you," said Ivor, fussing across the room to the dresser.

Roger gave him a rueful, forgiving look and said, "Yes, all right, if you like."

CHAPTER
TWENTY-NINE

Bacteriologists have to be both painstaking and thorough. The laboratory at Sandcliff General conducted its own series of tests on Sam's crab remains and on Sam himself, plate and broth culturing, restreaking and incubating, staining and examining until they were satisfied. Specimens had been sent to the Ministry of Agriculture, Fisheries, and Food, and to the London School of Hygiene and Tropical Medicine. The Environmental Health Department also conducted its own precise survey and tests, collecting shellfish, crabs, seaweed, sludge, domestic and river water and sea water from Half Moon Bay.

In all, it cost a lot of people a lot of time, and everyone a lot of money.

Dr. Blair telephoned Steve Wilder at Antlercraft. "We have some interesting news about Mr. Antler's infection," he said calmly. "Would you care to come and see me in my office at three o'clock?"

"Of course," said Steve. "How is he today?"

"There has been an improvement and he is comfortable," said Dr. Blair.

There was a needle in his tone that snagged upon Steve's sensitivities, no more than a speck of dust on the cilia of the lungs, but enough to cause a small mental cough. It became difficult for him to concentrate on his work. He cut a mahogany stringer two inches short, swore at Trix when he put his foot in her water bowl, and also at Stotty when she asked him for a decision on a delivery date. The cadence of his day was wrong, yet he could not isolate a reason for its temper-itching paces.

Dr. Blair was as immaculate as before, and he revealed no other emotion than affability when Steve entered his office in stained jeans and sweater, shedding sawdust on the Wilton. "Do sit down," he said. Before him on his well-kept desk lay a stack of papers, some black-and-white micrographs, and a tray of stained slides. He looked up and smiled. "You will, I hope, be pleased to hear that Mr. Antler does not have cholera."

Steve's jaw slackened. There was joy, heartfelt relief deep as the sea, but there was, oh God, shock and ridicule and "Someone has blundered" pounding loud as hooves across his mind. "Not cholera?" he mouthed.

"No."

"Then what?"

"It's very interesting." There was a glint of a laugh and a hint of compassion about Dr. Blair. "The ministry people knew something of it and they have confirmed the other findings. Mr. Antler is suffering from an infection of a similar bacterium to the cholera vibrio. It is called *Vibrio parahaemolyticus*. The symptoms can be parallel."

Steve blinked. "But will he be all right?"

"Oh, yes, we think so. He's on the mend. Cases of this sort are, to say the least, rare. That is why we mistook the diagnosis in the first place. I am sorry, Mr. Wilder."

"You are? Have you heard all the publicity?" Steve rubbed his scalp with his fingers, stimulating his numbed thought processes. Blair's dry little smile and nod did nothing to encourage. "Tell me about it," said Steve finally.

"All right. This is the probable train of events. The *Vibrio parahaemolyticus* is found quite commonly in shellfish such as crabs, certainly around parts of this coastline. It would seem to be a regular inhabitant, so to speak. It has a high resistance to salt water and also to heat. The general conclusion, arrived at by all of us who have studied this case, is that Mr. Antler's crab carried a few of these bugs, in among all the other usual flora and fauna. When Mr. Antler cooked his crab, the cooking time and temperature were sufficient to destroy all the less resistant bacteria, but insufficient to destroy our *Vibrio*. He left the crab . . . what, twenty-four hours or so before he ate it, and in that time the bacteria had multiplied enormously in its germ-free environment, an ideal medium. Mr. Antler probably consumed a substantial amount of bacteria and toxin. I think that about covers it."

Steve's face hung heavily, the wide mouth compressed. "Can you state positively that this bug is not present in sewage?"

The doctor shook his head. "There is nothing absolute in bacteriology," he said. "But I am reliably informed, and there has been a paper on the subject if you'd care to read it, that this bacterium can be found in concentrations that do not necessarily correspond to the presence of sewage or any other pollutant in the water."

"Oh, boy," said Steve quietly. "What a tangled web."

"You did not practice to deceive, did you?" said Dr. Blair thoughtfully.

"No, no. In truth I did not, Dr. Blair. But who will believe that? I was only angry. I was only angry, but I was wrong." He eased out of the chair, let his hands fall to his sides.

The doctor stood too. "I was with you," he said. "But in medicine we can't go off half-cocked. Every avenue, all that sort of thing. Mr. Wilder, be glad we were wrong. I have worked in India during floods and famines. Cholera is a terrible disease. Be glad you were wrong."

They shook hands, and Steve nodded twice before leaving the office. He had intended visiting Sam, but he knew that the burden upon his back was so large and obscene of shape that even old Sam in his illness could not fail to perceive the outline of calumny.

Up on the High Moor a lone kestrel hung in the west wind, his gray black-barred tail spread wide, his head on its short neck seeking from side to side. Winter coming on, and below, the tanning bracken, the drying heather. Time for feeding and fattening to sustain through the cold months. His chill, invincible eye scanned like a laser for the tiny movements that were not natural; the twitch of grass blades, the turning of a leaf. No bird sang near. Even the big gulls are scared by the predatory shape of a falcon.

Sparrows had swarmed away and were silent, larks dropped like stones into camouflage, laughing chaffinches had ceased their bobbing dances. The kestrel hovered alone and proudly over an acre of mute fear. There was no compassion in his small brain, no vulnerability, no notion but the hunt and hunger.

Down in the mystery of undergrowth a small mousy creature followed its pointed, sensitive nose on the trail of food, thistle seeds, grasses. It was not a fussy eater. It paused and sniffed and sent out a squeak or two to relay its position. High above, in a world the mousy creature knew naught of, the glint of early sunlight upon whiskers was observed and fixed. The creature moved on its erratic, snuffling way, unaware of the folding of wings and the sharp plummet until the shadow froze it and the accurate yellow talons pinned it to the ground in a split second of death agony.

The kestrel beat back toward the town, its wings rapid and its progress leisurely. There is a tall red-brick chimney in St. Jude's, attached to the old swimming baths that were heated by coal. Both the baths and the chimney are disused now, but the town still has to find the money for demolition, so they stand, and for the kestrel provide a fine luncheon base and nighttime roost.

He took his meal to the topmost decorative ledge of the chimney, arranged it carefully under his talons, and began to pull delicately at its flesh with a beak that was a curved ferocious hook. His head constantly turned as he watched over the town and its little movements, and he tugged and tore and swallowed until every scrap was gone, bones and fur and feet and all.

On the first Saturday of December, three weeks after his admission to hospital, Sam sat up in his bed, perky and pink, flannelette pajamas buttoned up to the neck, reading glasses on his nose, studying the techniques of elderberry-wine production. Discarded on the bedspread was a copy of the Sandcliff and Penquay *Gazette* of the previous day. The headlines ran, "DISTRICT ENGINEER DEMANDS FULL APOLOGY—RUMORS OF LAWSUIT." Sam had absorbed the details of his illness from it, having missed the earlier publicity, had snorted a couple of times, shaken his head over Steve's impulsiveness, and resolved to find out the truth at visiting time. "I don't trust bloody newspapers," he says frequently, while surveying at arm's length the naked breasts of some young hopeful.

He looked up with a wide grin that pulled his chin up to his nose as Jo, Steve, Ivor, and Jacko trooped shyly into his room. Jo's shopping basket contained tobacco and cigarette papers, four cans of beer (permitted by the good Dr. Blair), a carton of yogurt, and clean pajamas. Everyone smiled, as at a bonny baby.

Jo said, "Sam, you look so much better, even since yesterday."

"Aye, you won't be rid of me so easily. Get yourselves some chairs, then. How's the work coming, Steve lad?"

"Pretty good, but we miss you. I . . . uh . . . I got some advice from Jem about that vinyl liner he suggested for deck-head insulation. That's about all."

"No, it isn't," said Sam sternly. "What's all this?" He picked up the *Gazette* and waved it like a threat.

Jo linked her arm through her brother's. "Steve was awfully upset about you, Sam," she said. "We were told you had cholera, and it frightened us to death. I think he was right to do what he did."

"He wasn't, though, was he?" said Sam waspishly. "Still, it made me famous."

"You were already," said Ivor tartly. "And if you'd cooked your crab properly, you wouldn't be in here and none of it would have happened."

Jacko said, "Ssh!"

But Sam was explaining, "Now, I think I know how that came about. You see, I left the pan on the simmer and went off to do something, I can't remember what it was now, and when I came back . . ." His voice vanished in their laughter.

"Anyway," he added later, "I'll never touch crab again, I swear." As always, the last word.

Steve left the hospital for a meeting he did not want to attend. The thin cold strands of its probable outcome were already reaching his mind, and no matter how he fought for the sunlight, eyes on the empty blue sky, the darkness pulled him down. Ossie was in the public bar of the Anchor as usual, sitting as usual in the sunlit corner with a pint of diesel before him. It is a lethal mixture of cider and stout, for which, come winter, he develops a yen. He says it stops him catching colds. Steve reckoned it would stop a normal man breathing.

Ossie gave a nod and a straight look, but waited until Steve had bought a drink and seated himself before he spoke. "We're in trouble," he said.

Steve stirred thoughts that were both bloody and negative. "Not you, Ossie."

"Yes, me too. What the bloody hell did you think you were at?"

Steve was silent for a long while, fine cutting replies unspoken, turning to acid in his mouth. Eventually he said, "I used to go fossil hunting with Sam when I was younger, up at Lyme Regis. We spent hours doubled over in the cold, up to our knees in the blue clay. Your eyes become trained, set at short focus. But sometimes I wondered whether there wasn't a great eye in the sky above me, or the eagle of serendipity, and I was missing a vast eternal clue."

"What are you going to do about this?" demanded Ossie peremptorily. "I have been tarred with the same brush, being a colleague and . . . friend in the pollution campaign. My students are getting a rough time too. Some have been asked to leave their accommodation."

"Shit," said Steve quietly. "I'm sorry, Ossie. I'll try to clear them."

Ossie swallowed angrily. "Sorry," he mocked. "Why couldn't you wait until you got your facts straight? Damn fool! You've blown it, Steve, the whole show. Look at these. They are the end of the standing committee." He handed over three crumpled letters from his jeans pocket.

Steve's hand was unsteady. He read aloud from under the shadow of his fallen hair. "Withdrawing support" . . . "withdrawing offer of support" . . . "able no longer to support your campaign" . . . "They haven't the perspicuity to say why."

"No lawsuits for them," said Ossie nastily. "You'll

notice who they are from. The Department of Trade has authorized quite substantial compensation for those people who lost their livelihood."

"I came through the market," said Steve. "No one would speak to me. I've known them all my life."

"What do you expect, a pat on the back? Penquay is a laughingstock." Ossie glanced at Steve's face, white, harrowed, shapeless in self-contempt, and at his hands, rolled into fists studded with the knuckles of failure.

"I have to write an apology to the District Engineer, to be printed in the *Gazette*. I pray it will forfend prosecution. Ever since Dr. Blair told me I was wrong, I have turned myself inside out for a way to repair the damage. Ossie, I cannot find one."

"Leave it alone," said Ossie cruelly. "You've done enough. No one will listen to you again." He went to the bar and returned with two whiskeys. "I aim to get pissed and let the world go to the bloody hell it deserves. After a while I shan't smell the oil, and I sure won't drink the water."

Steve knocked back the Scotch in one go. It burned in his stomach and was as one with the burning of guilt. The strong hearth, full once of laughter, contained only ashes in the aftermath. The torques and stresses had been too great; like the Lias cliffs that crumble gently, gently, then collapse, his eroded soul slumped with a sound that blurred his vision. He who had only wanted to take the world in protective arms was outcast, without desire or ambition. Faintly, his Indian girl flickered like a flame, but he could not resolve her face, and in trying to build it, made it ugly. I could go back, marry, raise children, he thought, but the dream was abstract and dissipated like smoke on the south wind. And there is Jo, he thought. I cannot run.

He sat quietly, eyeless and listless.

CHAPTER THIRTY

Sam came home from hospital, having refused all offers of convalescence in country mansions, saying that he had already been regimented enough, and grateful as he was for his treatment, he did not intend to prolong his association with the medical world. His actual words were, "Steve, for Chrissake get me home!"

Jo visited Antlercraft every evening after work. Her vigil was ended, but it had revised her attitude to Sam. Always he had been in her life, never had she been forced to imagine a world without him; now he was precious. She did not dare reveal her feeling. Independence is a watchword for Sam, and a touchstone for his value of others. But Jo turned up, day after day, just to talk, bake jam tarts or make a milk jelly, to watch TV or read aloud to Sam, and she did not care if the new routine was queried. It was not. Such questions can destroy affection.

"I haven't seen Steve for nearly two weeks," she told Sam one evening. They were in the kitchen, Jo at the ironing board, Sam rolling a cigarette at the table, his elbows deep in the scattered entrails of an old radio he was revitalizing.

"I don't know where he goes," said Sam. "None o' my business. He's out quite late most nights." He squinted at a number on a transistor.

"A girl?" suggested Jo.

"He's miserable enough. But she'd have to be married, or cross-eyed, or twice his age."

Jo smiled. "Why?"

"Because he's normally so forthright. There must be some reason to keep it quiet. I don't think it's a woman, though. This is a small town."

Jo nodded, flipping a shirt over to iron the front onto the back, as Frances had taught her, many, many shirts ago. "I've never seen him so shaken," she said. "When all those people withdrew their support for the antipollution campaign, I thought he was going to break. My poor sweet brother. He's been so good to me since Jem left."

"Ah," said Sam. "He's a good lad, always has been. But very intense. I told him he'd bring trouble on himself." He got up to plug in the soldering iron, then sat and smoked while it heated. "Gone for good, has he?"

Jo looked into the old faded eyes that held a sympathy contrary to the harshness of the words. "Jem?" she said. "I don't know, Sam. It's getting on for two months. He did phone to say—"

"No, no," Sam interrupted. "You don't have to tell me. As long as you're managing."

Joe folded the last shirt, front to back, sleeves in, into three with the collar square. "Tell you what we'll do," she said suddenly. "I'll drive you up to the Pola. They're showing *Modern Times* as part of a Chaplin season. If you feel fit enough," she added quickly.

"Nothing wrong with me," said Sam. "I'll get my coat. What time does it start?"

Sam felt fit enough for a couple of beers in the Black Horse after the film, and was still bright and breezy and reminiscing enthusiastically about the art of Charlie Chaplin when Jo stopped the Transit outside Antlercraft. When Sam put the key in the lock, the wicket door swung ajar. He paused. "Did you leave this open, Jo?"

"No. Definitely not. I slammed it and pushed it to make sure. Perhaps Steve has come in."

Sam stepped over the sill and quickly knocked down the light switches. The high bright neon revealed nothing untoward. They crossed the floor into the workshop, where the lights already blazed. Jo frowned at Sam. "Steve!" she called, running to the foot of the spiral stairs. "Steve, are you there?"

No answer, but a soft thud from the attic rooms. Jo climbed the stairs, followed more slowly by Sam. Jem's landing office was unlit, his old room locked, but the kitchen door was open, and the door to Steve's room. A prickle of apprehension raised the hairs on Jo's forearms, and her hand on the doorjamb left a damp print. She could hear nothing but Sam's heavy footsteps and the slight wheezing of his breath. Cautiously she stepped into the kitchen and onto a broken plate. The room was devastated, cupboard doors all wide open and the contents strewn across the floor. Pans, glassware, cups and saucers, tinned food, flour and sugar bags with the contents cascading among broken eggs and trodden-in butter from the fridge. It was one hell of a cake mix.

Bemused, Jo picked her way through the mess. "Stay there, Sam," she called. "It's very slippery."

"What the bloody hell's been going on?" he demanded from the door.

Jo went into Steve's room, where the light, unshaded, burned down brutally upon an even worse sight. The pale wooden walls were splashed with aerosol paint in red and black, and the scathing, ill-spelled words filled Jo with blank disbelief. The books were torn and broken, injured to the point of death, the records ravaged, the desk raped, the stereo unit mugged. Steve's precious window was no more, assaulted into the sea far below, and the curtains hung only by their last fingertips. It defied imagination that one small room could sustain such an attack and still stand. Steve could not stand. He sat hunched on the bed in the center of the debris. The torn scraps of a shiny blue notebook lay at his feet.

Jo absorbed the vandalism unwillingly, with shocked eyes. "Steve?" she said. "Did you do this?"

"No," he mumbled. "Found it." He was very drunk.

Sam's invective when he saw the havoc was akin to that so liberally executed on the walls. "You all right?" he said gruffly to Steve.

"He's drunk," said Jo. "He didn't do it."

"Didn't think he did," said Sam. "Christ, what a mess! Why would anyone do this, Jo? Why here, what for?"

"Me," said Steve, unable to lift his head.

"Him," said Jo. "Some very nasty little minds obviously resent what Steve has been doing recently. It makes a change from ripping out the plumbing in public lavatories." She thumbed at the wall.

Sam read slowly. " 'You fuking bastard, leave aw town alone.' If I could get hold of them I'd wring their slimy little necks. I'll phone Sergeant Cassell, for all the good it will do. We can't just ignore it."

"Right. Oh, Sam, you'd better make some strong black coffee while you're there." Jo turned to Steve, still bowed, shivering now, and stroked his hair gently. "Never mind, brother," she said softly. A high wind keened across the sea, moaning in through the broken window.

"I do," he whispered. "I do."

Jo knelt among the broken records and looked up into his face, a fine, sensitive, slightly animal face of unusual beauty. All her girlfriends had pestered Jo for dates with her brother. And he had never realized his advantage, never known his effect, unlikely as it seems. Jo knew his innocence of pride or vanity. They had always been close, perhaps because there had been no father since Jo's birth. They had rolled and romped like puppies when children; he had fought on her behalf, and she on his if given half a chance. And later, when he had gone through the strange metamorphosis of puberty, shutting her out in a way she could not understand, they had preserved a respect and a gentleness. I know you better than I know anyone on this earth, thought Jo. Your thoughts are my thoughts, though our actions may differ. Your reasons are never alien to me. "Brother," she said. "We love you. If your heart is too big for your head, that is no sin."

Steve's head drooped until it touched hers, and for a moment their pains mingled and they took each other's cares. Jo felt tears upon her face and could not tell from whose eyes they fell.

"Come on downstairs," she said later. "Get you some coffee." They staggered and slid toward the landing. "I'll take a day off and give you a hand to clear this up tomorrow. You stink of beer. Where have you been? You'd better sleep on Sam's sofa tonight."

Steve arrested their progress with a hand on the stair

rail. "It can't be done, can it, Jo?" he said. "This bloody, bloody tide can't be turned. Can it?"

Jo shook her head. "Ask of the wind," she said gently.

It has never been Jacko's habit to go walking. He drives a sit-up-and-beg Ford Popular of fifties vintage that he maintains to a better standard than it ever acquired on the production line. It's black body gleams like a beetle in the sunshine, and its spanking engine whispers in contentment. But Jacko scarcely glanced in its direction as he left his house and turned to the left along St. Jude's Cresent toward the docks.

Jacko's walk was unpracticed. He moved in the manner of a lame hippopotamus, his head in advance of his feet, his steps unmeasured, one long, two short, and his mind was not on his perambulation.

He had arrived early at Antlercraft on the morning after the vandalism, had drifted upstairs toward the faint rustle of voices, and had seen that which pained his heart greatly. Jo and Steve had not yet removed the graffiti. They were working without words, except, "Oh, not my Karelia Suite," and "I've lost a page of *Murder in the Cathedral*" and "I'll repair those curtains on my sewing machine."

Jacko was too fazed even to say "Christ!" He read the crude aerosol accusations, his lips moving over each word. "Oh, no!" he said finally. "Oh, no! Have the police caught anyone?"

"Not so far," said Jo. "They promised to phone if they do, but I think we might as well forget it."

"Steve?" said Jacko.

"Yes, Jacko?"

Jacko's lips folded to a negative line, and he left the room, head down and moving from side to side, like that of a wounded animal. He found his beloved work very tedious for the rest of the day.

Jacko ceased his effortful walking and sat upon a front garden wall to concentrate. Someone had to carry the blame for all of these disasters. There had to be a rotten apple, a fly in the ointment. If only Steve had held on through, Steve who chose the jewels from the paste. Those defeated eyes; Jacko saw them clear again and again. His valiance was muddied, a fallen shield, and if the world had broken his spirit, what chance had they all? "Lost and wandering sheep" came to Jacko from youthful Sunday school.

Steve was sick, and Steve had to sing again; Jacko knew that as surely as he knew that a diesel has no spark plugs. What did a person do for sick people? Jacko kicked at the wall with his heel until a lump of brick fell out and the wall's owner hurried down to complain. Jacko shambled away without a word, even ignoring the shaking fist.

Presents, he thought. Like we brought for Sam to cheer him up. Gifts to make them smile. Of course! The idea so enlivened him that he almost ran down into St. Jude's, where a short row of shops that sell everything from toothpaste to gold watches provide a last trading post before the starkness of the docks.

The good Jacko mumbled and fumbled along the row before climbing back up the hill toward home carrying a large brown-paper parcel.

By ten o'clock on Saturday evening Steve's room was back to something approaching its former shape. The records, much depleted, stood gap-toothed in the rack; the books, shiny with tape, convalesced in the shelves. The stereo was in Jacko's workshop, the curtains, shorter but whole, hung evenly at the window. Old Sam had personally collected a new unwrinkled pane from Penquay Glass and had spent the afternoon applying putty. "If we don't get a blow tonight, we should be safe enough," he said.

Steve lay on the bed, slumped against the single pillow, trying to read. The walls closed in and resented him. Even after the use of a special solvent, the shadows of the sprayed paint remained. The old varnish would have to be sanded off. Steve wondered bleakly whether he should bother. Maybe the ghostly reminders of unforgivable stupidity would be sackcloth and ashes for his soul. "I shall remember while the light lives yet, And in the nighttime I shall not forget." The lines from Swinburne shone up at him as if freshly writ.

"God, I'm lonely," he said.

As if in answer there was a whisper of confusion outside, and the door was tapped firmly, twice. "Come in!" called Steve, folding the mended book carefully so as not to hurt it more.

A hand containing a bottle of wine waved around, there was a clink of glass, a nudge of laughter. "Please come in," said Steve.

Jo, Ivor, and Jacko tumbled in, pushing. "Party," said Jo. "Jacko had a lovely idea, so here we all are." She began wrestling with a corkscrew, Ivor laid out glasses, Jacko sat on the bed hugging his brown-paper parcel. Steve swung his feet to the floor. "What is it for?" he asked, with a sketch of the old smile.

"You," said Jo. "Tell him, Jacko." But Jacko grinned sheepishly and lost his tongue. "Well . . ." Jo poured the wine and handed out glasses. "Jacko decided that you were under the weather and in need of fun and laughter and attention, and we agreed."

"I'm . . . I don't know what to say," said Steve.

Jo bent and kissed his cheek soundly. "There's a first time for everything," she said. "To render you speechless is to make history. Cheers! To Steve, bless his good soul!"

"To Steve!" echoed Ivor and Jacko.

The glasses were filled again. "To old Sam!" said Ivor. "Long may his whatsit reek."

"To Sam!" they chanted. "And his whatsit."

"To Jo!" said Steve, holding out his glass for more. "My friend and confidante."

"To Jo!"

They descended a list that included Stotty and her cat; Roland Kemp and his wine shop, Irish Steve, Mick the Artist's latest period—stone and feather; absent friends— Jo closed her eyes; Andy Wain, his cornet, and the PPCC brass band both individually and collectively; and the early demise of the District Council en masse.

Steve and Jo were demonstrating the tango in a brilliant improvisation, and Ivor was admiring profusely—"You dance so well together" and Jo saying, "We always did . . . just lucky, I guess"—when Jacko decided to offer his gift.

"What is it?" asked Jo.

"It's for Steve. I thought he . . . it's for you, Steve." Jacko pushed the parcel into his arms.

"Why, Jacko?" he asked, flopping onto the bed.

"Because it's what you do when people are . . . it's what you do."

"Thank you, my old friend. Thank you." Steve opened the parcel slowly. He brought out and laid on the bed at his side an apple, an orange, two comics, a small pack of cigars, a squat colored candle, a screwdriver, and a ball of twine. He looked at Jacko, at all their warm faces, and back to the gifts spread on his checkered blanket. Then he gulped twice, and muttering "Excuse me," fled from the room.

"Oh, hell!" said Jacko. "What did I do? It was supposed to cheer him up, make him happy. Dammit, it was supposed to make him blinkin' happy!"

"It did." Jo gave him a hug. "It did."

It was the first frost of the season. The night was fierce, in its coldness brittle, and the stars so low they meshed with the house lights along Gypsy Lane. Steve knew he could not breathe deeply or his lungs would seize up and his nose would ache for weeks. The low hedges creaked as he passed, freezing to the sap, to the roots, the earth going to stone around them. His boots skidded and scraped over the beads of frozen sweat on the tarmac, and rhythmic shafts of steam from his nostrils preceded him. And there was Jo, as a child. "We're dragons. Let's be dragons," and getting dizzy from trying to blow the longest plume. And she whispered because you can shout only in rain or fog, but not in frost. The sound of his boots echoed back from the last of the houses.

Soon he would pass the cottage, long his home, long loved but seldom seen because familiarity breeds a certain blindness. Only when it had been sold, "a desirable old-world property in half an acre, with one acre of orchard, overlooking sea," had he realized his childhood privileges. It had been repainted now, pale cream, and the neglected garden brushed and combed. He thought of the strangers, a middle-aged wealthy couple, warming their hands at the sitting-room fireplace, where he had made toast and seen castles in the flames.

He had forgotten Trix, the click-click of her nails drowned by his thoughts, until she bolted in front of him with a delighted bark down a favorite track through the dunes. He lost sight of her quickly, but he could hear her snuffles and burrowings after imagined rabbits, and he followed. There was a glow ahead, lifting the black sky. Trix yapped loudly several times, then became ominously quiet. Steve called her, but she made no answer. Worried, he stumbled toward the glow.

The fire crackled gently, sparks spiraling up, and the smoke bore the scent of pine. A pack stood beside the fire, and a cup and thermos flask on a flat rock. The man, dressed in a dark duffel coat and sea boots, was holding Trix on his knees, trying to evade her licks.

"Well!" said Steve.

Jem Merriman stood and came to shake hands. Steve said, "Have you come back?"

The words reverberated through Jem. "Yes," he said. "Oh, yes, I've come back. Sit down, Steve. Have a cup of tea." They were silent a long while, staring over plastic cups into the firelight. Jem broke it. "How is Sam? Ivor wrote to me about his illness."

"Did he? I didn't know. I guess I assumed you would have seen the newspapers. It made quite a splash." He grinned without humor. "Sam's doing fine now. He's back at home, but he has to take it easy."

Jem nodded. "I went to Antlercraft, but it was late and there were no lights and I didn't want to disturb anyone. I left the car and brought my camping gear along here."

"You have a tent?"

"And a sleeping bag."

"So, you are back?"

"Yes."

"To stay?"

"If Sam will let me. If all of you will."

Steve studied Jem's face as he bent over Trix, again on his knees. It was thinner and paler, even in the fireglow, as careworn as Jo's. Why do we do these things to each other, wondered Steve, what rag-bag impulses motivate us fools? He said, "I'll take a leaf from Jacko's book and be blunt, otherwise you and I could sit here all night with our bums freezing. What happened?"

"Not very much, but everything. After my wife had recovered from her nervous shock, she realized she still loved the other man and that money and security were no substitute. And I tried too, but I missed Jo more and more instead of less and less, as I had hoped. It wasn't long before the rows started, all the terrible recriminations on both sides. Eventually Susan suggested we shouldn't be together. My own daughter. We cried, all of us, that night, but she was right. At least I tried."

"So, you are back."

"Have you lost your gift for words, poet?"

"I have lost . . . something . . . faith. I blundered and I failed, and I have done so before, but this . . . this was different. The Protect Port Penquay campaign has fizzled out, and pollution has become a taboo word, and just when I had thought I could win." He took up a handful of sand and let it run through his fingers. "You wuz right, Jem, and I wuz wrong."

Jem shrugged. "It's a setback. You can start again."

"In this town? I haven't the courage. I shall be a pariah for years." He rang an imaginary bell. "Unclean! Unclean!"

"Nonsense. You can't keep a good man down."

Steve pondered the point. "Actually," he said, "if my view of history is correct, I should say the converse is true." His bright eyes flashed once in anger; then he turned his gaze toward the sea, and his face was introverted and melancholy.

Jem hummed to himself, fondling Trix's ears. He was becoming tired, and if not bored, disappointed. Steve's laughter and vitality, always inherent in Jem's mind image of him, were quiescent. Surely not because he had made rather an ass of himself over that pollution nonsense. "How are all the lads?" he said.

"The same. We are like beavers now; we miss Sam's hand."

Jem tucked his mouth and eyes down. "Do they, do you, resent what I did?"

Steve hunched nearer the reddening fire. "I think they felt partially responsible, if that is a cause for resentment. And I resent you because I have had to see my sister suffer, and because you see the cold side of truth. But you have come back. If you leave Jo again, you will have me to reckon with."

CHAPTER THIRTY-ONE

Jem ached desperately after Jo, longed to walk up to her door, sink into her soft mouth, down and down to where it was dark and warm, but there were ends to tie first and hashes to settle. In the glow from the fire he read again a letter written in black ink on white paper.

It was very nearly midnight, and the last stragglers were leaving the club, grumbling at the cold, punching gloved hands together, starting recalcitrant cars that coughed and snarled away along Gypsy Lane. Jem stood in the deep shadow under the tree as the figures passed in silhouette against the still-lighted windows. He felt extremely foolish and ridiculous. It was only a hunch.

Colin Whale was last out, and alone, his tall slender outline quite distinctive. He moved sinuously and slowly, as if he always expected eyes to be admiring. Jem waited, letting him stroll past until he reached the inky spot where the club roof, the cold black conifers, and the sky mingled. Then Jem walked out onto the path, allowing his footsteps to echo loudly on the frosted paving slabs. The sandstone rang like an ominous knell.

Colin stopped and peered behind him nervously. Jem came on, knowing he was invisible. Colin wavered. "Alex?" he said, high-pitched.

Jem closed in, smiling the snarl of a tiger. He could feel his face contracting. He stepped from the path to the grass and was only two feet from Colin when Colin sensed a presence. As he turned to run, Jem caught his arm and twisted it behind his back in a half nelson. It was not

Colin's scene. He is a devout coward, and violence of any sort turns his limbs to water. "Help!" he screamed, struggling against the wire grip and seeking a more pronounced mountain in the hills of his guilty past.

"Shut up or I'll break your arm," said Jem flatly.

"Okay," whispered Colin.

"You've been hanging around Jo Wilder," said Jem softly. His teeth were dry and his lips barely moved.

"No I haven't." Colin's voice rose sharply as Jem increased the pressure.

"Lying bastard," said Jem. "But listen. If I so much as see you in her street in future, I'll separate you from your breath."

"All right," agreed Colin hastily. "I'm not interested. She's weird, you're welcome to her, whoever you are." He tried to look over his shoulder, but Jem was too quick. He pushed, and Colin went forward at a bent, stumbling run. By the time he had recovered, Jem had blended into the trees, and Colin did not stop to search. He has a feminine sort of run, thought Jem contemptuously. He slept well that night.

The following day ended early, a day of cloud and drizzle, and no-name frustration. Yet it ended in a glorious winter sunset with brushstrokes of rose madder on plain, ordinary clouds, with a generous outpouring of thin yellow gold across the sea, with a roll of drums and a crash of brass and a general emblazoning of the structures that are Port Penquay. The spire of St. Peter's caught the last ray and shimmered with joy.

Jo reached home in time to stand at her window as the sea changed from gold to silver-green, and the first eager stars appeared. The telephone rang at her elbow.

"That you, Jo?"

She recognized the bark, as she recognized Trix's. "Yes, Sam, it's me."

"Who?"

"Me, Sam. Jo."

"Ah, Jo. It's Sam."

"Yes, I know. How are you, Sam?"

There was a thrum of machinery in the background. "Put that sander off," said Sam, aside.

"Pardon?" said Jo.

"Not you, love. Steve."

"Oh, how is he?"

"Fine. What is all this how-are-you, how-is-he?"

"What did you want?" said Jo placatingly. Sam's telephone fuse is pretty short.

His voice dropped to normal decibels. "I just thought you'd like to know. Jem is back."

There was no sound but the rapid clatter of Jo's heart. Her system went into overdrive. She could see the front of her sweater jumping. "He is?" she managed.

"Just thought you ought to know," said Sam. She could see his face—concerned, crafty.

"Has he asked you to call?"

"Nope."

"Has he said anything?"

"Not much. I think he's a bit tired, washed-out. I gather things didn't go too well in London."

Jo's fingers tangled in the telephone cord, slippery with cold sweat. "Uh . . . what should I do, Sam?"

"Up to you, love. I don't know why he's come back, none o' my business, but he's paid a month's rent and brought me some details for the schooner. Why don't you come over?"

"I don't know," said Jo. Her voice was vibrating beyond control. "Perhaps I ought to wait."

"Please yourself. You're always welcome, you know that."

"Yes, yes. Let me think, Sam."

"You do that, lass."

"Sam?"

"Mmm?"

"Thank you."

On the wall above the telephone Jo had written several numbers in pencil, intending to transfer them to the book. They had been there for months. She tried to place their owners. Her mind was squirming away from its future like a lugworm in the sand of Half Moon Bay. She took an eraser from the desk and rubbed out the numbers, but left a smudge, so that she had to fetch a damp cloth from the kitchen to clean the wall. As always, the window attracted her. Deep twilight now, the lights coming on in the dusky pits of the town, but still the bright viridian cast on the western horizon silhouetting the lighthouse, and beside it, the bulk of Antlercraft. Sandholm loomed gray and cetacean, fading fast into the black mist that crept from the east. Jo had wiped the windowsill so clean with her cloth that she had to do the rest of the frame. Her mother's clock hiccuped and bonged six gentle bongs.

He's down there. She peered closely at the place where Antlercraft must be, fancying she could see the light from Sam's kitchen. He has come back.

She went to feed the goldfish, sprinkling in food with a tremor-induced liberality. He came gobbling to the surface. "I've never seen a fish that wasn't graceful," said Jo. "Fishy fishy fish-face, he has come back. Does he still want me?"

"Why else?"

"He has not called or come."

"He is afraid."

"Jem is never afraid."

"He does not seem to be. Nothing is what it seems. Of all people, you should know that."

"God, I'm scared. Now that there are possibilities for life, I'm scared."

"Will you wait, then, and hope?"

"No, I am not strong enough, not when he is so close, like a magnet."

"Then go to him. Show your need. It is why he came."

"No! I have pride. It would be debasing."

"It would be human."

"But will he leave again?"

"I know no more than you."

" 'Is the secret secret still?' " said Jo.

"Ask . . ."

Jo did not afterward remember her route, the weather, the transport, the tide in the harbor, the moon, or the stars. She knew that her hands, shaking, marred her lipstick, that she mislaid her new leather boots, that she tore her scalp with the tense, mechanical spasms of the hairbrush. But on her journey, by bus, foot, taxicab, or dogcart, she said in her head, "Dammit to hell, I'm going. I shall go crazy else. Supposition and a vivid imagination are ugly bedfellows for the soul. I'm going, even if it means the liquidation of all hope. I'm going."

I'm there.

She paused outside the high double doors and her mind ran away along the shiny sliding tracks. She called it back, stepped through the wicket gate with it close against her chest, and ran silently through the building to the kitchen. Sam and Steve sat at the table playing chess. Used dinner plates had been pushed aside for the board. Steve smiled slowly and nodded. Sam raised a hand like Christ's hand in the old paintings and pointed at the ceiling. Wordlessly Jo left the room.

Before another moronic incubus could entrap her waking mind, she tapped loudly at the door of Jem's room. The seconds elapsing before he answered had the texture of chewing gum. And then he was there, solid in the doorway, round and real beneath the ceiling light, and Jo thought: Poor Jem—for he had shrunk and was as an autumn leaf, parched from within.

"Jo! Please come in." He took her right hand in his left and squeezed so hard her palm bruised. She smiled, hiding her eyes.

They sat, one in each of the two big armchairs that had been Jo's mother's. The familiar old fabric, its doggy smell, and the well-dented seat gave Jo comfort and strength. Jem toured the valleys and plains of her face, inspecting each ingrained detail for change. The hair waved back still like a titian breaker above the smooth and creamy forehead. The eyes were dark and sad as graves, the chin round and strong. She was brave and tough, and shaming. Jem stared down at his fingers. "How have you been, Jo?"

She fastened her eyes on the walls of wood, the warm grainy wood, and relived the glow of the room and bumped sharply into the spears guarding the hollow night of his going. "I have not been," she said. "I have missed you."

"Jo . . ." Jem leaned forward, took her hand, and

pressed it to his cheek. "My dear, I'm so sorry. I had to find out if it would work, for Susan, for my family. I think I did the right thing."

Turn the knife, turn the knife. Jo moved back, pulled her hand free. "Then why are you here? Have you come back?"

Jem was silent for so long that Jo feared he was refusing her an answer. He huddled in the big chair, rocking and small, like a child. Children had always liked that chair. Then he said, "It would not work. I tried, but you were like a fire to me, like food. I had no sustenance. And Annette tried, but it's hard to pretend love and passion for the sake of security, and she is not mercenary enough. One night she called me by his name, and for all I know I called her by yours. It's a very easy mistake, and so unkind. Eventually even Susan couldn't stand the squabbling. She told us the dirty truth of the impossible."

Jo thought awhile. "Then search only for the possible," she said slowly. "We have time for little else in our lives, that I have learned in my short experience." You do not know, do you, and never will, how iceberg lonely and how branding-iron tortured . . . The months of his absence were draining down suddenly, leaving the sides of her mind scoured and shiny, with just a sticky rim at the surface where the germs of tears grew, and the molds of loss. It was a clean ascension, better than anything she had formerly felt, almost a devil-may-care sensation. She lost control of the energy of patience. "We are alive, Jem," she said urgently. "You, me, Annette, Susan. We have our precious, precious lives. And there was a time when mine was sweet, with Mum and Denny, then you."

"We'll make it sweet again," said Jem. "I promise." Against the strength of his will, his emotions fought a winning battle. "I've come to stay, Jo."

My Jem, thought Jo. Lost, like we all are. A mature, clever, logical man with an echoing, lonesome pain that shows in your face clearly now. I know I love you.

But at the moment when Jem's heart was in his eyes, Jo's heart perversely became remote. I am me, she thought, Josephine Frances Wilder. You will not capture, imprison, or torture me. You will not bend me again until I

break. Not you. Not anyone. Not ever. There was a touch
of Fred the Red in her soft smile.

He said, "Would you start again, Jo? Can I come a-
courtin'?"

"My Jem. My blue-eyed Jem." You played it the way
you saw it, right down the line, straight as a die and with
honesty. You did the right thing, regardless of me, of
friends, even of yourself. I pray we can live with your
decisions.

They smiled together. Jem took Jo's hand and pulled
her close, as if he pulled on a warm coat, and between
their palms, so real that Jo could feel the shaft of it press-
ing into her fingers, they held a key.

CHAPTER THIRTY-TWO

It was coming on Christmas, and despite events at Antler-craft the town was going about its Yuletide business of decorations, bells, lights, plastic reindeer, a tree from Norway in the Town Hall car park, gift shopping, cash counting, et-Christmas-stocking-cetera.

A few days after the reunion, as Jo termed it on a banner in her head, she took an extra hour for lunch and braved the throbbing town shops in search of a gift for Sam. A man who has everything is not any easy candidate. Having exhausted all the probabilities, she sought refuge in the lounge bar of the Roger de Coverly to consider the possibilities over a glass of sherry. It was not a bar her circle used, being overstuffed with rust-gold velvet, fox-hunting prints, and an enormous, perpetually hungry Labrador dog, as well as being impressively overpriced. So Jo could be forgiven for not at first recognizing, or even noticing, the figure slumped in a corner seat with a newspaper obscuring half of its frame. The shoes were familiar, but Jo was absorbed by her shopping list.

"Buy you a drink?"

She looked up, frowning darkly. "Steve! What are you doing here?"

"Imbibing. And you?"

"I'll have an amontillado."

"This isn't your usual scene, is it?" Jo took the refilled glass and moved her bags so that Steve could sit. "What's wrong with the Anchor?"

"At the risk of sounding pathetic, no one talks to me."

"I shall go into the garden and eat worms."

"Yes." Steve smiled. "How about you, fat face? Are you full of the joys now?"

"Over the moon. Jem has brought me flowers every night, and chocolates, and taken me out to dinner. We're courting, you see."

"What a lovely idea."

"Thank you, brother. Other comments have been a shade catty, remarking upon shutting stable doors after horses have bolted."

"I'm glad for you, Jo. I wish . . . I wish that I had a splendid thing to tell, so that I could reflect your happy face with mine."

Jo was quiet for a while, contemplating the guilt that rose, the apology quick behind her tongue for displaying the golden coins of happiness before a beggar whose hands were tied. To give, to justify, she shared her doubts. "It will be a long, long time before Jem and I will be at peace, if ever," she said calmly. "Love will see us through until we're old enough to relax, but I foresee traumas and fights and all sorts of difficulties."

Steve frowned at his sister. "You must not let him know this," he said.

Jo nodded. "Of course not. Some lessons are engraved in letters two feet high." She tapped her forehead. "But we will not live happily ever after. I shall not trust him, not for ages. I shall resent any communication with his wife, however insignificant or necessary. I shall detect worry in his eyes and be convinced its origin is another woman. I shall wonder when he uses after-shave whether it is to cover a scent I don't use. I shall scan his laundry minutely, read his letters, pick his pockets, ring him up at work too often, and I will be afraid, so afraid of losing him.

"And he will know my suspicions, and resent them, because Jem is good at sensing the weak and bad in people, and we shall fight about our insecurity. It's going to be hell at times." She grinned widely. "I always was a fool."

Steve stared at her. "You are remarkable," he said. "And a brave fool. I hope he is right for you. Is there a future for me too, Jo? It's like a sea-fog morning to me. I glimpse shapes that could be boats or dolphins and hear the thrum of engines and faint cries, but then it blots in and blots out."

Jo bit her lower lip gently, musing. "You are at the same point as I was," she said. "On the brink of a deep river, and the only bridge broken. Don't jump in, will you, Stevie. Promise me. It is worthwhile to wait."

"I hear you, Jo."

"You were my strength. I'd be yours if I knew how. Happiness is so selfish, and your problem is the world, not the individual. How can I help, Steve? Tell me."

"Kick my backside, maybe. Jem would concur."

Jo smiled. "And why should I treat chalk as cheese? You may need the help of love to recover. You can't fight the world alone, and your friends have proved fair-weather."

"You think I need a woman?"

"Your tendencies don't run to a man."

"I thought about Degonwadonti, but she rarely crosses my days now. I found an old poem I wrote for her, in a book when we were tidying my room, and it reminded me. I could go back, but in my heart I'm not sure I want to. There is no love that spans worlds and time, is there?"

Jo tucked away her cigarettes, gathered the handles and strings of her shopping bags. "I have always longed to believe in romantic love," she said. "But the evidence of life confounds the dream. If Jem had not come back, I would have eventually forgotten, and loved again. I did with Denny. We are only human, Stevie, and our capacity for endurance is only as great as our inadequate memories. Else how would we live? Now, the oracle has to hoist its parcels and get moving." She stood and smiled. "You always did make me say the oddest things."

"Good," said Steve. "And you have made me remember the yellow-dust-mote corners of reason. Here, you have more use for this than I." He fumbled under his sweater and brought out from his shirt pocket a gray folded paper, crumbling at the edges. "It's not very good, but it was meant for lovers."

"Thanks," said Jo, taking it carefully. "Steve, perhaps you should consider the weapons at your disposal. Power is necessary to achieve change, and the absence of a personal ulterior motive that powerful enemies could use against you. You have the latter, and you have your words. You could write it down. Who was it said, 'The pen is mightier than the sword'?"

It was during dinner at the Royal Grill that Jo, searching her handbag for a Kleenex, laid hand upon the folded paper again. She brought it out and placed it on the linen tablecloth beside her wineglass. Jem did not notice. He was involved with her presence, her hair, her eyes, her big white teeth daintily masticating steak, and absorbed in sharp memories of how she had been, those months ago, and how she would be again when the courting days were through. Her hair damp under his hands, a little sweat, a little soap from the shower. Her mixture, shine, smooth, slippery, hard points, furry bubbles, squirmy, silly, sexy Jo. Before his eyes, blind to chips and wine bottles, lay the prospect of life with a compliant woman, full of laughter, sharing, loving. The idyllic horizon was unclouded, and toward it ran the golden road along which he and the brown eyes lighting his heart would travel in perfection.

Jo blew her nose with a short honking sound, but Jem only loved her more. "I have never been so happy," he said.

"Nor me," sniffed Jo. Her nose was red now on the tip. She smiled, and the rose spot disappeared. "I love you, pooch," she said.

They only grounded when a waiter inquired about coffee. Jo remembered Steve's poem. She unfolded it like a flower and read silently. "This is for us," she said. "For all lovers. Listen."

> On the gray-green panorama slopes
> I tasted, smelled, touched by mouth
> The essence of all lovers through time.
> The empty trees trailed an empty
> Landscape, to an empty sea with
> Golden islands, where the sun shone.
>
> I will walk with you hand in hand
> Where the sky collides with land,
> Through old villages of pain, leaving
> Them ruined, through the quarries of

Trial, leaving soft sand. Through the
Woods of love, leaving them green.

Under the faded sepia print of the *Eleanor*, united in
amicable harmony, crowded old Sam Antler, Jacko, Ivor,
Stotty, Jo, and Jem. The club crooned softly to itself in the
latter hours, peaceful in the windless, moonless, inoffensive night. Red and blue festoons sagged from the beams,
gold and silver shemoggles dangled over the bar. Irish
Steve had raised glazed and wondering eyes, like a shep-
herd startled by an angel, to the fantastically shaped decorations, and had said, "What's tem tings?"

And Alex, expressionless, had replied, "Shemoggles."

Wrinkling balloons lodged in every window, and artifi-
cial snow prevented much of the light from filtering
through the panes. A huge "Merry Christmas" poster
beckoned folks to the dance floor, "And there are still
two weeks to go," Sam had remarked pungently.

Jem sighed contentedly. "Ah, this is nice. . . ."

Jo nodded and Sam said, "Aye," soberly.

"Everything seems to be coming back to normal," said
Ivor. "I feel like a plant that's been in a darkened room for
months, and now I've been put out in the sun." He sighed
and crossed his legs, twitching up the knees of his new all-
wool worsteds.

Roger Payne joined them, sat, and pushed his glasses up
the bridge of his nose with his middle finger. "I'm not a
man for upheaval," he said. "It does my heart good to see
Sam here, and fit, and Jo and Jem so happy. But some
things never change. My Elsie went to all those classes,
and she still can't cook."

"And I never get the bloody jackpot on that fruit
machine," said Stotty ruefully.

"Good," said Sam. "You spend enough time shoving my
money down its throat already."

"Your money!" Stotty stopped when she caught the dull
gleam of one of Sam's teeth. "Cheeky sod," she said.

"Do you have a Christmas dance here?" asked Jem. "I
want to take this one dancing." His fingers gently mussed
the curled ends of Jo's hair.

"And how." Roger laughed. "Last year, someone—we
never discovered who—caught the decorations on fire."

"That big bird from Blenchin's did a strip," reminisced Sam. "She is a big girl, too."

"Browny Law threw a stone through his own greenhouse because he thought he'd found a prowler," put in Ivor. "It turned out to be his reflection."

Jacko had been listening agitatedly to the humdrum, self-satisfied conversation with a growing indignation and disgruntlement. His beer stood untouched and his fists worked rhythmically over his knees in the throes of stress. The inane, happy faces set his teeth on edge, and down in his belly anger rumbled, contained only by the governor of quandary. Finally he growled, "You're all pretty pleased with yourselves."

Ivor was concerned. "What's upsetting the good Jacko?" he said. "Haven't we reason to be happy?"

"No, you bloody haven't." Jacko's eyes were sullen red in their fat sockets. "Aren't you all forgetting somethin'?"

"It's not your birthday, is it?" said Jo.

"No, it's not." Jacko was short, like Grumpy, thought Jo.

"Then tell us, do." Ivor waved his slender hands encouragingly. "Your blood pressure must be enormous."

"Yes, do," said Stotty firmly. "We don't want our Jacko troubled."

"You should all be troubled," he said. "About Steve."

A wary silence fell like a hammer. Eyes darted, face to ear to nose to eyebrows. Jacko glared at all of them in turn, "Defiance on a monument," said Sam afterward. "I'm very worried about Steve," said Jacko. "We ought to do somethin' about him."

Sam dwelt slowly upon the company, the characters he knew and loved and hated and manipulated and served, the personalities that were a large part of his very existence. Jo, and her head close to Jem's, after so much anguish; elegant, studious Ivor; simple, brilliant Jacko; mainstay Stotty; patient, meticulous Roger. He dwelt upon them as a zoologist might upon a batch of tadpoles, as God may dwell upon his creations.

His chin lifted determinedly. With the clarity and finality of the last trump, he said, "No!"

He had the last word.

The Story
All America
Took To Its Heart

A Woman of Independent Means

A Novel by
Elizabeth
Forsythe
Hailey

THE SPLENDID
NATIONAL BESTSELLER

"Nothing about it is ordinary . . . irresistible."
Los Angeles Times

"Bares the soul of an independent American housewife . . .
a woman to respect . . . a writer to remember."
John Barkham Reviews

AVON $2.50

WIM-7/79

AVON ◆ THE BEST IN BESTSELLING ENTERTAINMENT

He is happily married to another woman.
She is happily married to another man.

ADJACENT LIVES

How do you
choose between
the love of
your life and
the passion of
a lifetime?

Find out in
one of the most
beautifully
written love
stories in years.

"FINE AND
PASSIONATE....
Her gift is for
evoking desire...
a serious and
important writer."
The New Republic

ELLEN SCHWAMM

AVON  45211 $2.50

ADJ-9/79